CANADIAN
FOLKLORE

Perspectives on Canadian Culture

JUDITH SALTMAN
Modern Canadian Children's Books

EUGENE BENSON & L.W. CONOLLY
English-Canadian Theatre

DAVID CLANDFIELD
Canadian Film

MICHELLE GADPAILLE
The Canadian Short Story

EDITH FOWKE
Canadian Folklore

Forthcoming:

PENNY PETRONE
Canadian Indian Literature

MERVIN BUTOVSKY
Canadian Jewish Writers

DAVID KETTERER
Canadian Science Fiction and Fantasy

ALICE VAN WART
Canadian Diaries and Journals

DONNA BENNETT
Canadian Literary Criticism

DOUG FETHERLING
The Press in Canada

DAVID MATTISON
Canadian Photography

CANADIAN FOLKLORE

Edith Fowke

Toronto OXFORD UNIVERSITY PRESS 1988

Oxford University Press, 70 Wynford Drive, Don Mills, Ontario, M3C 1J9

Toronto Oxford New York Delhi Bombay Calcutta Madras Karachi
Petaling Jaya Singapore Hong Kong Tokyo Nairobi Dar es Salaam
Cape Town Melbourne Auckland

and associated companies in
Berlin Ibadan

Canadian Cataloguing in Publication Data

Fowke, Edith, 1913–
Canadian folklore

(Perspectives on Canadian culture)
Bibliography: p.
Includes index.
ISBN 0-19-540671-0

1. Folklore – Canada. 2. Canada – Social life and
customs. 3. Folklorists – Canada. 4. Folklore –
Canada – Methodology. I. Title. II. Series.

GR113.F69 1988   398'.0971   C88-094621-0

CONTENTS

Introduction 1

DEFINITIONS 1

LIMITS OF THIS SURVEY 3

THE SOURCES OF OUR FOLKLORE 4

THE STUDY OF FOLKLORE 5

THE BIBLIOGRAPHIES 8

1. Beginnings 9

2. The Pioneers 14

MARIUS BARBEAU 14

LUC LACOURCIÈRE 16

W. ROY MACKENZIE 17

HELEN CREIGHTON 18

LOUISE MANNY 20

ELISABETH BRISTOL GREENLEAF 21

W. J. WINTEMBERG 22

MARY L. FRASER AND ARTHUR HUFF FAUSET 24

3. Tales 26

TYPES OF FOLKTALES 26

TALES OF THE NATIVE PEOPLES 31

FRENCH-CANADIAN TALES 34

TALES OF ANGLO-CANADIANS 37

TALES OF OTHER ETHNIC GROUPS 43

LITERARY FORMS 46

4. Song, Music, and Dance 48

    SONGS OF THE NATIVE PEOPLES 48

    FRENCH-CANADIAN SONGS 49

    ANGLO-CANADIAN SONGS 51

    SONGS COMPOSED IN CANADA 54

    ANGLO-CANADIAN COLLECTIONS 58

    SONGS OF OTHER GROUPS 63

    INSTRUMENTAL MUSIC 64

    DANCING 66

    THE SINGERS 69

    THE SINGER-SONGMAKERS 74

5. Minor Genres 76

    FOLK SPEECH 76

    PLACE NAMES 79

    PROVERBS 80

    RIDDLES 81

    CHILDLORE 84

    ADULT GAMES 88

6. Popular Beliefs and Superstitions 90

7. Folklife and Customs 98

    CUSTOMS 101

8. Folk Arts and Crafts 106

    THE NATIVE PEOPLES 108

FRENCH CANADIANS 108

ANGLO-CANADIANS 109

OTHER ETHNIC GROUPS 110

GENERAL 111

9. A Few Final Words 114

Selected Bibliographies 117

ABBREVIATIONS 117

GENERAL 117

BIOGRAPHIES 119

TALES 120

SONGS, MUSIC, AND DANCE 124

RECORDS 130

MINOR GENRES 131

POPULAR BELIEFS AND SUPERSTITIONS 134

FOLKLIFE AND CUSTOMS 135

FOLK ARTS AND CRAFTS 138

Selective Indexes 143

AUTHORS, INFORMANTS, PERSONALITIES 143

SUBJECTS 147

'Loon Quilt' by Alice Olsen Williams

INTRODUCTION

DEFINITIONS

The term folklore is difficult to define, partly because it refers both to the materials involved and to the method of studying them. There are many different approaches, which result in almost as many definitions as there are folklorists; *The Standard Dictionary of Folklore, Mythology, and Legend* gives twenty-one. The term dates from 1848 when the Englishman William Thoms introduced it to cover what was then known as 'Popular Antiquities': 'manners, customs, observances, superstitions, ballads, proverbs, etc. of the olden times'. Many since have tried to define it more exactly, but often, like Thoms, have been reduced to listing the things they consider folklore. Today the emphasis is less on 'olden times' and more on present traditions, but Thoms' list still covers much of the material involved in folklore.

Some think primarily of tales and songs that are handed down orally from one generation to another, often termed 'oral literature' or 'the verbal arts', but that leaves out the many things that are not transmitted orally. The renowned American folklorist Archer Taylor gave a good general definition: 'Folklore is the material that is handed on by tradition, either by word of mouth or by custom and practice.' Dr Marius Barbeau, the only Canadian among the twenty-one folklorists quoted in the folklore dictionary, gave a more poetic description:

> Whenever a lullaby is sung to a child; whenever a ditty, a riddle, a tongue-twister, or a counting-out rhyme is used in the nursery or at

1

school; whenever sayings, proverbs, fables, noodle-stories, folktales, reminiscences of the fireside are retold; whenever, out of habit or inclination, the folk indulge in songs and dances, in ancient games, in merry-making, to mark the passing of the year or the usual festivities; whenever a mother shows her daughter how to sew, knot, spin, weave, embroider, make a coverlet, braid a sash, bake an old-fashioned pie; whenever a farmer on the ancestral plot trains his son in the ways long familiar, or shows him how to read the moon and winds to forecast the weather at sowing or harvest time; whenever a village craftsman—carpenter, carver, shoemaker, cooper, blacksmith, builder of wooden ships—trains his apprentice in the use of tools . . . whenever in many callings the knowledge, experience, wisdom, skill, the habits and practices of the past are handed down by example or spoken word, by the older to the new generations, without reference to book, print, or schoolteacher; then we have folklore in its own perennial domain, at work as ever, alive and shifting, always apt to grasp and assimilate new elements on its way. . . . It is the born opponent of the serial number, the stamped product, and the patented standard. . . .

The things Barbeau lists are still important, and his emphasis on folklore's variety and shifting nature is even more important today than when he wrote. But today the concept has been extended to cover many things that are not old, and that were not thought of as folklore in previous times. Where earlier folklorists looked to the past, to rural areas, and to those with little education, modern scholars find folklore everywhere and among all peoples.

Folklore Forum (Nov. 1968) quoted a more general definition by the American folklorist Richard Dorson:

Folklore is the culture of the people. It is the hidden submerged culture lying in the shadow of the official civilization about which historians write. Schools and churches, legislatures and courts, books and concerts represent the institutions of civilization. But surrounding them are other cultural systems that directly govern the ideas, beliefs, and behavior of most of the world's peoples . . . The written literature of classic authors stands in contrast to the subterranean oral expression and the lowly channels of print that permeate civilized as well as less literate societies. Medical doctors, drugstore prescriptions, and hospitals share the solution of health problems with faith healers and home remedies. . . . Early in the nineteenth century intellectuals in Germany and England stumbled on and began to study this hidden culture that lay all around them.

Anthropologists would discover faraway cultures. Folkorists were discovering their own, and finding unsuspected revelations and rewards.

Two shorter definitions are: 'Folklore is communication in small groups', and 'Folklore is anything that you don't get from books'. Important in recognizing it is the fact that it involves variation. If a tale or song is standardized—always presented in the same form—it is unlikely to be folklore. Another dominant characteristic is repetition. Where literary compositions use description for emphasis, oral compositions use repetition, particularly repetition by threes.

Today folklorists think of folklore as circulating within any group of people who have something in common. The main folk groups are linked by age, occupation, region, or nationality. Children, teenagers, and seniors have lore peculiar to them. People in every occupation share common traditions, whether they are fishermen, lumbermen, miners, cowboys, farmers, factory workers, truck drivers, writers, students, professors, doctors, lawyers, or criminals. The lore of maritimers differs from that of prairie residents, as does that of Indians, Inuit, and English, French, German, Doukhobor, Jewish, or Mennonite Canadians. Sex, religion, and political ideology are other bonds, and many minor groups—square-dancers, drug users, those who collect antiques or stamps, play particular games, or go to dog or horse shows—all share certain lore that is not common to other groups. The lore that circulates among members of a group is termed esoteric; the beliefs that outsiders hold about a particular group are termed exoteric.

LIMITS OF THIS SURVEY

In Canada ethnic groups constitute one of the major divisions, and much of their published lore is in languages other than English. (Strangely, the term ethnic has come to mean groups other than English, although strictly speaking all racial groups are ethnic.) This survey emphasizes primarily the folklore of English-speaking Canadians, but it also includes material from other groups that has been published in English or exists in English translations. This covers only a small part of the great mass of French-Canadian lore, although some of the most significant of the publications in French are also noted. Those interested in exploring this important aspect of our heritage in detail may refer to certain key works and reference tools listed in the bibliographies. Folklore of the other non-English groups is surveyed only when it appears in translation.

The lore of the Indians and Inuit is not discussed extensively. Literature relating to the native peoples is so vast that it requires separate treatment, and many of the multitudinous publications about them belong more properly to anthropology. Again, some of the major books are mentioned, and the bibliographies list general references and surveys for those wishing to study this lore. Penny Petrone's *Canadian Indian Literature*, which will appear in this series in 1989, will contain more information.

Folklorists distinguish between authentic folklore presented in the form used by the folk and folklore that has been rewritten by those who present it. In this survey the emphasis is on genuine folklore rather than on adaptations. Of the genres, I have covered the verbal arts, especially tales and songs, more fully than the others. So many publications relate to folklife, customs, folk arts, and material culture that these cannot be considered in detail. Again, further information can be found in the major references listed.

THE SOURCES OF OUR FOLKLORE

The greater part of our Canadian folklore came to this country with the people who left their native homes to settle in the new land. Comparatively little folklore actually originated here. A large proportion is international, existing in slightly different forms in many countries. The early British settlers brought their tales and songs with them and handed them down from generation to generation, and some preserved here are older and more complete than ones now found in their original homelands. The same, of course, is true of French-Canadian lore, and to a lesser extent of the lore of later immigrants, although that brought to Canada in recent years has not had time to be assimilated and hence can hardly yet be termed Canadian.

Although most of our folklore comes from old-world sources, much of it takes on a new form in its new home. Tales and songs acquire local references—songs sung by British sailors are adapted to describe Canadian shantyboys; tales of French princes are revised to tell of the *habitant* lad Ti-Jean; tall tales that in Europe told of Baron Munchausen are here attributed to Paul Bunyan or Joe Mufferaw. There are also quite a few stories, songs, and jokes inspired by Canadian events, many customs and sayings reflect the conditions of the new world, and some artifacts—like the prairie schooners, York boats, sod shanties, and bark canoes—result from particular conditions existing in this country.

Most of the Anglo-Canadian lore collected comes from eastern Canada, particularly from the Maritime provinces and New-foundland. It is fortunate for folklorists that Newfoundland final-ly joined Confederation, thus enabling us to claim its amazingly rich lore as Canadian. As the American folklorist MacEdward Leach wrote in his foreword to Greenleaf's song collection,

> If a folklorist should be given the opportunity to create an ideal folk region, he could hardly do better than to duplicate Newfoundland. It is an island and until recently an island difficult of access. It has always been thinly populated. From earliest times the folk have lived in tiny out-ports at the heads of the deep fjord-like harbours that serrate the coast. All of this developed a culture turned in on itself and a highly self-sufficient one.

No other province except Quebec has anything to compare with it. In both provinces the reason for their wealth is obvious. Isolation fosters the preservation and creation of folklore; Quebec is isolated as a francophone island surrounded by anglophones; New-foundland is isolated from the mainland by water, and the hundreds of tiny outports scattered around its winding coast are isolated even from each other.

THE STUDY OF FOLKLORE

Until some forty odd years ago Canada lagged behind other countries in its study of folklore. Although the nineteenth and early twentieth centuries saw some lore collected, there was little organized attempt to study it. Some early folklore societies were organized, but they lasted only briefly. The anthropologists and folklorists who did the early collecting published their material in the *Journal of American Folklore*; no comparable Canadian journal existed.

When Marius Barbeau joined the National Museum in 1911, it became the major centre of folklore activity for the next thirty years. The folklore section he headed formed part of the National Museum of Man, later becoming a division titled the Canadian Centre for Folk Culture Studies (CCFCS) under the direction of Carmen Roy. It acquired an extensive archive of manuscripts, recordings, films, photographs, and artifacts, and published numerous books and pamphlets, including a Mercury Series of typed and photocopied papers by the folklorists who collected material for the Museum. The National Museum is now called the Canadian Museum of Civilization, and the emphasis is shifting from research and publications to exhibitions.

French Canada had the greatest interest in its cultural heritage, and in 1944 Université Laval established a chair in folklore, the first academic recognition of the discipline. Under Luc Lacourcière, Laval began to develop an extensive archive and to publish a journal, *Les Archives de Folklore*, that became the major medium for scholarly studies of French-Canadian lore. Originally presenting a variety of articles, it soon began publishing monographs on single subjects by different francophone scholars. Laval's archives developed so greatly that they have become one of the most important folklore centres in North America, and the publications growing out of them have won international acclaim. In 1976 Les Archives took on a broader function to co-ordinate studies of all North American francophone culture under the title 'le Centre d'études sur la langue, les arts et les traditions populaires des francophones en Amerique du Nord', popularly known as CELAT. When Lacourcière retired he was succeeded by Jean-Claude Dupont who has published numerous books and articles on folktales and material culture.

Later, several other francophone universities developed folklore sections. Father Germain Lemieux established the Centre franco-ontarien de folklore at l'Université de Sudbury to house his extensive collection of songs and tales; Anselme Chiasson's collecting in New Brunswick led to the Centre d'études Acadiennes at l'Université de Moncton, and Memorial University in St John's, Newfoundland, has a Centre d'études franco-terreneuviennes.

It was not until 1968 that Memorial University established the first Anglo-Canadian folklore department. Its founder was the American folklorist Herbert Halpert, who had joined Memorial's English Department to teach folklore in 1962. He also established the Memorial University of Newfoundland Folklore and Language Archive (known as MUNFLA), which has become one of North America's major collections of anglophone lore.

Since then a number of universities across Canada have introduced one or more folklore courses, but Memorial remains the only anglophone university with a complete department offering both undergraduate and post-graduate courses leading to masters' and doctors' degrees.

In 1960 Dr Barbeau founded the Canadian Folk Music Society as a branch of the International Folk Music Council, and 1976 saw the formation of the Folklore Studies Association of Canada. These organizations led to the launching of three academic journals: the *Canadian Folk Music Journal* in 1973; *Culture and Tradition*, which folklore students at Laval and Memorial have published annually since 1976; and the journal of the Folklore Studies Association, *Canadian Folklore canadien*, started in 1979. Journals of related disciplines—*Ethnomusicology* and *Canadian Ethnic Studies*—have presented folklore material in special issues, and some university journals have published useful articles. Carole Carpenter's doctoral thesis, *Many Voices: A Study of Folklore Activities in Canada and Their Role in Canadian Culture,* published in the Mercury Series in 1979, is an extensive survey and analysis of the field. Many other folklore students have written theses on Canadian topics, and the bibliographies list those that are published.

THE BIBLIOGRAPHIES

The bibliographies are selective, aiming to list the most important books and articles dealing with authentic folklore. They omit some items because they are difficult to find, and include brief articles only if they deal with subjects where material is scarce. If two or more publications cover the same subject, the most complete one is listed. Emphasis is on publications since 1979 because they do not appear in the Fowke and Carpenter *Bibliography of Canadian Folklore in English*. All items mentioned in the text are included except for some cited as illustrations and identified by dates, and some noted as related material.

The bibliographies correspond to the chapters—on tales, songs, minor genres, beliefs, folklife and customs, arts and crafts—except for two: 'General' and 'Biographies'. The first gives periodicals, references, and items containing a number of genres—for example, the books by Creighton, Fauset, Fraser, and Halpert, and the articles by Bleakney, Waugh, and Wintemberg. This General bibliography should be kept in mind because its items contain material relating to several different chapters. The second, 'Biographies', includes material referring to the 'Pioneers' discussed in the third chapter and also to some of the other folklorists mentioned throughout the text. All items are Canadian except for a few general reference books marked with asterisks.

1

BEGINNINGS

From the earliest days of the European immigrants, writers have been noting some aspects of folklore in Canada. In the seventeenth century the Jesuits wrote of the Huron and Algonkian people's beliefs, tales, and customs in the *Jesuit Relations*, and later priests like Fathers Lacombe and Petitot noted tales of the western and northern tribes. Father Brébeuf composed the first Canadian Christmas carol, 'Jesous Ahatonhia', around 1642—originally sung in Huron, but later translated into both French and English.

Many of the early explorers—David Thompson, Alexander Mackenzie, George Vancouver, Henry Kelsey, and Sir John Franklin—described Indian customs and beliefs in their memoirs, and Paul Kane documented much Indian lore through his paintings and his book *Wanderings of an Artist among the Indians of North America* (1859).

The first person to record Indian tales in English was Henry Rowe Schoolcraft (1793-1864) who served as an Indian agent among the Ojibwas of the Great Lakes between 1812 and 1842. His books— the first published in 1850—inspired Longfellow's *Hiawatha*, resulting from Schoolcraft's confusion of the Ojibwa culture hero Nanabozho with a historical sixteenth-century Iroquois leader. In the next half-century many others—Indian agents, missionaries, doctors, and teachers—noted and published tales, sometimes simply translating them, but more often retelling them in a style they thought would make them more popular. The most important of these early collectors was Silas Rand (1810-89), a Baptist minister in Nova Scotia, who in his *Tales of the Micmacs* (1894) rendered the tales close to the way he had heard them.

Then towards the end of the last century the American anthropologist Franz Boas (1852-1942) began to record the myths, legends, songs, and customs of Canada's native peoples, and other anthropologists soon followed—like James A. Teit, A.F. Chamberlain, and James Deans, who began writing about Indian culture in the 1880s. The early twentieth century saw more anthropological works by Charles Hill-Tout, Alanson Skinner, George Laidlaw, John R. Swanton, Frank Speck, William Mechling, Vilhjalmur Stefansson, and Paul Radin, followed a little later by Marius Barbeau, Knud Rasmussen, Leonard Bloomfield, Richard Preston, Diamond Jenness, and Wilson Wallis. They provide remarkably detailed studies of the traditions of Canadian tribes that far outnumber the publications on other segments of our population.

Second only to the wealth of native lore is that of the French Canadians. Records exist from the time of the early settlements. Marc Lescarbot, a French lawyer, described the life and customs at Port Royal, and various accounts recall L'Ordre du Bon Temps, which Champlain founded in the winter of 1606-7. Visitors and travellers—like Mrs John Graves Simcoe, whose husband was governor of Upper Canada in the 1790s; the Irish poet Thomas Moore, who went down the St Lawrence by canoe in 1803; and John Bigsby, who travelled in Canada before 1850—recorded their impressions of the *voyageurs* and *coureurs de bois*. (Barbeau quotes these and others in an article on 'The Ermatinger Collection of Voyageur Songs'.)

The *nationaliste* movement in Quebec aimed to preserve the French-Canadian culture through literature. Various early writers described folk traditions in books such as Philippe-Aubert de Gaspé's *Les anciens canadiens* and J.C. Taché's *Forestiers et voyageurs*, both published in 1863. Some literary works in English also reflected aspects of French-Canadian lore, like J.M. LeMoine's *The Chronicles of the St Lawrence* (1878) and *The Legends of the St Lawrence* (1898), and Honoré Beaugrand's *La Chasse-Galerie and Other Canadian Stories* (1900) and *New Studies in Canadian Folklore* (1904).

The earliest songs collected in Canada were also French-

Canadian. During Franklin's first Arctic expedition (1819-22), Lieutenant Back noted some songs that Edward Knight published as *Canadian Airs* in 1832, and the fur-trader Edward Ermatinger collected *voyageur* songs while serving with the Hudson's Bay Company between 1818 and 1828. In 1863 Hubert LaRue published a number of songs in *Le Foyer canadien*, and throughout the nineteenth century several other small collections appeared, some in English translations, like William McLennan's *Songs of Old Canada* (1886).

In 1865 Ernest Gagnon (1834-1915) published the first major Canadian folklore collection, *Chansons populaires du Canada*, containing a hundred of the best-known French-Canadian songs. It was reprinted several times and served as a source for many later publications. Not only is it the first major book devoted to Canadian folklore: it is a landmark in nineteenth-century folksong research, and is still studied today. Gagnon noted his melodies with great precision and also included data on his informants and the regions where he collected, thus introducing techniques that only later became accepted as necessary to place folklore items in their proper perspective. Modern musicologists find his work of interest—Jay Rahn writes of the 'Text Underlay in Gagnon's French-Canadian Songs' and Gordon Smith discusses his songs as 'an argument for plainchant and folksong'.

A particularly valuable book from this early period is W.P. Greenough's *Canadian Folk-Life and Folk-Lore*, published in 1897. It is the first book to report in English on various folklore genres—tales, songs, customs, and games—and it gives an excellent account of *habitant* life in Quebec during the nineteenth century.

In 'The Present State of French-Canadian Folklore Studies', Luc Lacourcière explains why the French-Canadian heritage is so rich:

> From the beginning of Canadian history to the middle of the nineteenth century folklore and oral tradition were in what we could call *un âge d'or*. They continued developing naturally and spontaneously. Even the Seven Years' War and the cession of Canada to the English offered no obstacles; quite the contrary, these important historical events created a new climate in which the peasant's attachment to the soil became more

pronounced and his French traditions more deeply rooted. Because of the attitude of the king of France who never allowed the establishment of a press in New France, and the English government which consistently after the conquest of Canada used English as an instrument of propaganda for introducing that language and Protestantism, there was a complete lack of publication in French and a scarcity of French schools. This period, which appears to some historians as a new dark age, was truly the golden age of oral literature.

Then in the early twentieth century Marius Barbeau began his life work, which was to make him the undisputed father of Canadian folklore. During the next half-century, he and his collaborators collected and published a remarkable stock of tales and songs.

Thus the early documentation of Canadian folklore focused on the native peoples and the French-Canadians. Very little Anglo-Canadian lore appeared until well into the twentieth century, except for incidental folklife descriptions in diaries, autobiographies, early histories, and accounts of pioneer life. Some of the earliest is in books reflecting life in nineteenth-century Ontario, when it was still Upper Canada. The best known are Anna Jameson's *Winter Studies and Summer Rambles in Canada* (1830), Catharine Parr Traill's *The Backwoods of Canada* (1836) and *The Canadian Settler's Guide* (1855), and Susanna Moodie's *Roughing It in the Bush* (1852) and *Life in the Clearings* (1853). Because of their literary value, these books have been kept in print while many other accounts of that period have long disappeared.

There were some early attempts to organize folklore societies. A Canadian branch of the American Folklore Society existed in Montreal from 1892 to 1898, a Canadian Folk-Lore Society met in Toronto from 1908 to 1911, and a Canadian branch of the American Folklore Society was re-established in 1917, mainly to produce Canadian numbers of the *Journal of American Folklore*. But none of these organizations were very active.

In the 1890s Alice Leon, Alexander Chamberlain, George Patterson, and Alice Leeson contributed a few Canadian items on children's lore, dialect, and superstitions to the *Journal of American Folklore*, and the 1918 Canadian issue contained several important articles. David Boyle and Laura Durand published some early items on folklore in the Toronto *Globe* around the turn of the century; songs appeared early in *The Family Herald and Weekly Star* and some Newfoundland papers, and John Burke and James Murphy published numerous small song books in the early 1900s. The first major Anglo-Canadian book, however, did not appear until 1919, long after major works on native peoples and French Canadians.

2

THE PIONEERS

Canadian folklore really began with the pioneer work of Marius Barbeau (1884-1969). Born in Quebec, he was educated at the universities of Laval, Oxford, and the Sorbonne, and joined the National Museum as an ethnologist in 1911. There he worked until his death, collecting, publishing, and encouraging others to collect and publish. As F. J. Alcock , chief curator of the Museum, wrote in the *Journal of American Folklore* in 1950:

> Dr Barbeau has been responsible for the development of folklore research in Canada, and the wealth of folklore material in the possession of the National Museum of Canada was largely collected by him and the numerous students to whom he has transmitted his enthusiasm for this type of study.... Scholars and laymen alike are giving increasing recognition to the importance of Canadian folklore, and credit for this must go chiefly to Dr Barbeau.

Luc Lacourcière, his disciple and distinguished colleague, also paid hommage to him in *Les Archives de Folklore*: 'En effet, depuis son retour des grandes écoles de Paris et d'Oxford, vers 1912, Monsieur Barbeau a consacré sa vie et ses études à nos traditions populaires. Grace à lui, le folklore canadien occupe sa place dans l'étude scientifique des traditions comparées.'

Conrad Laforte quotes Frédéric Pelletier's comment on Barbeau's *Romancero du Canada* of 1937: 'Let us salute the man who has made us aware of the true nature of the treasure inherited from France—a treasure the French have forgotten they possess, and one which we have transformed in accordance with our own genius.'

After Barbeau's death the Canadian Press noted:

During fifty years of research, much of it on long and arduous field trips, he produced a wealth of knowledge concerning the Asiatic migrations to North America. He delved deeply into French-Canadian folklore and into the story of the Indian peoples, their legends and culture. He gave the National Museum a collection of 195 Eskimo songs, more than 3,000 Indian, close to 7,000 French-Canadian, and 1,500 old English songs. Many of them are still on the old tube-like records that came off his Edison recorder. . . . 'I would need two lives to process all my research,' he once said.

The work Barbeau achieved in one lifetime is almost unbelievable. In an age of increasing specialization he ranged over the whole field of folklore and anthropology, collecting and studying and describing Indian myths, ceremonials, language, music, arts, and culture; French-Canadian folktales, songs, games, handicrafts, a rt, and architecture; and English-Canadian songs and art. Totem poles and Indian masks, Assomption sashes and religious carvings, butter and maple-sugar moulds, sculptures and water-colour—they all fell within his purview. A prolific writer and completely bilingual, he published some fifty major books, as many more pamphlets and monographs, and some seven hundred articles in over a hundred different periodicals ranging from scientific journals to popular magazines and daily papers.

He took an active part in the American Folklore Society, serving as president and as associate editor of the *Journal of American Folklore*. With collaborators like Marcel Rioux, E.-Z. Massicotte, and Gustave Lanctôt he prepared eight special Canadian issues of the *Journal* between 1916 and 1940. In 1957 he organized the Canadian Folk Music Society, and in 1961 entertained the world's major folksong authorities as host of the Congress of the International Folk Music Council in Quebec City.

Far from being an ivory-tower scholar, Barbeau spared no effort to preserve and promote folklore in as many ways as he could. In addition to his scientific works he wrote several books designed for the general public, and he encouraged other writers to use his materials. However busy he was, he always found time to answer the many people who wrote him for information and to receive cordially the many others who visited him at the Museum or his Ottawa home. He gave warm encouragement to anyone developing an interest in folklore and was quick to praise their achievements. He lectured at universities, spoke before numerous organizations, and appeared frequently on radio and television. He prepared several records on Canadian folk music, including one that he called 'My Life in Recording Canadian-Indian Folk-Lore'. He worked tirelessly to make Canadian folklore known abroad and to promote friendly relations between folklorists throughout the world. His contribution to Canadian folklore can hardly be overestimated.

LUC LACOURCIÈRE

Luc Lacourcière, Barbeau's disciple and worthy successor, was born in Quebec's Beauce County in 1910 and educated at Laval and McGill Universities. He taught in France and Switzerland before returning to Canada to begin teaching in Laval's French summer courses. In 1939 the Royal Society of Canada gave him a scholarship to study anthropology and folklore with Dr Barbeau at the National Museum in Ottawa. In 1944 he began teaching folklore and ethnography at Laval and established the Archives de folklore. Soon he initiated a series of scholarly publications under the title of *Les Archives de Folklore*, contributing many articles himself and publishing the researches of those who became his collaborators.

Throughout the next forty years Lacourcière continued collecting, building up the most important archive of French lore in North America, and documenting and classifying it. As Richard Dorson wrote in Luc's 1978 *festschrift*:

> Luc Lacourcière is the complete folklorist of his area, the folklore of the French-speaking peoples of North America, whose traditions he has collected, classified, published, edited, taught, directed doctoral dissertation on, and developed a great archives to store.... And in each of these areas he has contributed with equal mastery. Some folklorists achieve as collectors, some as scholars, some as teachers, some as archivists,

some as indexers, but Luc has done it all. Over a thirty-year span he gathered 4,500 tales, songs, and other folklore texts. His magnum opus, in process of publication, will index some two hundred thousand entries on the French folklore of America.

W. ROY MACKENZIE

W. Roy Mackenzie (1883-1957) was born in River John, Pictou County, Nova Scotia, graduated from Dalhousie University, and took graduate work at Harvard. Encouraged by George Kittredge, Harvard's leading ballad scholar, he began collecting from his summer cottage at River John in 1908. After receiving his Ph.D. he became a professor of English at Washington University in St Louis, but he returned to Nova Scotia each summer where he continued his search for traditional singers.

Mackenzie published some of the first songs he collected in the *Journal of American Folklore* in 1908 and 1910, and went on to produce a fascinating account of his experiences in *The Quest of the Ballad*—the first and still the best description of the adventures of a Canadian collector. In it he wrote:

> My constant purpose has been to portray, as faithfully as in me lies, the popular ballads which it has been my high privilege to encounter in their natural state and the reserved but simple and profoundly human old men and women who are still maintaining them in that state.

As the American folklorist Malcolm Laws noted, *The Quest* is 'a book full of profound insights into the nature of folksong and folksingers'. Mackenzie's vivid descriptions of his singers are a delight to read. His sympathy for them and his colourful accounts of the way they felt about their songs help us to understand how important the songs were to the folk who preserved them. He went on to publish *Ballads and Sea Songs from Nova Scotia* in 1929. Not only is this the first major Anglo-Canadian collection, but it is notable in two ways. Unlike some collectors who were tempted to tamper with their texts to 'improve' them, Mackenzie printed as accurately as possible what the singers sang, thus providing an example for those who followed him.

He was also a pioneer in the lengths to which he went to locate previously collected or printed versions of each song. Quite a number of British collections had appeared in the late nineteenth and early twentieth centuries, and a dozen or more were published in the United States in the 1920s. Checking those was not too onerous, and was customary among most serious collectors of the time. What was different in Mackenzie's approach was his determination to locate broadside versions of his songs. This involved searching through North America's major broadside collection at Harvard where, as Mrs Mackenzie reported, 'He spent one whole vacation in a basement of Harvard sorting and arranging the dustiest, dirtiest lot of broadsides you can imagine—probably not touched since the days of Child.' Saluting this diligence, Malcolm Laws noted: 'The Mackenzie headnotes remain of unique value to anyone making a serious study of these songs.'

HELEN CREIGHTON

Just as Luc Lacourcière succeeded Marius Barbeau in collecting and studying French-Canadian lore, so Helen Creighton followed Roy Mackenzie in collecting Nova Scotia songs, and she went on to document other types of Maritime traditions as well.

Born in Dartmouth in 1899, Helen Creighton graduated from Halifax Ladies' College in 1916, worked briefly as a social worker and teacher, and told stories as 'Aunt Helen' on a children's radio show. When she was searching for something to write about, Nova Scotia's Superintendent of Education Dr Henry Munroe suggested that she look for ballads. Then one evening a villager mentioned that people in a region near Halifax knew pirate songs, and that started her collecting. She had trouble noting the tunes so she began recording them on a melodeon that she transported in a wheelbarrow; later she switched to a dictaphone. For a time the English musician Doreen Senior helped her to transcribe the tunes, and then in 1943 she acquired her first tape recorder.

Creighton took a summer course in folklore at the University of Indiana, and won three Rockefeller fellowships to finance her collecting. She had several contracts from the United States Library of Congress, and between 1947 and 1967 she worked for Canada's

National Museum, where the bulk of her collection is stored. (Copies are also in Nova Scotia's Public Archives.)

She collected over four thousand songs and their variants. Most came originally from Britain, but Creighton also recorded some in French, Gaelic, Micmac, and German, as well as some composed in Canada. Several Canadian musicians have written compositions based on her songs, which also form the basis of Michael Perrault's ballet *Sea Gallows* and Trevor Jones's opera *The Broken Ring*. She has appeared on various radio and television programs and in films—two are titled *Songs of Nova Scotia* and *The Nova Scotia Song*.

In addition to songs, Dr Creighton collected many other types of folklore: tales, superstitions, games, riddles, proverbs, and customs. She assembled the most extensive Anglo-Canadian folklore collection of any single individual—a collection that was unequalled until Memorial University established its folkore department.

Dr Creighton has published five major books of songs, beginning with *Songs and Ballads from Nova Scotia* in 1931. In preparing it she consulted Dr John Robins of Toronto's Victoria College, who wrote in the introduction: 'There is an academic, clinical approach to folk-songs, and there is a sentimental approach, maudlin or mocking as the case may be, but the ideal is a combination of the scientific and the sympathetic, and that is the one Miss Creighton has shown.'

She writes vividly and with great warmth of some of her experiences, as when she describes—in her introduction to her first book, *Songs and Ballads from Nova Scotia*—her first visit to Devil's Island in Halifax Harbour:

> Picture the little island at your back with its miniature hills and dales, its houses perched so insecurely that you feel a breath of wind might come at any moment and blow them all away. . . . Behind the log on which the men are sitting the Devil's Island harbour lies, the fishing boats rocking cosily in the soft cradle of the sea. . . . Far, far away is Citadel Hill at Halifax. . . . Behind Citadel Hill is the setting sun. . . . All is quiet among the islanders, save for the voice of Mr Henneberry. His theme is the long, sad story of 'Meagher's Children', the tale of two little tots lost in the woods near Dartmouth. The island listeners all know the song, and their sympathy is felt as the hardships of the children are related....

One by one other islanders join the group attracted by the beloved voice of Mr Ben. . . . The air is tense and vibrant, for the ballad singer is an artist among his people, but upon this occasion the islanders are divided in thought between pleasure in hearing this dear old song again, and pride in the one who is singing it. Often have I wished I might repeat that precious moment.

As her collecting progressed, she published *Traditional Songs from Nova Scotia*, *Maritime Folk Songs*, *Gaelic Songs in Nova Scotia*, and *Folksongs from Southern New Brunswick*. In addition to the songs, she produced a comprehensive collection of lore from Lunenburg County, the first major books of Canadian superstitions and ghost stories—*Bluenose Magic* and *Bluenose Ghosts*—and a number of articles.

Dr Creighton has been honoured nationally, internationally, and locally—she is a Fellow of the American Folklore Society and a member of the Order of Canada; she has half a dozen honorary degrees, and several Nova Scotia festivals have celebrated her. Her autobiography, *A Life in Folklore*, gives a good account of her colourful and productive career.

LOUISE MANNY

Another Maritime collector, Louise Manny (1890-1970), did not collect or publish as extensively as Helen Creighton, but her work in New Brunswick is noteworthy. Although she was born in Maine, she was educated in Canada, earning a history degree at McGill and spending most of her life in Newcastle on the Miramichi River. She became interested in local history, and began publishing and broadcasting about it, one of her books being *Ships of Miramichi* (1960). In 1947 Lord Beaverbrook, who remembered fondly the songs he had heard in his youth in New Brunswick, commissioned her to collect songs from the Miramichi lumbermen.

Manny soon began broadcasting on Newcastle's radio station CKMR the songs she discovered, and in 1958 she founded the Miramichi Folk Festival, which she continued to direct until 1969. It is the only festival in Canada that can truly be called folk, for Manny insisted that only traditional singers should perform, while other festivals feature mainly professional or semi-professional singers, most of whom sing contemporary compositions rather than traditional songs.

In 1962 the record *Folksongs of the Miramichi* presented some of the songs Dr Manny collected, and later she worked with Edward Ives to annotate a record of the important New Brunswick singer Marie Hare. In 1968 she published her major book *Songs of Miramichi*, with tunes transcribd by J.R. Wilson. It includes many pictures of the region and of the lumbering industry, and provides a useful glossary identifying references and defining unusual lumbering terms that turn up in the songs. On the title page she quotes Victor Hugo: 'What is a tree without its roots? What is a people without its songs?' and in her preface she writes: 'Our singers *believe* in these songs which have become an extension of their personalities. And so we have been able to record and research a living part of a great tradition.'

Dr Manny received two honorary doctorates and in 1967 the National Council of Jewish Women awarded her their Woman of the Century medal. She shares with Dr Barbeau the honour of having a mountain named for her—Mount Manny in New Brunswick's Historians' Range.

ELISABETH BRISTOL GREENLEAF

Elisabeth Bristol (1895-1980) was born in New York and graduated from Vassar College in 1917. In 1920 she volunteered to teach for the Grenfell Mission Summer School in Newfoundland and went to Sally's Cove on the west coast. There she heard traditional singing for the first time. When she reported this, Vassar's president H.N. MacCracken and Martha W. Beckwith, a professor of the Vassar College Folk-Lore Foundation, encouraged her to continue her collecting the following summer. After this second visit she married and retired from teaching for a time, but in 1929 she revisited Newfoundland to make a more complete song collection, and took with her a musicologist, Grace Yarrow (later Mrs Mansfield). Their field trip was successful, and in 1933 Harvard published their *Ballads and Sea Songs of Newfoundland.*

Mrs Greenleaf delighted in the Newfoundland songs and singers, describing them warmly in her introduction, and showing how the songs grew out of the people's culture. Not only is her book the first scholarly collection of Newfoundland songs; it is one of the first North American collections to give the tunes equal emphasis with the texts. Writing in the *Canadian Historical Review*, Dr John Robins described it as 'the finest body of regional folksong in English-speaking America' and praised the scholarly notes and references. Later, in a preface to the reprint edition, the American folklorist MacEdward Leach wrote:

> Although these collectors may have been amateurs, yet they had an instinct for the right approach. The songs were collected in context, that is, in the natural social situation. Mrs Greenleaf tells of singing for the informants, of trading songs, of recording songs in the long evenings as the group sat around socializing at the end of the day.... It is furnished with a very full and informative Introduction which gives the reader detailed information about the informants, social backgrounds, and clinical details of the problems of collecting. It is an enjoyable essay because it recreates by concrete illustration, by anecdote and by characterization, the people and their lives. It puts the reader in the experience. As a part of this, the folkways of the Newfoundlanders are detailed so skillfully that the ballads become for the reader a part of a living culture.

Elisabeth Greenleaf also collected and published an extensive article on the Newfoundland riddles that she collected. As she notes, 'I heard the riddles in the long evenings, or while on a "cruise" in the berry patches. (Even a simple walk takes on a nautical name in sea-going Newfoundland.) Soon I heard them even in school.' As a means of improving the children's diction she had them repeat riddles in class. Later on the wharf while waiting for a boat she offered a crowd of youngsters 'a penny for every riddle we haven't heard', and reaped a plentiful harvest.

W. J. WINTEMBERG

William John Wintemberg (1876-1941), born in New Dundee, Waterloo County, Ontario, was the first important Ontario collector, recording a variety of folklore from both Pennsylvania Germans and Anglo-Canadians. Professionally he worked as an archeologist, first for the Ontario Provincial Museum and then for the federal Geological Survey of Canada. He carried out archeological surveys and excavations from Ontario to Newfoundland, and the articles he published threw light on the prehistory of eastern Canada, especially the prehistoric Iroquoian farmers.

Wintemberg was active in the various short-lived folklore societies formed early in the century. In 1911 he was secretary of the Ottawa-based Canadian Folk-Lore Society, and in 1918 he served as vice-president of the Ontario Branch of the American Folklore Society.

His personal interest was in the lore of his native region which had been settled by Pennsylvania Germans. Douglas Leechman noted that 'The German dialect spoken in Waterloo County attracted Wintemberg's attention from his early youth.' He began to collect items in that dialect and by 1899 was publishing brief articles in the *Journal of American Folklore*. After his death Leechman gathered all of Wintemberg's available material on the Pennsylvania Germans for a National Museum bulletin, *Folk-Lore of Waterloo County, Ontario*. It includes a surprising variety of items: beliefs and sayings about the heavenly bodies, natural phenomena, weather lore, animal and plant lore, folk medicine, death signs, burial customs, good and bad luck, charms, proverbs, folk names, stories about ghosts and witches, folk rhymes, folk songs, and folktales.

In addition to the German lore from Waterloo, Wintemberg collected English items from friends and relatives in nearby counties, and some he noted during the course of his archeological fieldwork. These form important articles in the 1918 Canadian issue of the *Journal of American Folklore*. As Dr Barbeau notes in his introduction, the collections presented 'are the result, not of systematic, subsidized investigation in a well-selected field, but merely of assiduity, chance, and perspicacity'. Nevertheless, they are the most extensive reports of Anglo-Canadian folklore in Ontario up to that time and for the next half century. In addition, Wintemberg published a number of short items in the *Journal* on such diverse subjects as French-Canadian folktales, German folktales, Negro-

Canadian folklore, Alsatian witch stories, Algonkian words in American English, weather terms—'squaw winter', 'Indian winter', and 'dogwood winter'—and the use of shells by Ontario Indians.

MARY L. FRASER and ARTHUR HUFF FAUSET

Two other writers, Mary L. Fraser and Arthur Huff Fauset, are also pioneers, although they contributed less to Canadian folklore than the collectors described above. In 1931 both published important books based on their university theses—the first general folklore books presenting anglophone material.

Mary Fraser, a nun from Antigonish whose religious name was Mother St Thomas of the Angels, took her Ph.D. at Fordham University in New York State, where the Rev. John Monaghan, a professor of English, directed her work. It consisted of collecting in Cape Breton and eastern Nova Scotia the material she published as *Folklore of Nova Scotia*. She noted Micmac, Gaelic, Acadian, and English lore—mainly beliefs, superstitions, legends, and customs—and her book is significant for the emphasis it places on the intermingling of these traditions.

Arthur Fauset was an anthropology student at the University of Pennsylvania when American folklorist Elsie Clews Parsons arranged for him to collect among the blacks in Nova Scotia. Fauset, who was himself half-black, did fieldwork in the summer of 1923, collecting throughout the southern half of the province. He noted many kinds of folklore, mainly from blacks, but some also from whites and Indians. This collection formed his master's thesis and was published as *Folklore from Nova Scotia*. It is the only major book of black folklore in Canada, and it presents a remarkably varied collection, including tales of many kinds: *märchen*, animal stories, tall tales, tales of witches, devils, preachers, and treasure; ballads and songs, games and counting-out rhymes, riddles, and many folk beliefs: omens, charms, weather signs, folk medicine, and superstitions relating to pregnancy, birth, childhood, and death. Fauset's only other publication of Canadian material is an article,

'Folklore from the Half-Breeds in Nova Scotia', in the *Journal of American Folklore* in 1925.

Fauset is an example of the many foreigners who have collected Canadian lore, from some of the early anthropologists through Greenleaf and Mansfield, Maud Karpeles, MacEdward Leach, and Edward Ives. Others have collected for the National Museum, including Rolf Brednich, Linda Degh, Jan Brunvand, and Michael Jones, and several have joined Memorial's folklore staff, including Herbert Halpert, Gerald Pocius, J.D.A.Widdowson, and Neil Rosenberg.

3

TALES

Folktales include all types of traditional narratives that circulate orally—myths, legends, fairy tales, animal stories, jokes, anecdotes, formula tales, and personal narratives. Most of those told in Canada have parallels in other countries, but many have been adapted and localized here.

TYPES OF FOLKTALES

The tales that came to Canada from the Old World fall into the categories that Antii Aarne and Stith Thompson classify in *The Types of the Folktale*. The first group, 'Animal Tales', are mainly fables—animal stories used to teach lessons—and stories in which animals take on human characteristics. Apart from Indian legends, few of these have been told in Canada, although Fauset found some among the blacks in Nova Scotia, and a few have come here more recently with immigrants from the West Indies.

In the second and largest group, labeled simply 'Ordinary Folktales', most of the plots have supernatural elements. These are what most people think of when folktales are mentioned—the kind of stories that the Germans call *Märchen*, the French *contes populaires*, and the English fairy-tales—although they are better termed wonder tales, for few are about fairies. Some have their roots in a pre-Christian era; most date back hundreds of years; many came originally from the Orient or Egypt; and nearly all have international plots.

These tales have certain typical features, of which the most important is repetition—particularly repetition by threes. Many feature three sons who have to perform three tasks to win three princesses; the hero often has three helpers who may give him three gifts that help him to perform his tasks. They emphasize trials and quests, supernatural enemies and supernatural helpers, magic objects, and marvellous transformations. Frequently they describe the triumph of the youngest son, or the weakest character, and most have happy endings.

The plots contain a number of motifs—small elements that may be characters, events, objects, or incidents. Examples are the fairy godmother, giants, dragons, the devil; talking birds or animals, a magic ring, a cloak that makes its wearer invisible, boots that carry their wearer swiftly over vast distances, a magic table that produces food and drink; transformations, contests, and deceptions. Typical wonder tales told in Canada include 'Jack and the Beanstalk', 'Open Sesame', 'Bluebeard', 'Cinderella', and 'The Dragon Slayer'. Such plots are known all over the world, and people from many lands have brought them here. We usually think of them as stories parents tell to children, but in earlier times adults told them, and they served much the same function as fantasy and science fiction do today. Folklorists, psychiatrists, and sociologists analyse them to show their effect on children and to explain their meaning and importance. Bruno Bettelheim's *The Uses of Enchantment* (1976) is one famous study based on a Freudian approach.

Much more common than the wonder tales are 'Jokes and Anecdotes', the third of the four Aarne and Thompson types. Where comparatively few tell the old supernatural stories today, practically everyone occasionally tells a joke or anecdote. The two most common groups are tales of lying and numskull jokes.

Particularly popular are tales of lying—termed tall tales—that depend on exaggeration for their humour. They are often linked to legendary or semi-legendary characters like Paul Bunyan or Joe Mufferaw, or occasionally to less well-known local characters. Common themes are extraordinary weather, enormous insects, or the fantastic exploits of hunters or fishermen.

Many tell bawdy jokes, but they are rarely printed. More often noted are the so-called ethnic jokes or *blasons populaires*. Originally known as fool, numskull, or moron jokes, people now tell them of some minority that differs from the norm. They are commonly directed against immigrant groups—there used to be many 'Pat and Mike' or 'fool Irishman' jokes, and in the United States the generic name is 'Polack jokes'. In Canada the same slanders are directed against the French-Canadians ('Frogs'), Ukrainians ('Ukies'), Newfoundlanders ('Newfies'), and more recently Pakistanis ('Pakis'). Although they are usually termed 'ethnic jokes', the group slandered is not always ethnic, as the numerous 'Newfie' jokes indicate. There are also 'Aggie' jokes ridiculing Agriculture students.

The fourth and smallest section in the Aarne and Thompson classification covers formula tales. In these the form rather than the subject matter is the identifying factor, and the most common are cumulative, like 'The House That Jack Built' or 'The Old Woman and Her Pig'. Others are endless, involving repetitive actions that go on forever—for example, grasshoppers begin to remove corn from a barn: 'One grasshopper enters, takes out a grain; one grasshopper enters, takes out a grain, one grasshopper enters, takes out a grain . . . *ad infinitum.*' Then there are circular tales that start over from the beginning and go on repeating: 'It was a dark and stormy night. A band of Indians was sitting around the camp fire and the chief said, "Tell me a story." The tallest brave stood up and said, "It was a dark and stormy night. A band of Indians was sitting around a campfire. . . ." ' There are also catch tales that fool or startle the listeners—in an Alberta yarn the teller ends his story about a bear by saying that the bear ate him.

Distinct from the four classified types are myths and legends. Myths—tales believed to be true accounts of a pre-historic world and featuring gods and demigod—hardly exist in Canada except for the religious narratives of the Indians and Inuit. Most myths deal with the creation of the world and its peoples, and with the origins of religious rituals. Strangely, people often use the term 'myth' for anything that is obviously untrue, but in folklore it means tales believed to be true by the people who tell them.

Legends, like myths, are believed by the people who tell them—

or at least were originally believed. But where myths deal with supernatural beings, other worlds, and prehistoric times, legends are usually set in this world and feature human beings, although they may also involve supernatural creatures like the Devil, ghosts, fairies, or witches. Some supposedly explain certain animal characteristics or geographical features. Others may deal with weather peculiarities, rites or customs, strange happenings, unusual people, miracles, buried treasure, or strange creatures like vampires or werewolves.

While most folktales told in this country came from other lands and have international parallels, legends are more apt to be linked to a particular place or a particular situation, and hence may be more distinctively Canadian. Many legends involve superstitions (which are discussed in Chapter 7), but stories based on the superstitions are also folktales. There are, for example, many tales of Canadian ghosts or poltergeists, of ghost ships, and of treasure supposedly buried by pirates.

Stories about monsters are common all over the world, but Canada seems to have more than its share. The French-Canadian stories of *lutins* (mischievious goblins) and *loups-garous* parallel European beliefs in fairies and werewolves, but Sedna, the hag of Inuit myth, and D'Sonoqua, the cannibal woman of the Pacific Coast Indians, are more unusual. Still better known is the Windigo, the most feared supernatural creature in Indian folklore, sometimes a demon and sometimes a man who has become crazed by hunger and turned cannibal.

Canadians also tell many stories about the Sasquatch, the Canadian version of the monster known elsewhere as Bigfoot, the Abominable Snowman, or the Yeti. Hundreds of witnesses have reported seeing a monster who conforms to the Sasquatch concept—a huge animal-like being who walks like a man—and many of the accounts are detailed and convincing. But most scientists remain skeptical,and it appears that the Sasquatch will not move from the field of legend to that of historical truth until one is produced either dead or alive.

Another distinctive Canadian creature, the Ogopogo, is regarded less seriously. It is a sea serpent supposed to live in Lake Okanagan in British Columbia, and seems to parallel Scotland's famous Loch Ness monster. From early times to the present many people have reported seeing it; originally it was feared, but today it is regarded as a mascot of the region. We also have tales of many other lake monsters—a result of Canada's superabundance of lakes.

Some fairly modern stories—termed urban legends or belief tales—are very popular among teenagers, who sometimes call them 'scary stories'. Most of them are rather gruesome accounts of misadventures, or strange happenings involving ghosts. These tales, usually told as true, flourish at social gatherings—slumber parties, camp-fires, pub meetings, camp reunions—and spread rapidly from one place to another. They are usually said to have happened to someone in the vicinity, but most are known all over North America and some in other parts of the world as well.

Somewhat similar to the urban legends are a group of stories that circulate in summer camps. Each region is likely to have a yarn that spreads from one camp to another, changing a bit as it goes. The counsellors usually tell them, probably partly with the aim of keeping the campers from wandering at night.

Also of interest are personal-experience narratives. These may be accounts of dramatic events or local incidents told by people who were present, or reminiscences about pioneer life—the kind of material often termed oral history. They also include stories about their lives that parents or grandparents relate to the children until they become part of the family tradition.

Folklorists are also beginning to study a group of folktales referred to as monologues or recitations. Until recently these were not considered folktales because they have a set form, but they do circulate orally. Wilfred Wareham, a folklore professor at Memorial University, notes that they have long formed part of the traditional Newfoundland 'times'. Some people are noted for singing or storytelling, and some for 'saying recitations'. Monologue is the general term, but rhymed stories are usually termed recitations.

TALES OF THE NATIVE PEOPLES

The greatest number of traditional tales that have been told in Canada are those of the Indians. All the tribes have their own creation myths—sacred stories telling of their beginnings, usually featuring a culture hero who makes the world from sand brought up out of the primeval waters, and procures light and fire for his people. Many tribes have tales of a flood resembling the Biblical narrative of Noah, and they also tell of other calamities that destroy, or almost destroy, the world by fire, storms, or drought. A widespread story tells how various animals try to free the sun that has been trapped by some hostile power. Other stories explain the characteristics of animals and birds, features of the landscape, and the origin of the sun, moon, seasons, and winds. Tales describing the origin and history of a particular tribe are common.

The culture hero has a different name in different localities. Among the Algonkians of eastern Canada he is Nanabozho and among the Micmacs of the Maritimes he is Glooscap; the plains Indians call him the Old Man, and to the Salish Indians of interior British Columbia he is Coyote; among most of the Pacific Coast tribes he is Raven, and among the Yukon tribes he is Crow.

The culture heroes usually have a dual personality: they are gods who supply various needed things for their people, and they are also tricksters who trick and are tricked. Paul Radin has analysed this duality in *The Trickster: A Study in American Indian Mythology.* The Indians seem to combine in their culture heroes the characteristics Europeans assign to God and Satan. This throws light on the different ways whites and Indians look at the world and themselves. The whites tend to regard the people in their tales as either good or bad, as heroes or villains, but to the Indians the same person can be at times hero, at times trickster, at times victim, thus embodying different aspects of personality in the one character. Also, the Indians see themselves as part of the natural world and kin to the animals, beliefs that shape their tales and their religion.

Many Indian stories resemble familiar European tales. One from the West Coast is reminiscent of 'Hansel and Gretel'; others suggest the classical tales of Phaeton, Cupid and Psyche, and the Swan Maiden. The Indians also borrowed some European wonder tales from the early French settlers: 'The Seven-headed Dragon', 'John the Bear', 'The White Cat', 'Cinderella', and 'The Master Thief'.

As noted earlier, Indian tales were the first collected in Canada, with records dating from the seventeenth century, and expanding into the numerous anthropological works of the late nineteenth and early twentieth centuries. Some of the most important of these are James Teit's *Traditions of the Thompson River Indians of British Columbia* (1898), *Malecite Tales* by William Mechling (1914), *Folk Tales of Salishan and Sahaptin Tribes* edited by Franz Boaz (1917), *Sacred Stories of the Sweet Grass Cree* by Leonard Bloomfield (1930); *Tsimshian Texts* (1902), *Kwakiutl Tales* (1935), and *Kwakiutl Culture as Reflected in Mythology* (1936) by Franz Boas; Marius Barbeau's *Huron and Wyandot Mythology* (1915), *Haida Myths Illustrated in Argillite Carvings* (1953), and *Huron-Wyandot Traditional Narratives in Translations and Native Texts* (1960); and *The Micmac Indians of Eastern Canada* by W.D. and R.S. Wallis (1955). Other anthropologists who recorded Indian tales include Alexander Chamberlain, Diamond Jenness, George Laidlaw, Douglas Leechman, Edward Sapir, Frank Speck, and John Swanton.

The last quarter-century has seen an interesting development. Where earlier native tales were compiled largely by whites, the natives themselves are now publishing stories of their own peoples. Norval Morrisseau's *Legends of My People: The Great Ojibway* (1965) was one of the earliest. Other books by Indians include *The Great Leader of the Ojibway: Mis-Quono-Quab* (1972) by James Redsky, *Cree Legends* (1973) by Beth Ahenakew and Sam Hardlotte, *Tales of Nokomis* (1975) by Petronella Johnston, *Son of Raven, Son of Deer* (1975) by George Clutesi, *Ojibway Heritage* (1976) by Basil Johnston, and *The Raven Steals the Light* (1984) by the famous Haida artist Bill Reid. From the North come *Eskimo Stories—Unikkaatuat* (1969) by Zebedee Nungak and Eugene Arima, Mark Kalluak's *How Kabloonat Became and Other Inuit Legends* (1974), and Leoni Kappi's *Inuit Legends* (1977).

Lillooet Stories (1973) and *Shuswap Stories* (1979), edited by Randy Bouchard and Dorothy Kennedy, are literal transcriptions, and *Tales from the Longhouse* (1973) by Indian children of British

Columbia and *Stories from Pangnirtung* (1976) also represent the authentic oral tradition. Particularly valuable is *Visitors Who Never Left: The Origin of the People of Damelahamid* (1974) in which Kenneth Harris shows the relationship of their myths to the history and culture of his people.

The subject of the Windigo has produced an enormous number of tales. The dread cannibal turns up in early writings of missionaries and explorers, and in more recent articles by anthropologists and Indians. John Robert Colombo has assembled forty-four reports dating from 1636 to 1976 in *Windigo: An Anthology of Fact and Fantastic Fiction.*

Using the tales collected from the Indians as their basis, many writers have published books in which they rewrite or adapt the original stories. These are not considered folktales, which should be reproduced as closely as possible to the way they were told, but some of them have proved popular with children and are noted in an earlier volume in this series, Judith Saltman's *Modern Canadian Children's Books* (1987).

One reason why the Indian tales are usually rewritten is that many of them deal frankly with sexual and scatological themes. Incest, intercourse with animals, and cannibalism are common, as are also accounts of procreation and evacuation. Usually only anthropologists present the tales as they are actually told—and even some of the early collectors felt obliged to render sexual episodes in Latin. Herbert Schwartz's *Tales from the Smokehouse* (1974) is one of the few books intended for the general reader that offers unexpurgated texts.

Penny Petrone and Robin Gedalof McGrath give useful bibliographies of Indian and Inuit tales in *The Oxford Companion to Canadian Literature* (1983); and Robin Gedalof's earlier volumes, *An Annotated Bibliography of Canadian Inuit Literature* and *Paper Stays Put: A Collection of Inuit Writing*, give more extensive listings.

FRENCH-CANADIAN TALES

Next to the native peoples, the French-Canadians have the largest and most interesting body of folktales. The early settlers brought with them most of the old *contes populaires* that circulated in France during the sixteenth and seventeenth centuries, and many of them continue to be told, with their original princely heroes transformed into the *habitant* lad Ti-Jean of rural Quebec. These are supplemented by many legends, often featuring the Devil or such elements of *habitant* folklore as the *feux-follets*, *lutins*, *loups-garous*, and the *chasse-galerie*. Luc Lacourcière's *Catalogue raisonné du conte populaire français en Amerique du nord* lists the multitude of French tales in North America.

The important French-Canadian collections appear in French and there are few literal translations. Most of the English versions of the tales are rewritten or adapted, and, like the rewritten Indian tales, some are noted in Judith Saltman's *Modern Canadian Children's Books*. A few early authors writing in English give their versions of stories they heard—like LeMoine, Beaugrand, and Greenough mentioned in Chapter 2. Beaugrand gives an early description of the flying canoe, one of the most colourful Canadian legends. In an introductory note he writes:

> The story is based on a popular belief from the time of the coureurs de bois and voyageurs of the northwest. The shantyboys continued the tradition and it is essentially in the river parishes of the St Lawrence that the legends of the chasse-galerie are known. I have met more than one old voyageur who claimed to have seen the bark canoes travel in the air filled with the possessed, going to see their sweethearts, under the sponsorship of Beelzebub.

W.P. Greenough gives a good account of his guide, Nazaire, whom he calls 'a prince among story-tellers'. Nazaire told many tall tales about a famous hunter called Dalbec, and he also told lengthy *contes*. As Greenough notes:

> I have heard a good raconteur go on two hours with one of his stories, and there are some stories that occupy two evenings in the telling. They are mostly fairy stories in which there is almost always a *'jeune prince'*

and a *'jeune princesse'*. Where they come from I do not know, but a few are from the *Thousand and One Nights*.

Later books that adapt familiar tales are Paul Wallace's *Baptiste Larocque: Legends of French Canada* (1923), E.C. Woodley's *Legends of French Canada* (1931), Natalie Carlson's *The Talking Cat and Other Stories of French Canada* (1952), and Hazel Boswell's *Legends of Quebec* (1966).

Alice Kane translated a more recent and more elaborate book, Claude Aubry's *The Magic Fiddler and Other Legends of French Canada*, which has imaginative illustrations by Saul Field. The title story retells one of the most famous French-Canadian legends, usually titled 'Rose Latulippe' or 'The Devil at a Dance'. It first appeared in print in 1837 when Philippe Aubert de Gaspé published it as 'L'Étranger'—The Stranger—attributing it to an old farmer. He may have originated the name Rose Latulippe for the girl who danced with the Devil, but the story was already widespread along the St Lawrence—variants locate it in half a dozen different communities.

Aubry's book also presents one of the few English accounts of 'La Corriveau' which, as he notes, is 'without doubt one of the most macabre of our legends and moreover it is one that has its basis in real life'. Luc Lacoucière has studied the stories linked to La Corriveau—an eighteenth-century woman of Saint-Vallier who was sentenced to be executed for poisoning her two husbands and was then hung up in an iron cage. Her ghost is said to have terrorized the settlers in the region over the next century. She appears in fictionalized accounts like Aubert de Gaspe's *Les Anciens Canadiens* (1863) and Gilbert Parker's *Seats of the Mighty* (1896).

Many of the books that adapt French-Canadian tales are based on Marius Barbeau's collections. One of the best of these, *The Golden Phoenix and Other French-Canadian Fairy Tales*—which is really Michael Hornyasky's retelling of stories in Barbeau's *Les Contes du grand'pere Sept-heures* (12 vols)—is a good sampling of the old European tales preserved in Quebec. Writing 'About the Stories', Dr Barbeau notes:

Folk tales like 'The Golden Phoenix', 'The Princess of Tomboso', and others here belong to all European nations more or less. Yet in their present form they are French-Canadian from the lower St Lawrence River. They were brought over from France to America by the early colonists three hundred years ago, and are part of the spoken traditions of the country. . . . I collected them at first hand from *raconteurs* in the course of many years; in their authentic text they are now filed away in the collections of the National Museum of Canada. They are presented here in a polished retelling by Michael Hornyansky. . . .

In *The Tree of Dreams,* a book featuring legends, Dr Barbeau writes:

Some of these legends are very brief, almost inarticulate; others are lengthy and replete with colourful details. Here the folk paint themselves as they are, with humour or in the grip of fear. Among the best in the Quebec repertory we count: The Handsome Dancer (or Rose Latulippe), The Black Hen (about a soul for sale at the crossroads), The Witch Canoe (La Chasse-Gallery), The Black Horse (the Devil helps to build a parish church), The Buried Treasures of Portneuf County, The Church Bell of Caughnawaga, Père de la Brosse, and the Great Serpent of Lorette (or Wolverine. . .

The same themes turn up in many other collections.

Literal translations of French-Canadian tales are scarce. The largest collection is Gerald Thomas's *Les Deux Traditions: Le conte populaire chez les Franco-Terreneuviens*—tales he collected in Newfoundland for which he gives both the original texts and literal translations; a few were told in English. *Folktales from Western Newfoundland* collected by Marie-Angélique Desplanques presents French-Canadian tales that Angela Kerfont told in English. In *Tales of French Canada* I provide translations of a representative group chosen largely from Barbeau's collections in the *Journal of American Folklore*, and Margaret Low translates seven collected by Luc Lacourcière for Richard Dorson's *Folktales of the World*. Dorson himself collected and published tales he heard from French Canadians living in Michigan's Upper Peninsula, some of which involve Joe Mufferaw.

Mufferaw is a popular French-Canadian figure featured in numerous tall tales. Unlike Paul Bunyan, he has a historical basis in a famous athlete whose career Benjamin Sulte described in *His-*

toire de Jos. Montferrand: L'Athlète canadien, but the tales told of him are the typical exaggerations associated with characters like Baron Munchausen in Europe and Bunyan in America. He is also known in English Canada: Bernie Bedore has popularized him in a number of books, and Jeanne Pattison collected various anecdotes in northern Ontario, where people say of anything strange, 'It must have been Joe Mufferaw.' George Monteiro discusses the relationship between Joseph Montferrand and Joe Mufferaw.

Folklorists have begun to analyse some of the French-Canadian tales. Several volumes of Laval's *Archives de Folklore* are detailed studies of particular folktale types. Articles in English include John Bemer's report on 'Nineteenth Century French-Canadian Folk Tales' and Margaret Low's discussion of 'The Motif of the External Soul in French-Canadian Folktales'. Gerald Thomas writes of the French Newfoundlanders' folktales and folktale style, and Geraldine Barter of their folktales in relation to children. In 'Participant Reaction, Truth, and Belief in the Legend Process' Gary Butler quotes taped conversations among French-speaking Newfoundlanders to show that their discussion of legends often reveals various degrees of belief or non-belief.

TALES OF ANGLO-CANADIANS

Among Canadians other than native or French-speaking, tales seem to have been less popular than songs, although this may be partly because folklorists have been less diligent in collecting them. The largest number of tales from the British Isles noted in Canada came with the Gaelic-speaking Scots; these are discussed in the following section. To date very few books are devoted entirely to tales that were told in English. One of the few is *Eight Folktales from Miramichi As Told by Wilmot MacDonald,* collected by Helen Creighton and Edward Ives. Wilmot MacDonald first became known as a fine traditional singer; then Creighton and Ives discovered that he was also a master of the folktale. His songs came from his family, but his tales he learned in the lumbercamps— probably from Irish or French Canadians, for most are common in Irish and French tradition. Almost all are supernatural, the best known being 'Jack and the Beanstalk', while another resembles 'The Dragon Slayer'.

Carole Spray's *Will o' the Wisp: Folk Tales and Legends of New Brunswick* has a remarkable cross-section of different story types. Her introduction gives an interesting account of her collecting experiences along with samples of New Brunswick's varied lore. The tales include several international *Märchen*; east-coast legends like 'The Burning Ship', 'The Dungarvon Whooper', and 'The Man Who Plucked the Gorbey'; local ghost stories; tall tales; and a couple of examples of verses given as recitations.

Some general folklore collections from the east coast include important sections on tales: Fauset's *Folklore from Nova Scotia* drawn largely from blacks, Mary Fraser's *Folklore of Nova Scotia* drawn from Scots and Acadians, and Helen Creighton's *Folklore of Lunenburg County* drawn largely from people of German ancestry. Creighton has a group of amusing anecdotes and tall tales, along with two longer stories and some legends, and Fraser gives a number of supernatural legends. Fauset's collection is the most varied—he lists *Märchen*, Animal Tales, Pat and Mike Stories and Tall Tales, Witch, Devil, and Ghost Tales, Tales of Treasure, Preacher Tales and Other Neighborhood Stories—172 altogether—and he also has some cante fables—narratives including verses—and riddle stories.

Helen Creighton's *Bluenose Ghosts* concentrates on a specialized type: tales of the supernatural. She has heard a great many stories about ghosts, haunted houses, poltergeists, phantom ships, buried gold, and witches, and her narrative indicates that many Nova Scotians firmly believe in such tales. Mary Fraser's *Folklore of Nova Scotia* also has many short accounts of the second sight, forerunners, ghosts, witches, fairy lore, and buried treasure. Creighton's *Bluenose Magic* has supernatural legends and personal experience narratives, but it is perhaps more relevant to the chapter on superstitions. L.W. Janes compiled a smaller collection, *A Treasury of Newfoundland Stories*, from items submitted by listeners to a radio program. Other legends and anecdotes occur in some historical and autobiographical books.

Herbert Halpert's more recent *A Folklore Sampler from the*

Maritimes presents a group of folk narratives along with a useful 'Bibliographical Essay on the Folktale in English'. He notes:

> This chapter has a surprisingly varied collection of folk narratives con-
> tributed by Mount Allison students: didactic stories for children; an un-
> usual Canadian-Italian *Märchen*; a Canadian-Polish grandfather's
> personal-experience narrative; a Cree Indian myth; a New Brunswick
> trickster cycle; Maritime supernatural legends; and so on.

The main tale publications from western Canada concentrate on one particular type: the tall tale. In the 1940s the American folklorist Robert Gard organized the Alberta Folklore and Local History Project, out of which came a short-lived *Alberta Folklore Quarterly* and his book *Johnny Chinook: Tall Tales and True from the Canadian West*. During the Second World War Dr Halpert was stationed for a time in Calgary, where he collected 'Tall Tales and Other Yarns from Calgary, Alberta', and more recently Michael Taft collected *Tall Tales of British Columbia*. All of these, and several other collections, give yarns that dwell on huge animals and insects, strange hunting and fishing adventures, and extremes of weather. They tell how they used to hitch up mosquitoes and plough with them; how a man shot at a goose that was flying so high it didn't come down till the next morning; how sounds freeze in the winter and thaw out in the spring; how one summer it was so hot that a dog was chasing a cat and both were walking.

While many of the tall tales are international, some reflect aspects of Canada. In Alberta they tell many stories about the chinook—how it makes the snow melt so fast that a man in a bobsleigh driving east finds his front runners on snow and his back ones in mud; and about a winter in Banff so cold that ice froze on the Hot Springs pool and when a boy's feet went through the ice his foot was scalded. In Ontario's 'Muddy York' a man sank in the mud and when his friends tried to pull him out he asked them to wait till he got his feet out of the stirrups. In Nova Scotia they tell of a boy who left a toy boat on the shore, and when he went for it in the spring it had grown into a four-masted schooner.

Many tall tales are attached to particular characters, some legendary and some real. Ontario and Quebec have their stories of Joe

Mufferaw, almost every province has some Paul Bunyan yarns, andNewfoundlanders tell stories of Joey Smallwood. In addition to these, various stories feature less well-known local characters who have become the focus for jokes and anecdotes. In Alberta Dave McDougall is mentioned in Gard's *Johnny Chinook* and Halpert's 'Tall Tales from Calgary'. In New Brunswick Carole Spray tells some stories of an old trapper named Geordie Brown; in Nova Scotia, Fauset reports stories about Jim Grey, who is portrayed as a foolish yokel; in Quebec's Eastern Townships Margaret Bennett Knight heard anecdotes about the outlaw Donald Morrison; and in the Ottawa Valley Sheldon Posen heard jokes about the Couvrettes.

There are also some political jokes. For example, in Nova Scotia they tell of a Conservative member of Parliament visiting a Liberal, who announces, 'My beautiful Angora has just had five little Conservative kittens.' The next time he visits the Liberal he is shown 'Five little Liberal kittens'. When he says, 'I thought you said they were Conservatives', the Liberal replies, 'So they were, but now they've got their eyes open.'

A few articles explore particular tales or legends. Dr Halpert amasses international versions of two stories—'The Cut-Off Head Frozen On' and 'Ireland, Sheila, and Newfoundland'—popular in Newfoundland. 'The Cut-Off Head' is an international tall tale that first appeared in a sixteenth-century German joke book and was heard and recorded in Newfoundland as early as 1795. The story— told with many different details—is about a man whose head is cut off and then put back on his shoulders. There it freezes in place, remaining until he comes into a warm room and thaws out. The other article traces many references to 'Sheila' or 'Sheelagh', who is somehow linked to St Patrick—she is often referred to as his wife. March 18 was said to be her day, and she is associated with snow storms or bad weather. Snow just after St Patrick's Day is called 'Sheila's gown' and inspired a couplet:

> Patty walks the shores around
> And Sheila follows in a long white gown.

Another legend that has been popular in New Brunswick and

Maine lumbercamps tells of 'The Man Who Plucked the Gorbey'. Edward Ives collected over a hundred versions, some of which mention the person supposed to have committed the act and suffered appropriate retribution—usually he wakes up the next morning to find himself completely bald.

Because American folklorists termed Paul Bunyan 'fakelore'— meaning that the tales about him were created by writers rather than told by the folk—I wrote 'In Defence of Paul Bunyan', showing that oral tales about him had circulated in the lumberwoods before the printed stories that prompted the fakelore designation. In the *Canadian Forum* Dr John Robins told of hearing Bunyan yarns in Northern Ontario between 1900 and 1909, before the first 'fakelore' tales appeared.

Gerald Thomas has assembled a collection of 'Newfie Jokes', and Robert Klymasz describes and analyses 'Ethnic Jokes in Canada Today', citing examples from seven different joke cycles directed against the English, French, Ukrainians, Jews, Newfoundlanders, Italians, and Icelanders. Many such jokes are interchangeable, but some crystallize popular notions about certain ethnic groups—for example: to kill five thousand Ukrainians at once you plant mushrooms on the freeway; to break up an Italian wedding you say 'The cement's here'. Dr Klymasz finds some merit in this unpleasant type of story, suggesting that such jokes may heighten ethnic sensitivity and help to revitalize the ethnic community.

Susan Smith collected some of the urban belief legends so popular among teenagers, showing that typical modern ones like 'The Hook', 'The Boy-Friend's Death', and 'The Baby-Sitter' are very widespread. 'The Baby-Sitter' is a typical example. Parents go out for an evening, leaving a baby-sitter in charge of their infant. Later the mother phones to see if everything is all right. The baby-sitter says everything is fine; she has just put the turkey in the oven. This puzzles the mother because she didn't have a turkey. The couple return home to find the baby-sitter, high on drugs, has put the baby in the oven.

Judy Wagner found similar ones among girls in a junior high school in Manitoba. Children in public schools also know many such stories, including some older ones like 'The Vanishing

Hitchhiker' and others related to an ancient international tale of a dead lover who returns to his sweetheart as a ghost and is later found in his grave with her handkerchief wound around his head. Three of these from Toronto children appear in *Tales Told in Canada*.

Certain legends told in summer camps are more distinctive. They resemble the urban legends except that those are international while the camp legends are usually peculiar to a particular region. But most of them fall into a similar pattern, telling of violent accidents or gruesome deaths, and they are always said to have happened in the particular locality where they are told. The most widespread one in Ontario features a character called Anson Minor, or some variation of that name, who gets his foot caught in a tractor, develops gangrene, and dies—or sometimes goes insane and murders his wife. He is said to return to the camp area on the anniversary of his accident, dragging his leg and carrying a green lantern. In Manitoba they tell about Old Man Gimli who is supposed to have drowned; they say his ghost chopped off the fingers of a young boy living in his house, and anyone staying there at night hears the sound of chopping and screaming.

The publications devoted to tales should shortly be augmented by two major volumes. Herbert Halpert and J.D.A. Widdowson are compiling a collection from Newfoundland, and Helen Creighton has been preparing for publication the tales she collected in Nova Scotia.

Oral histories have become very popular recently. Foremost among the recorders are Bill McNeil with *Voice of the Pioneer* drawn from his CBC radio program 'Fresh Air', and Barry Broadfoot with his series including *The Lost Years*, *The War Years*, and *The Pioneer Years*. Heather Robertson's *Salt of the Earth* and Moira Farrow's *Nobody Here But Us: Pioneers of the North* are based largely on old-timers' reminiscences, and there are many similar books. In 'The Family Album' Pauline Greenhill discusses a special type: family narratives inspired by photograph albums.

Folklorists are now studying the contexts in which tales are told. For example, Wayne Fanning discusses 'Storytelling at a Nova Scotia General Store', and Martin Laba writes of 'The Jokes and Joke-Telling of Jim Dawe', an eleven-year-old boy who developed his narrative skills by telling jokes in his family living-room. Gerald Pocius presents an extended study of one joke-teller, Frank Williams, describing how he learned jokes, hearing some as a child from older men and his schoolmates, others in the army, and more later when working on building projects, as a fisherman, and as a garage attendant and handyman. He analyses the situations in which Frank tells his jokes, his reasons for telling them, and their effect on his audiences. Pocius urges folklorists to study folklore in contemporary society rather than concentrating on the past.

A problem that confronts folklorists preparing oral tales for publication is how best to present them. They recognize that tales should not be rewritten or have anything added, that all the words should come from the original story-teller. However, most editors make minor changes when publishing stories. They often eliminate false starts and repetitive words, particularly phrases like 'he said' and 'she said' that sound natural when heard but clutter up a printed narrative. They have to decide whether to reproduce dialect and mispronunciations, and what to do about obvious slips such as changes in the names of characters. Drs Halpert and Widdowson discuss this problem in 'Folk-Narrative Performance and Tape Transcription: Theory versus Practice', showing that exact transcriptions are rare.

TALES OF OTHER ETHNIC GROUPS

As mentioned earlier, the largest number of tales from the British Isles noted in Canada came with the Gaelic-speaking Scots. Three fine collections exist in the original Gaelic and in English translations: *Luirgean Eachainn Nill: Folktales from Cape Breton* told by Hector Campbell and translated by Margaret MacDonell and John Shaw; *Tales until Dawn: The World of a Cape Breton Gaelic Story-Teller* by Joe Neil MacNeil, translated by John Shaw; and Calum MacLeod's *Stories from Nova Scotia*, his translation of his Gaelic collection.

The first two volumes feature exceptionally fine traditional Gaelic storytellers. Margaret MacDonell has described Hector Campbell (1888-1975), who lived in Inverness County, as 'one of the finest traditional Gaelic storytellers in Cape Breton during our time'. She tells us that his ancestors emigrated from South Uist in 1823 and that 'In his home, as in almost every other Highland home in Cape Breton, there was Gaelic singing, fiddling, and piping.' Campbell learned his stories mainly from an older Gaelic storyteller, Hector MacEachen, who died in the mid-1920s. They are largely international types—some listed in the Aarne-Thompson index as 'The Rich and the Poor Peasant', 'The Clever Peasant Girl', 'The Brave Little Tailor', and 'The Table, the Ass and the Stick'. Others describe the tricks of Mac Crùslain, a well-known character in Highland Gaelic tradition, and the adventures of the Fenian hero Ceudach.

Joe Neil MacNeil, born in 1908, is one of the few active tradition-bearers in Cape Breton today. His fame has spread beyond his home community—he has told his Gaelic tales at the last two Storytellers' Festivals in Toronto. The gems of his collection are some of the ancient Fenian tales recounting the adventures of the legendary warrior Fionn MacCumhail. The variety of the stories is suggested by such intriguing titles as 'The Woman Who Was Awarded a Pair of Shoes by the Devil', 'The Night It Rained Porridge', and 'Angus MacIsaac's Trip to the Moon'. The tales of both Campbell and McNeill spring from the rich Highland stock that incorporates more than stories. Joe Neil cites not only tales but proverbs, children's rhymes, games, and superstitions that he knew.

Calum MacLeod's collection comes from the same area but is drawn from different sources. In addition to stories he collected and translated, he includes tales from two unpublished manuscripts, some of which are unusual and striking. They tell of fairies and changelings, and describe the experiences of early immigrants, legendary events, and famous Nova Scotia characters like Black Neil and Angus MacAskill, the Cape Breton giant. MacAskill, known as Big Boy, is said to have been seven feet nine inches tall, weighing some five hundred pounds. They tell how he hauled a tree from the woods that oxen could not move, and how he gave a stranger directions by lifting his plough and pointing with it.

Two important articles also present Gaelic tales in English. Mac-Edward Leach's 'Celtic Tales from Cape Breton' draws on the same sources as the books cited above, but James Teit's 'Water-Beings in Shetlandic Folk-Lore' taps a different source. Instead of the *Märchen* of the Scottish Highlands this article notes the many sea legends of Scotland's northern islands—about mermen and mermaids, silkies and sea trolls, sea monsters and sea phantoms, sea witches and water horses—remembered in British Columbia. Still another article, the inaccurately titled 'Scottish Myths from Ontario', describes the ghost stories and other supernatural legends that C.A. Fraser heard from third-generation Highland Scots in the nineteenth century.

Groups other than British and French brought numerous tales from their homelands; many have been collected but only a few are published. One of the most important books is Robert Klymasz's *Folk Narrative Among Ukrainian-Canadians in Western Canada*, tales he collected for his doctoral dissertation. By showing what changes took place in the traditional Ukrainian folktales some eighty years after the storytellers began settling on the prairies, Dr Klymasz throws light on the factors that cause changes in folklore and the trends these changes reflect. Earlier collections of Ukrainian tales in English translation appear in some of Jaroslav Rudnyc'kyj's publications.

André E. Elbaz's *Folktales of the Canadian Sephardim* comes from a smaller ethnic group—the Moroccan Jewish immigrants whose heritage stems from the Spanish Jews who settled in Africa when they were expelled from Spain in 1492. Of the eighty tales Dr Elbaz collected and translated, the largest number describe the exploits of miracle-working rabbis, indicating the popularity of the cult of saints. Others concern Biblical heroes and harmful spirits known as *djun*; there are also a few fairy tales, and many stories about extraordinary personal experiences.

Those two books are the only ones devoted entirely to tales from the Canadian Centre for Folk Culture Studies, which has tales from many ethnic groups, although some appear in the Mercury publications cited later in the chapter on folklife. Fauset's *Folklore from Nova Scotia* contains a good sampling of tales from black informants. Representative tales from sixteen ethnic groups appear in Fowke's *Tales Told in Canada*, and Kay Stone's *Prairie Folklore* includes a number of Polish and Russian tales.

An important article showing how storytelling can be used to affect social situations is Barbara Kirchenblatt-Gimblett's 'A Parable in Context: A Social Interactional Analysis of Storytelling Performance'. Parables—didactic stories told to illustrate a moral—are popular in Jewish folklore because of the rabbinical tradition, and Dr Kirshenblatt-Gimblett shows how they can be used to ease tension and resolve conflicts.

LITERARY FORMS

Related to folktales are many Canadian novels and other literary forms that make use of various kinds of folklore. William Kirby's *The Golden Dog* uses the legend of the Golden Dog, and Aubert de Gaspé's *Les Anciens Canadiens* uses the legend of La Corriveau, among others. In *Mountain Cloud* Dr Barbeau bases his story of an Indian brave on the ritual and customs of the West Coast Indians, and Emily Carr depicts them vividly in *Klee Wyck*. Thomas Chandler Haliburton borrows traditional New England yarns for his books about the Yankee peddler Sam Slick, and Bob Edwards localizes and embroiders various tall tales in his newspaper the *Calgary Eye-Opener*. Sheila Watson uses trickster myths in *The Double Hook*. James Reaney uses many forms of folklore in his poems and plays, notably in *Sticks and Stones*, the first of his Donnelly trilogy, where a Canadian version of the old ballad of 'John Barleycorn' forms a motif running through the drama.

Margaret Laurence had a lively interest in folklore, using songs, tales, superstitions, and children's rhymes in her novels. The titles of *A Bird in the House* and *The Diviners* come from folk beliefs, and *The Diviners* includes cowboy songs, children's taunts, old Scottish songs, and some Métis songs that she composed, using folk patterns. Roch Carrier and Antonine Maillet also have many folklore elements in their novels. Margaret Atwood uses two *Golden Phoenix* stories, plus one other fairy story, in *Surfacing*.

Robert Service's verses have traditional patterns that reflect the Yukon's gold-rush atmosphere, and one of them engendered a folk version—'When the Ice Worms Nest Again'. Isabella Valancy

Crawford's poem 'Malcolm's Katie' has many of the qualities of the old ballads. Pauline Johnson's 'The Legend of the Qu'Appelle' is close to folklore, and Anne Wilkinson uses traditional echoes to achieve a modern effect in such poems as 'Dirge', 'Christmas Eve', and 'A Folk Tale'. Several poems by Canadian poets acquired tunes and passed into oral tradition—notably W.H. Drummond's 'The Wreck of the *Julie Plante*', C.D. Shanly's 'The Walker of the Snow', and Fred Coyne's 'Ballad of the Raftmen'.

Novels that illustrate the folklife of various ethnic groups include Louis Hémon's *Maria Chapdelaine* and Hugh MacLennan's *Two Solitudes* (French); Ralph Connor's *The Man from Glengarry* (Scottish); James Houston's *The White Dawn* (Inuit); Laura Salverson's *The Viking Heart* (Icelandic); Rudy Wiebe's *Peace Shall Destroy Many* and Ann Konrad's *The Blue Glass* (Mennonite); Adele Wiseman's *The Sacrifice* and Fredelle Maynard's *Raisins and Almonds* (Jewish); and Patrick Slater's *The Yellow Briar* (Irish). Many novels depict folklife aspects of pioneer days: Mary Hiemstra's *Gully Farm,* Frederick Philip Grove's *The Settlers of the Marsh*, and Wallace Stegner's *Wolf Willow*, to mention a few.

Folklorists are beginning to study the way folklore is incorporated in Canadian fiction. Among recent articles are Roberta Buchanan's 'Some Aspects of the Use of Folklore in Harold Horwood's *Tomorrow Will Be Sunday*', Joyce Coldwell's 'Folklore as Fiction: The Writings of L.M. Montgomery', Edith Fowke's ' "Blind MacNair": A Canadian Short Story and Its Sources', Terry Goldie's 'Folklore in the Canadian Novel', Clara Murphy's 'The Use of Fairy Lore in Margaret Duley's Novel *Cold Pastoral*', and Nancy Watson's '*Rockbound*, by Frank Parker Day: Novel and Ethnography'.

4

SONGS, MUSIC, AND DANCE

The first songs sung in Canada were those of the native peoples to whom music was an essential part of their lives. An early collector, Alice Fletcher, wrote: 'In his sports, in his games, when he wooed, and when he mourned . . . the Indian sang in every experience of life from the cradle to the grave.' Most native songs were short and made up of either a few words repeated many times or of meaningless syllables. Usually they formed part of a story or a ceremony: there were prayers for rain, warriors' songs, hunting songs, dirges for the dead, songs of welcome, and chants of victory. Most of them sound strange to non-natives who are used to different harmonic patterns.

Collectors have noted an enormous number of Indian and Inuit songs, and most are available in translation. John Robert Colombo has performed a remarkable service by compiling two extensive anthologies—*Poems of the Inuit* and *Songs of the Indians*—that survey the songs found in the numerous collections, with informative comments and useful bibliographies. Also useful are the articles on 'Indians' and 'Inuit' in the *Encyclopedia of Music in Canada*. Collectors—Gertrude Kurath, Laura Boulton, Kenneth Peacock, and Ida Halpern—have produced records of native songs that give a much better impression of them than the printed texts do alone.

FRENCH-CANADIAN SONGS

The pioneer settlers of New France brought with them the thousands of songs that were then being sung in Europe, and made them part of their everyday life. In Marius Barbeau's words, 'Threshing and winnowing in the barns moved to the rhythm of work tunes, as did spinning, weaving, and beating the wash by the fireside.' Barbeau notes that these French songs collected in Canada represent every type—chronicles, canticles, love lyrics, shepherd tunes, workaday songs, dances, rigmaroles, drinking chants, lullabies, carols. Many were a legacy from the *jongleurs* of medieval France and have remained unchanged since the sixteenth or seventeenth centuries. Even the *chansons* reflecting the artificial court life survived intact in the somewhat incongruous setting of rural Quebec. The pioneer clearing his land with an axe sang of knights and princesses, and the *coureurs de bois* made the woods echo to the strains of a ballad about three damsels in beautiful old Rochelle.

The *coureurs de bois* and fur traders adapted the ancient ballads to the rhythm of their paddles. One old French song about a king's son who goes hunting and kills a white duck—known as 'Trois beaux canards'—has over a hundred Canadian versions, the best known being 'En roulant ma boule' and 'V'là l'bon vent'. The simple story remains constant, but the tunes and the refrains vary. Similarly, one of French-Canada's best-loved songs, 'A la claire fontaine', about a lad whose sweetheart spurns him for failing to give her roses, has several different forms. The *canadiens* also set new words to old tunes: for example, the paddling song 'Youpe, Youpe, sur la rivière'—about a *habitant* lad who goes to call on his girl and is rebuffed for being too fickle—goes to the tune of the old French song 'Le p'ti bois d' l'ail'; and the well-loved lament of 'Un canadien errant', dating from the Rebellions of 1837, is set to the folk tune 'Si tu te mets anguille'.

Only a comparatively few *canadien* songs are completely new, and most are about the *coureurs de bois* and the *forestiers*. The earliest French song composed in Canada is probably 'La complainte de Cadieux' (also known as 'Petit rocher'), based on one of the ear liest and most widespread native French-Canadian legends. Cadieux, a *coureur de bois*, is said to have died in 1709; by 1800 almost every *voyageur* knew his story. When an Iroquois war party threatened an Algonkin village, Cadieux sent the families down the Grand River in canoes while he and a companion held off the Iroquois. He succeeded, but then died of hunger and exhaustion, first writing his song on bark that is said to have been found on his breast.

Of the many French-Canadian song collections, only a few exist in English translation. The most important are Marius Barbeau's *Folk Songs of French Canada, Folk Songs of Old Quebec*, and *Jongleur Songs of Old Quebec*, which has an extensive bibliography. Fowke and Johnston's *Folk Songs of Quebec* gives singable translations for some of the well-known French songs. Most of the other collections—by Luc Lacourcière and François Brassard in Quebec, Père Anselme Chiasson and Frère Daniel Boudreau, Charlotte Cormier, Donald Deschênes, Georges Arsenault, and Ronald Labelle in Acadia, and Germain Lemieux in Ontario—appear only in French. So do many studies of particular songs and analyses of their relation to French-Canadian culture. Two in English are Gary Butler's 'Folksong Performance in French-Newfoundland Culture', discussing the practices of the singer Josephine Costard, and Mary-Ann Griggs' *The Folk-Song in the Traditional Society of French-Canada*.

Some of the distinctive French-Canadian songs of the Métis are available in translation, notably in *Songs of Old Manitoba* by Margaret MacLeod (1877-1966). The most interesting are by the prairie bard Pierre Falcon (1793-1876), whose 'La Chanson de la Grenouillère'—describing the Battle of Seven Oaks in which the Métis under Cuthbert Grant defeated a band of Red River settlers led by Governor Semple—is best known. Barbara Cass-Beggs collected and published *Seven Métis Songs*, including two said to have been composed by Louis Riel.

The *Encyclopedia of Music in Canada* gives a good survey of French-Canadian music. Those wishing to explore it in more detail may refer to Conrad Laforte's extensive six-volume *Catalogue folklorique de la chanson française*.

ANGLO-CANADIAN SONGS

Somewhat later than the French, the early English, Scottish, and Irish settlers brought with them the ancient ballads, broadsides, and love songs current in the British Isles, and handed them down from one generation to the next, providing the largest part of our Anglo-Canadian folksong heritage.

For a considerable period after Anglo-Canadian folklore began to develop, collectors concentrated on folksongs more than on any other genre, with the result that this aspect is much better documented than any other. This emphasis is rather difficult to explain, for stories were probably as common as songs; perhaps collectors found the songs more attractive because they combine the features of both poetry and music. Also, major international folksong studies served to emphasize their importance. Francis James Child's five-volume *The English and Scottish Popular Ballads* (1882-98) and, nearly a century later, Bertrand Bronson's four-volume *The Traditional Tunes of the Child Ballads* (1959-72) focused attention on the old ballads.

At least seventy-seven of the famous 305 English and Scottish ballads Dr Child catalogued have survived in Canada, some in better versions than in their homelands. They are simple dramatic stories plunging right into the action, leaping from scene to scene and lingering on the dramatic parts. Their most characteristic feature is repetition, usually in threes, and they use many 'commonplaces'—words and phrases like 'milk-white steed', 'lily-white hands', 'tinkling on the ring', 'little penknife'—that float from one ballad to another. They are completely objective—one critic says it is as if the story was telling itself. They feature kings and queens, knights and ladies; many have supernatural elements; and the most famous tell tragic stories of love that leads to death. As David Buchan shows in *The Ballad and the Folk*, they are carefully structured, with parallel and framing stanzas, and a chiastic pattern that applies to stanzas, characters, and action.

The most popular ballad in Canada, as throughout the English-speaking world, is 'the little Scotch song of Barbary Allen' that

Samuel Pepys praised. Next in popularity is the ancient international tale of 'Lady Isabel and the Elf Knight', in which a woman
thwarts a suitor who has killed six other maidens and plans to kill
her. After these come 'The Cruel Mother', 'The Gypsy Laddie',
'Lord Randall', 'The Sweet Trinity', and 'Young Beichan'—all of
which have been collected at least twenty-five times. Some of the
old ballads preserved in Canada have been more popular here than
in the United States, and Newfoundlanders favour more supernatural songs—like 'Sweet William's Ghost', 'The Unquiet
Grave', and 'Fair Margaret and Sweet William'—than people elsewhere in North America.

More numerous than the old ballads are the somewhat later British
broadsides—songs originally printed on single sheets—that stroll-
ing balladmongers sold on the streets or from stalls at country fairs.
Using tried and true formulas, hack journalists churned out most of
them for money. They weren't so much composed as patched
together from well-known elements—the same story told again and
again in slightly different forms. Instead of the dramatic 'leaping
and lingering' of the Child ballads, they begin at the beginning and
follow through to the end, giving all the details; instead of lords and
ladies they feature soldiers and sailors, merchants and merchants'
daughters; they make little use of repetition; and where the older
ballads tell the story objectively, without praise or blame, the broadsides are subjective, often told in the first person, and frequently
end with a moral.

Canadian pioneers brought over hundreds of these ballads and
lovingly sang them, feeling that printed ballads were better than the
ones they got from their grandfathers. Some were improved
through oral tradition, and the folk tended to select the better ones
to sing. Maritime and Ontario singers remember tales of pirates
('Captain Kidd' and 'Kelly the Pirate') and highwaymen ('Bren-
nan on the Moor' and 'Bold Jack Donaghue') and famous battles
('The Plains of Waterloo' and 'The Heights of Alma'). They
delight particularly in the many romantic tales of true love ('Burns
and His Highland Mary' and 'The Lass of Glenshee') and false love
('Rogers the Miller' and 'The Butcher Boy'). They dwell on sad
stories of girls seduced and deserted ('The Dawning of the Day'

and 'The Nightingale') and of others seduced and murdered ('The Cruel Ship's Carpenter' and 'The Wexford Girl').

The most popular of all ballads were the numerous broadsides that tell the unlikely story of a man—usually a soldier or sailor—who returns to his sweetheart after seven years' absence; when she does not recognize him, he tells her that her lover is dead; she proclaims her continued loyalty, and he then reveals his identity, usually by producing his half of a ring they had divided between them. This simple story, often referred to as 'The Broken Ring', was repeated in dozens of different ballads, of which the most common are 'A Fair Maid Walked in Her Father's Garden' and 'The Dark-Eyed Sailor'. In several of these the lover is said to have died at Waterloo.

This, of course, is one of the world's oldest and most popular plots, retold again and again, from the classic tale of Ulysses, through the medieval romance of 'Hind Horn', to the modern ballad of 'The Cowboy's Wedding Ring'. Its amazing popularity in Canada throws light on our pioneer society in which lovers were often parted when the man came to the New World, or went off to gold rushes in California or the Klondike, or to the Prairies to take up a homestead, leaving his sweetheart behind. Pioneer society naturally prized loyalty and feared infidelity, so it found the story of the faithful sweetheart reassuring.

In addition to the many popular and broadsides ballads, the British colonists brought with them many beautiful love songs. As Northrop Frye comments in *The Bush Garden*: 'The unpredictable genius of oral transmission occasionally turns into a breath-taking beauty, as in the last line of:

> She's like the swallow that flies so high,
> She's like the river that never runs dry,
> She's like the sunshine on the lee shore,
> I love my love and love is no more.'

So many songs and ballads about love came over from Britain that very few were composed in Canada. Our native songs for the most part deal with sterner topics.

SONGS COMPOSED IN CANADA

At least three-quarters of the traditional songs sung in Canada came originally from the Old World, but it is the smaller number composed in this country that best reflect our culture and throw light on our history. To hear a ballad composed at the time of an event gives a more vivid impression of that event than many pages of print. Few of our native Canadian songs rate high as poetry: by literary standards they are inferior to the old British ballads that have been polished by their passage through the centuries. But those that have survived appeal to ordinary Canadians, who continue to sing them because they say something the people feel is worth remembering.

In style the native North American ballads are akin to the broadsides; but where most broadsides are fictional and deal mainly with love, the native ballads are more realistic, dealing with the lives of fishermen and cowboys and lumbermen, and with actual murders, tragedies, and disasters. To generalize, the Child ballads may be compared to plays, the broadsides to Harlequin romances, and the native North American ballads to newspaper reports.

An early ballad, 'Brave Wolfe', telling of Wolfe's victory and death on the Plains of Abraham, is among the finest of our native compositions. Elisabeth Greenleaf, who collected it in Newfoundland, notes: 'This martial and moving song burst on us suddenly in the midst of an evening devoted mainly to the woes of the love-lorn. Its stately measures linger in one's memory, with some of its striking lines.'

The United Empire Loyalists brought some songs to Canada, like 'Revolutionary Tea', which describes the American Revolution as a scrap between mother and daughter. The Canadians' pride in General Brock's victory over General Hull at the Battle of Detroit—voiced in the boastful ballad, 'Come All You Bold Canadians'—reveals an early feeling of national identity. Those who routed William Lyon Mackenzie's American supporters boasted of their victory at 'The Battle of the Windmill' in 1838, and 'A Fenian Song' and 'An Anti-Fenian Song' recall the clashes of 1866. There are Newfoundlanders who can still recall 'An Anti-Confederation Song' from the election of 1869 that helped defeat those who wanted the island to join the new Canadian confederation—an event that would not come to pass for another eighty years.

Those songs express the feelings of people who took part in dramatic historical events, but most native Canadian songs reflect the daily lives of ordinary people. The largest number sprang from men who worked on the sea or in the woods. The sea dominates the lives of all who live in the small outport villages of Newfoundland and along the Atlantic coast, and this dominance led to innumerable songs. The sailors knew many shanties, most of which came from Britain, but the songs they composed are largely about fishing, sealing, and whaling. Typical are 'The Old Polina', about a whaling ship that sailed from Dundee to St John's; 'The Sealing Cruise of the *Lone Flyer*'; and 'The Crowd of Bold Sharemen' who went cod-fishing. Others record tragic shipwrecks—'The *Greenland* Disaster', 'The Loss of the *Atlantic*', 'The *Newfoundland* Disaster', and 'The *Southern Cross*', to name a few. Even the dance songs sung on land—like 'I'se the B'y That Builds the Boat' or 'Lots of Fish in Bonavist' Harbour'—reflect the dependence on the sea.

Lumbercamps were the other major source of native songs. Just as men of the sea were isolated on their ships during long voyages, so men in the camps were isolated in their snow-swept shanties during the long winters. Particularly in Ontario it was the lumbercamps that preserved and spread the traditional songs. Before radio and television, men from all over the province, and many from outside, went into the camps in the fall, and throughout the long months until the spring break-up they had to provide their own entertainment. They sang all the songs they knew, and in the spring they took home with them the ones they had learned from other singers, thus spreading them throughout the province.

When they ran out of old songs the shantyboys made up new ones based on their own lives. These fall into three main groups. The first describe the work: practically every year, in every camp, the men would compose a song, usually basing it on a familiar pattern and incorporating the names of the camp boss and the men who worked there that year. Sometimes known simply as 'The Lumbercamp Song', this often had a more specific title—'Jim Murphy's Camp', 'Turner's Camp', or 'Hogan's Lake', for example.

Another large group describe tragic accidents in the woods or on the river drives. The shantyboys probably composed a ballad about every one of their comrades who was killed, but many of these compositions did not survive. A score or more did, however, and one, 'The Jam on Gerry's Rocks', is familiar to almost every man who ever worked in the camps. We don't know where that tragedy occurred, but other ballads—like 'Jimmy Whelan' and 'Peter Amberley'—document known accidents.

A third and smaller group tells what happened when the shantyboys left the camps in the spring with their winter's pay in their pockets. 'The Lumberman in Town' is patterned on the English song about 'Jack Tar Ashore', telling how the men spend their money on liquor and women. Others—like 'The Farmer's Son and the Shantyboy' and 'Ye Maidens of Ontario'—describe the girls' fondness for the roving lumbering men.

Other occupations produced fewer songs, mainly because they did not provide the same conditions of isolation. A few mining songs, however, follow a similar pattern—some describing the work and others recalling tragic accidents. Canadian cowboys rarely composed songs because they inherited many from the Americans who drove cattle from Texas up to the early Canadian ranches. The homesteaders on our Prairies also borrowed songs from Americans, whose western plains were settled before ours. Farmers produced few songs because their work was largely solitary, but those they did sing—like 'The Little Old Sod Shanty' and 'The Alberta Homesteader'—offer graphic descriptions of the hardships they endured, usually treated in a semi-humorous way that reveals much about the courage and determination of those who settled the West.

Some songs make graphic comments on social and economic conditions. In 'The Poor Little Girls of Ontario' the women lament the loss of their beaux who head for the great Northwest, 'thinking to better themselves, no doubt'; the Newfoundland fishermen sing of 'Hard, Hard Times' and note that

> Fish is low and flour is high
> So Geordie Smith he can't have I;

while Saskatchewan farmers comment on 'the dirty thirties':

> We sit and gaze across the plains
> And wonder why it never rains,
> And Gabriel blows his trumpet sound:
> He says: 'The rain she's gone around.'

Although occupations inspired most of Canada's native songs, a miscellaneous group feature other subjects. The gold-seekers of the Cariboo and the Klondike sang of their hopes and disappointments, and quite a few ballads document local murders —there are at least two about the famous Ontario case of J.R. Birchall who killed F.C. Benwell and was hanged in Woodstock jail in 1890, and several about William Millman's murder of Maggie Tuplin in Prince Edward Island in 1887. Some humorous ditties feature jails—two Ontario songs, 'The Don Jail' in Toronto and 'Johnson's Hotel' in Peterborough, were patterned on one about 'The Mountjoy Hotel' in Dublin. Some ballads record local happenings, like 'The Miramichi Fire' of 1825, 'The *Saladin* Mutiny' in the 1840s, 'The Twelfth of July' riot in Montreal in 1877, and 'The Halifax Explosion' of 1917. These are a kind of local history that gained more than local currency by being spread through the fishing fleets or the lumbercamps.

One striking feature of the Anglo-Canadian songs is their predominantly Irish character. A remarkable number of the British broadsides sung in Canada are Irish, and almost all the songs composed here have Irish patterns and Irish tunes. Dance tunes like 'The Crooked Stovepipe', 'Rosin the Beau', and 'Larry O'Gaff' are popular; while some songs borrow more distinctive Irish tunes, from 'The Cruiskeen Lawn', 'The Wild Colonial Boy', 'The Bonny Laboring Boy', 'Youghal Harbour', 'Erin's Green Shore', and 'The Leprehaun'. They commonly fall into the 'come-all-ye' pattern— so-called because they begin 'Come all you young fellows and listen to me', or some similar phrase. The popularity of this form is evident in the index of practically every Canadian song collection. Canadian traditional singers usually *speak* the last word or phrase of a song—another Irish characteristic.

The songs are usually sung solo and unaccompanied. The idea

that folksingers play guitars and sing in chorus is a very modern concept. Providing instrumental arrangements for folksongs is not only untraditional, it tends to corrupt the tunes. Many old songs have modal melodies that do not lend themselves to harmonic accompaniment. These modal tunes—'Brave Wolfe' is aeolian, 'The Blooming Bright Star of Belle Isle' is mixolydian, 'The Lumbercamp Song' is dorian—are among the most beautiful in our collections, and when accompanied they tend to become major or minor.

ANGLO-CANADIAN COLLECTIONS

Some of the first published Anglo-Canadian folk songs appeared in a section titled 'Old Favourites' in *The Family Herald and Weekly Star*, a rural newspaper published in Montreal. This feature—which included poems, popular songs, and traditional songs—ran from 1895 to 1968. Readers requested particular songs and submitted ones they knew, thus serving to spread them throughout Canada. *The Western Producer*, published in Saskatoon since 1923, had a somewhat similar section. Collectors found that many singers clipped the columns and pasted them in scrapbooks. Also, singers often wrote out the songs they heard, thus helping to preserve them. Neil Rosenberg has discussed the manuscript book of a New Brunswick singer and has commented on the place of such books in tradition.

Apart from such columns, nearly all the early publications of Anglo-Canadian folksongs came from the Atlantic provinces. Some Newfoundland verses appeared in newspapers in the nineteenth century, and various songsters were printed in the early years of this century. Paul Mercer listed numerous pamphlets in *Newfoundland Songs and Ballads in Print: 1842-1974*, and compiled *The Ballads of Johnny Burke* (1974). In 1927 Gerald S. Doyle, a St John's merchant interested in local folklore, issued the first of his series of booklets titled *Old-Time Songs and Poetry of Newfoundland*, with the songs interspersed between advertisements for cod-liver oil, Dodd's Kidney Pills, and Salada tea. Doyle distributed these little booklets widely and they became a major factor in preserving and spreading local songs. Combining ads and songs was common in Newfoundland, as Paul Mercer and Mac Swackhammer have demonstrated in their article about 'Folklore and " Tradition" in Newfoundland Advertising'.

It has already been noted that Professor Kittredge inspired the first scholarly approach to Anglo-Canadian lore by encouraging Roy Mackenzie to return to his native province to collect songs, and the resulting publications— cited in 'The Pioneers'—were our first major books on Anglo-Canadian folklore. The 162 songs in *Ballads and Sea Songs from Nova Scotia* include 16 Child ballads, about 90 broadsides, a dozen shanties, a few native American ballads, and some local songs.

Mackenzie shared with earlier and later folklorists the belief that ballad-singing was a dying art. In 1919 he wrote: 'The mournful truth that most constantly obtrudes itself upon the collector is that the oral propagation of ballads has in our day and generation almost ceased.' That opinion had already been voiced in Britain in the middle of the nineteenth century, and Gavin Greig titled his 1925 collection *Last Leaves of Traditional Ballads*. It has become more difficult to find traditional singers, but since 1929 when Mackenzie's *Ballads and Sea Songs* appeared, Canadian collectors have published some two dozen books, many containing versions of the very songs Mackenzie found earlier. Radio, records, and television have reduced the folk's desire to create their own entertainment, but the ballad has proved a much hardier specimen than anyone suspected.

Although Mackenzie thought he had collected the last of the Nova Scotia ballads, his successor, Helen Creighton, went on to find thousands more, publishing many in the books mentioned in the chapter on 'The Pioneers'. Later, in 1979, Ron MacEachern edited a small collection of Amby Thomas's *Songs and Stories from Deep Cove, Cape Breton.*

Meanwhile women from Britain and the United States were exploring Newfoundland's musical wealth. 'The Pioneers' chapter described the collecting of Elisabeth Greenleaf and Grace Mansfield, whose *Ballads and Sea Songs of Newfoundland* was the first, and is still the best, scholarly collection of the island's songs. In addition to fine versions of old English and Scottish ballads and the somewhat more recent British broadsides, the many local songs that Greenleaf noted provide a valuable reflection of the island's culture.

In 1928 Maud Karpeles (1886-1976)—a renowned English scholar who had been Cecil Sharp's assistant during his collecting in the Appalachians—decided to make the trip to Newfoundland that Sharp had planned before his death. Unlike Elisabeth Greenleaf, Dr Karpeles was interested only in the songs of British origin that had survived. Because she ignored the many local compositions that form such an important part of the island's tradition, her book *Folk Songs from Newfoundland* is less valuable than Greenleaf's.

Two decades after the Greenleaf and Karpeles expeditions, the National Museum of Canada sent the Canadian musician Kenneth Peacock to collect in Newfoundland. He made six trips between 1951 and 1961, and in 1965 published his three-volume set of *Songs from the Newfoundland Outports*, the largest single publication of Canadian songs to date. That same year the American folklorist MacEdward Leach published *Folk Ballads and Songs of the Lower Labrador Coast*, which he had collected on a contract for the National Museum.

Greenleaf, Karpeles, Leach, and Peacock were all visitors from outside, but in 1985 two Newfoundlanders, Genevieve Lehr and Anita Best, brought out their songbook *Come and I Will Sing You*. Featuring mainly local Newfoundland songs, it shows that the songwriting tradition is still flourishing. Other evidence of this is in *Haulin' Rope and Gaff: Songs and Poetry in the History of the Newfoundland Seal Fishery*, compiled by Shannon Ryan and Larry Small, which consists entirely of local songs.

Newfoundland continues to be a particularly rich source of folksong. Students in Memorial University's folklore department are amassing an extensive archive of songs as well as other types of folklore, and Dr Kenneth Goldstein, a well-known American folklorist, has spent several summers collecting systematically throughout the province.

New Brunswick too has yielded a rich harvest. The prime collector there was Louise Manny, another pioneer, who joined with

James Wilson to publish *Songs of Miramichi*. It features songs from the north of the province and emphasizes the local compositions, while Helen Creighton's *Folksongs from Southern New Brunswick* concentrates on the older British ballads.

Prince Edward Island was largely neglected until 1963 when Edward Ives—a folklore professor from the University of Maine—published *Twenty-one Folksongs from Prince Edward Island.* Then in 1973 Christopher Gledhill and Randall and Dorothy Dibblee published two small Island collections.

Professor Ives has also produced three major books on Maritime singer-composers: Larry Gorman, Lawrence Doyle, and Joe Scott. These biographical and analytical studies pioneer a new approach that places the songs in their cultural context and throws light on the process by which folksongs are created. (Brief descriptions of the three singer-composers appear at the end of this chapter.)

Few songs from west of Quebec were noted before the second half of this century. In Ontario I began to record traditional singers around Peterborough and in the Ottawa Valley in the late 1950s, and documented my collecting in *Traditional Singers and Songs from Ontario* featuring ballads from the British Isles, and *Lumbering Songs from the Northern Woods* emphasizing the occupational songs. Believing that it is important to hear the songs as they were actually sung, I produced nine records by traditional Ontario singers, and I list records as well as books when giving references.

Singing Our History focuses on songs about important historical events and our early industries, and *The Penguin Book of Canadian Folk Songs* gives a sampling of songs from across Canada. Through the Nova Scotia novelist Thomas Raddall I obtained and published *Sea Songs and Ballads from Nineteenth-Century Nova Scotia: The William Smith and Fenwick Hatt Manuscripts.* William Smith preserved the greatest number of shanties noted in Canada, and Fenwick Hatt's notebook of songs written before 1883 contains the earliest Anglo-Canadian songs to come to light.

A special group of Ontario songs describes voyages and shipwrecks on the Great Lakes. Ivan H. Walton (1893-1968), a Michigan authority on marine lore, collected many of these and stored them in the University of Michigan's library. C.H.J. Snider, a Canadian who wrote extensively of naval history, also collected Great Lakes songs; he and Stanley Bâby (whose father captained sailing ships on the Lakes) sing some of them on Folkways record 4018.

Two collections present songs from the Ottawa Valley. Russell Leach put together *The Rusty Leach Collection of Shanty Songs and Recollections of the Upper Ottawa Valley*, and Venetia Crawford assembled *Pontiac Treasures in Song and Story*. Both emphasize lumbering songs.

On the Prairies, Anglo-Canadian songs are scarce. Barbara Cass-Beggs did some collecting in the 1960s and published *Eight Songs of Saskatchewan*. The main collector in British Columbia is Philip Thomas, who has concentrated on finding songs and verses that reflect the history of the West Coast. His major book is *Songs of the Pacific Northwest*.

Several folklorists have written about particular songs. Sheldon Posen has made the most extensive study of one song, 'The Chapeau Boys', and he discusses its origin and history in a book based on his doctoral dissertation: *For singing and dancing and all sorts of fun: The Story of the Chapeau Boys*. John Moulden, an Irish folklorist, proves that 'The Blooming Bright Star of Belle Isle', thought to be a Newfoundland song, is actually transplanted from Ireland. I have shown that 'The Red River Valley', thought to be an American song, probably dates from the Red River Rebellion. John Szwed's article on Paul Hall analyses his 'Bachelor Song' to show how it reflects Newfoundland rural society. Tim Rogers discusses the ballad of 'The *Southern Cross*' as history. Edward Ives studies 'The Ballad of "John Ladner" ' to show what it reveals about life in the lumberwoods, and he also discusses many individual songs in his books about Gorman, Scott, and Doyle.

Other folklorists have published articles studying how songs relate to the singers and their audiences. Three Memorial University professors—George Casey, Neil Rosenberg, and Wilfred Wareham—discuss the way singers categorize their songs, and Kenneth Goldstein analyses the element of faith in a group of Newfoundland ballads to show that the fishermen's apparent fatalism is a recognition of the importance of a daily struggle that requires both faith and occupational skill.

SONGS OF OTHER GROUPS

The Highland Scots who settled Cape Breton preserved their Gaelic songs, and these appear with English translations in several collections. An early one is *Gaelic Songs in Nova Scotia* by Helen Creighton and Calum MacLeod. Two broader collections—both emphasizing songs about immigration—are Margaret MacDonell's *The Emigrant Experience: Songs of Highland Emigrants in North America* and Donald Fergusson's *Beyond the Hebrides.*

Although Anglo-Canadian music on the Prairies is poorly documented, the songs of the other ethnic communities have been more thoroughly explored. Florence Livesay—the mother of poet Dorothy Livesay—published a pioneer volume, *Songs of Ukrainia*, back in 1916, and Robert Klymasz produced two later collections: *The Ukrainian-Canadian Immigrant Folksong Cycle* and *The Ukrainian Winter Folksong Cycle in Canada.*

Kenneth Peacock wrote *A Survey of Ethnic Folk Music Across Canada* and compiled a small anthology, *Twenty Ethnic Songs from Western Canada.* He also documented the songs of two distinctive ethnic groups from the Prairies in *A Garland of Rue: Lithuanian Folksongs of Love and Betrothal* and *Songs of the Doukhobors.*

Peacock discusses the unique style of Doukhobor choral and part singing, which he is the first to transcribe. He notes that 'the key to the Doukhobor choral style lies in the old unison singing of men and women in octaves'. When that is embellished by counterpoint and extemporized harmonies, the result is a complex musical structure in which each person is a soloist, creating 'an edifice of choral sound unique in Canadian folkmusic'. And, he emphasizes, 'Doukhobor choral and part singing is done entirely by ear.'

Several volumes in the Mercury Series of the Canadian Centre for Folk Culture Studies record the songs of various ethnic groups. Paul McIntyre's *Black Pentecostal Music in Windsor* focuses on church music; Ban-Song Song gives an ethno-musicological study of Korean-Canadian folk songs; and John Michael Glofcheskie reports on the folk music of Canada's oldest Polish community in Ontario's Renfrew county. Also worth noting are Ramon Pelinski's survey of 'The Music of Canada's Ethnic Minorities' and Judith Cohen's reports on Judeo-Spanish traditional songs collected in Toronto and Montreal.

Many of the songs of these various groups are direct transplants from the country of origin, but the most interesting tell of immigrants' and settlers' experiences in the new land. Robert Klymasz emphasizes this distinction, pointing out that the twenty-eight songs in his immigrant cycle form only a small segment of the almost two thousand songs he collected. He based his selection on two criteria: 'The song is an original item composed in Canada; or it is a traditional item with obvious signs of "Canadianization" through contact with the new Canadian environment.' Much the same criteria apply to the two immigrant collections of Gaelic songs, and to *Many Are Strong among the Strangers: Canadian Songs of Immigration* compiled by Ellen Karp, which is of particular interest because its thirty-four songs stem from a wide variety of ethnic groups, including—as well as the Gaelic and Ukrainian documented earlier—Yiddish, Italian, Hungarian, Irish, Finnish, Polish, Norwegian, Rumanian, Latvian, Portuguese, Chilean, and Jamaican. Common themes in the immigrant songs are the reasons for emigrating, the expectation of a better life in the New World, the journey and arrival, the disenchantment and homesickness that usually follow, the reactions to conditions in Canada, and the gradual acceptance of the new homeland.

INSTRUMENTAL MUSIC

The fiddle is Canada's pre-eminent folk instrument and the only one that has been studied at all extensively. The most valuable articles are by George Proctor (1931-85), an ethnomusicologist who collected for the National Museum. In 'Old-Time Fiddling in Ontario' he describes the practices in several counties and gives a history of old-time fiddling, emphasizing the Scots style that has influenced many Canadian fiddlers. In 'Fiddle Music as a Manifestation of Regionalism' he discusses the differences that have developed in various parts of Canada. Dorothy and Homer Hogan also emphasize regional differences in their survey, 'Canadian Fiddle Culture', listing records that represent the regions. Another regional study is the special fiddling issue of the *Canadian Folk Music Bulletin* edited by Anne Lederman. Also valuable is the article on 'Fiddling' in the *Encyclopedia of Music in Canada*. Lisa Ornstein gives a more general historical survey of instrumental music and its relation to dance in Quebec, and Neil Rosenberg compiled 'A Preliminary Bibliography of Old-Time Music Books'.

The fiddle and the bagpipe—many of them home-made—were the instruments used to accompany dancing in early Canada; outside of Scottish communities the fiddle was the most common. Because of its use for dancing, rhythm is the most important element in fiddle music, and Scottish and Irish fiddling have influenced most Canadian styles. The Scottish style, predominant in Cape Breton and some parts of Ontario, is related to the bagpipe, with a reedy sound, use of the drone, and the embellishment characteristic of bagpipe tunes. Strathspeys and reels are the most popular dances, the first slow and the second fast. The Quebec style shows considerable Irish influence. The music—much of it based on Irish jigs and reels—is highly ornamented, very fast and strongly rhythmic, and often accompanied by clogging: the fiddler uses his feet to beat a heavy rhythm on the floor, sometimes with wooden-soled shoes. A simpler style stemming from Don Messer's long-running radio program is widespread in other regions, and some fiddlers are influenced by American western style. On the Prairies Métis and Slavic influences are also important.

The most famous of the old-time fiddlers was Jean Carignan (1916-88)—known affectionately as Ti-Jean. His father played fiddle in the French-Canadian style, and by the time he was five Jean had picked it up and begun playing in the streets to help support his family. He became a pupil of Joseph Allard (1873-1947), one of the finest French-Canadian fiddlers, and another important influence was the great Irish fiddler Michael Coleman. For some time Carignan toured with George Wade's country dance band, and then for years earned his living playing in a Montreal dance hall. Later he became a taxi driver, but continued to play at concerts and festivals and to make numerous records.

Other important folk fiddlers are Joseph Bouchard and Louis Boudreault from Quebec, Rufus Guinchard and Emile Benoit from Newfoundland, and Winston (Scotty) Fitzgerald and Joseph Cormier from Cape Breton. Philippe Bruneau is a well-known folk accordionist. All of these performers can be heard on records.

Most fiddle tunes are reels, jigs, or strathspeys used for dancing, and most came from Europe. Among the few traditional Canadian tunes are 'Le Reel du pendu' (The Hangman's Reel) from Quebec—said to have won a reprieve for a condemned man—and 'The Red River Jig' from the West. More recently Ward Allen's 'Maple Sugar' has become popular, and many other fiddlers have composed their own tunes.

DANCING

Folk dancing is an aspect of Canadian folklore that has received little attention. It is mentioned in books about pioneer life, but rarely described. One common form was the step dance. It was an individual dance usually performed by men: they stayed on one spot, tapping their feet alternately in intricate rhythms, but holding their body still. It was particularly popular in lumbercamps, and sometimes formed part of Christmas visits in Newfoundland.

The most widespread dance in Canada is the square dance, which, like most Canadian customs, had its roots in Europe. Somewhere around 1650 English country dancing took three forms: the round, the square, and the longways dance. A little later the round and the square forms died out in England, and the longways became the predominant country dance. But meanwhile the square had become popular in France, where its simple steps were prettified by the French dancing masters and thus transformed into a quadrille, whereupon it came back to England as a drawing-room dance.

So the North American square dance has two ancestors—the English country dance of the seventeenth century, and the quadrille, whose French influence is apparent in such common square-dance terms as 'do-si-do' and 'allemand left'. The early settlers brought these forms to the New World, where they became popular with both English and French. As Edwin Guillet wrote: 'In the towns dancing schools taught various fancy minuets and quadrilles, but the backwoods settlers were quite satisfied with the usual country dances.'

In England the dancers needed no directions once they had learned the steps, but in rural Canada there were no dancing masters to teach the patterns. Instead, farmers and their wives picked up a few common dance movements by watching others, and then followed the lead of someone who could guide them. So the habit grew of having a caller who would stand beside the fiddler and call out what steps to do next. He would often make up the order as he went along, thus providing the variations so typical of folklore.

Square-dance calls range from plain to fancy, and take three main forms: the prompt, the patter, and the singing calls. In the simplest, the prompt call, the caller briefly indicates the next movement—for example, 'Right hand gent with the right hand round,/Partner with the left hand round'—and there are many bars of music without any words. In the patter call the caller never stops talking. It still includes directions telling the dancers what to do, but in a more picturesque form and usually in rhyming couplets. Where a prompt call would say simply, 'Take the opposite lady', the patter call might run: 'Now we'll swap, now we'll trade,/Your old girl for my old maid.' The patter calls are more difficult to follow, but they are more fun once the dancers get used to them.

All square-dance tunes have either a four-four or six-eight rhythm, and a call in one rhythm can be used with any tune in that rhythm. However, the singing call is composed for one tune only. Like the patter call, it uses rhythm and rhyme, but carries them further so that a whole verse is made up to fit a familiar melody like 'Listen to the Mocking Bird', 'Darling Nellie Gray', or 'Life on the Ocean Wave'.

The colourful language of the calls often reflects the local community. On the farms of central Canada the call might run 'Swing your partner like swinging on a gate' or 'Couples turn like a stable door', while out west cowboys might shout 'Rope your cow and brand your calf,/Swing your honey for an hour and a half', and in east-coast fishing villages the favourite is 'Dip for the oyster, dip for the clam,/Now take a dip in the frying pan.'

French Canadians have studied dancing more extensively than Anglo-Canadians. The primary dance researcher is Simonne Voyer, who has published articles and an extensive book on traditional dances in eastern Canada; Robert Séguin has also written of traditional Quebec dances. The major Anglo-Canadian book on folk dance to date is Colin Quigley's *Close to the Floor: Folk Dance in Newfoundland*. He reports on step dancing and square dancing in some detail, mentions other single, couple, and group patterns, and describes the many social occasions that include dancing.

One reason why so little has been written about folk dancing is the difficulty of recording dance patterns. Some folklorists are beginning to develop methods to cope with this problem—for example, Ellen Shifrin in 'Traditional French-Canadian Dance Iconography: A Methodology for Analysis'. One of the few detailed articles is Frank Rhodes' account of 'Dancing in Cape Breton Island' showing that the Cape Bretoners have preserved dance elements older than those now alive in Scotland.

In pioneer societies when instruments were scarce dances were sometimes performed to mouth music. A person with stamina and a strong voice would provide the rhythm for the dance by singing, often just nonsense syllables but occasionally throwing in words. This had various names: in Cape Breton it was 'port a beul', in Newfoundland chin or gob music, in Nova Scotia cheek music, and sometimes simply mouth music. It has also been called 'lilting', 'dowdling', or 'diddling'. Originally used to substitute for instruments, it sometimes provided an amusing accompaniment to fiddle music with improvised verses. Colin Quigley notes that taunts between communities or about individuals were common in Newfoundland, and so were sexual verses such as:

> Some like the girls who are pretty in the face,
> Some like the girls who are neat around the waist,
> But I love the girls with a wriggle and a twist;
> In the bottom of her belly is the cuckoo's nest.

THE SINGERS

Although books preserve the words and melodies of our songs, they cannot convey the way traditional singers sang them. They sang solo and unaccompanied (except for the Doukhobor choral songs and some religious items), and freely adapted the melody to accommodate variations in the metre. It is fortunate that records now make available a good sampling of traditional singers, allowing us to hear how they sang, for it is almost impossible to transcribe their melodies exactly.

Most collectors celebrate the fine singers who provide them with the songs they have preserved. Of the hundreds responsible for our many song collections, a few outstanding ones are singled out here for brief notes. Nearly all of them can be heard on records.

Dr Barbeau has written extensively of **Louis Simard**, called l'Aveugle—the Blind Singer—who tramped his way all along the North Shore of the St Lawrence pulling the little cart that held his musical instruments. He always came to St Irenée for the feast of Ste Anne at the end of July, and there in 1916 Dr Barbeau caught up with him and recorded his songs and tales. As Barbeau writes in *The Tree of Dreams:*

> One song followed another, from Pyramus two thousand years ago to the wanderings of the Lord at the edge of the Sea of Gallilee—like his own on the North Shore—to the martyrdom of Ste Catherine of Rome, to the lamentable tragedies of the Middle Ages, to the drinking songs of all times, to the love lyrics of springtime and courtship, to the shortcomings of married life . . . to the hop and diddle of the folkdances, to the fun and nonsense dear to all because they blot out the common hardships and gild the pill of life.

Roy Mackenzie also writes glowingly of his fine Nova Scotia singers, particularly Ned Langille, Dick Hines, and Bob Langille. He heard **Ned Langille** in the 1890s before he became interested in folksongs. Of French descent, Ned was a cobbler in the village of River John, working in his small hut and entertaining visitors with his stock of ballads, which 'in age and variety was probaby without parallel in the whole countryside'. Mackenzie laments that at the time he did not note those songs, but he remembers his singing of 'Lord Thomas and Fair Elinor', 'Little Matha Grove', 'Bolender Martin', and 'Peter Amberley'.

When Mackenzie started collecting songs in 1909, **Bob Langille**, an octogenarian of Tatamagouche, was one of the first singers he found. Despite his French ancestry, he was intensely patriotic, delighting in songs of English victories. In *The Quest of the Ballad* Mackenzie gives this graphic description of his style:

> Bob leaned forward, fixed his gaze earnestly upon a knot in the floor and studied for a few moments; then throwing back his head and closing his eyes, he began with a suddenness and volume of sound that for the moment harrowed me with fear and wonder. . . . On the last line of the song he practiced the device which has been used by every ballad singer that I have ever listened to, that is, he sang the first part of the line in the regular way with eyes closed and head thrown back, then made a swift and sudden descent from the empyrean of music, opened his eyes, leaned forward, glared upon his audience, and pronounced the last few words in an emphatical conversational tone.

Dick Hinds, Able Seaman—'who in his time sailed the seven seas bearing his reputation as one of the most gifted and resourceful of shantymen'—was Mackenzie's major find in 1910. Dick learned traditional ballads in childhood, acquired further ballads and countless sea songs from his companions at sea, and added more from the streets and music halls of the various cities he visited. His favourites were 'Kelly the Pirate' and 'Jack Donahue'; he also sang of 'Brave Wolfe', 'Frank Fidd', 'Bold Dighton', and 'The Jolly Tars', and provided Mackenzie with his largest stock of shanties.

Helen Creighton also gives good descriptions of Nova Scotia singers. In 1928, when she met her first singer, **Enos Hartlan**, she said, 'I hear you sing old songs down here,' and he replied, 'We don't sing nothin' else. See them stars in the sky. As many stars as there are up there, that's as many songs as I used to know, but now me teeth is gone and me voice is rusty.' Nevertheless he sang for her. The Hartlans' German ancestors came to Canada in 1753, yet, Dr Creighton notes, 'Strangely enough it was among these people that some of my finest and oldest English songs were discovered.'

Ben Henneberry, the great singer she found on Devil's Island—her description of the first time she heard him is quoted in Chapter 3—sang no less than ninety songs. One, 'The Courtship of Willie Riley', contains seventy-eight verses. The wealth of songs from the Hartlans and the Henneberrys almost filled her first book.

Nathan Hatt, probably of German ancestry, owned a mill in Middle River near Chester, New Brunswick. When he became ill with pernicious anaemia he whiled away his days with songs, and sang over eighty for Dr Creighton in the 1950s. His version of the old Child ballad 'The Twa Brothers' is quite unusual, borrowing motifs from 'The Unquiet Grave'. He knew several other Child ballads and some lovely songs like 'The Banks of the Roses'. The enthusiasm with which he entered into the ballad story fascinated Alan Mills, who reproduced the way he sang 'Lady Isabel and the Elf Knight' on Folkways record 3532.

Angelo Dornan, of Irish descent on both sides of his family, lived on a farm in Alberta County, New Brunswick. He learned many songs from his father, and like him he embroidered his tunes with great skill. When he was nineteen he moved to Alberta, where he lived until his sixties; then he grew homesick and returned to New Brunswick, buying a farm near Elgin. In 1953 he heard of Helen Creighton and wrote to her suggesting that she record his songs. In a series of visits she collected some 135. She notes that 'he sang mostly of love as it is proposed, plighted, rejected, and bereaved', and she published so many of his songs in *Folksongs from Southern New Brunswick* that she said it might have been called 'The Dornan Book of Songs'.

Louise Manny also praised the New Brunswick singers she recorded in the 1940s and 1950s. She writes of 'the singing MacDonalds' of Black River Bridge and Glenwood, of whom **Wilmot MacDonald**—also a great storyteller—was the most famous, and tells how **Jared MacLean** of Strathadam took time off from his work at the fish hatchery to sing 'The Dungarvon Whooper', 'The Banks of the Miramichi', 'The Maid of Tidehead', and 'Peelhead'.

The best known New Brunswick singer, **Marie Hare,** was the youngest (thirteenth) child of Neville Whitney of Strathadam and

Janey Jones, whose ancestors' grist mill and saw mill inspired a favourite New Brunswick song, 'The Jones Boys':

> O the Jones Boys!
> They built a mill on the side of a hill
> And they worked all night and they worked all day,
> And they couldn't make that gosh-darned saw-mill pay.

Both Marie's parents were fine singers and she remembers many evenings of singing in her family kitchen. She has been a star performer at the Miramichi Folksong Festivals for many years and has also appeared at Mariposa and other festivals. She made a record in 1962; the songs on it are largely about love—mostly unhappy love—from the British broadside tradition. Her 'Green Valley', 'Patrick O'Donnell', and 'The Maid of the East' are quite rare.

Another New Brunswick singer, **Allan Kelly**, was born in an Acadian village in 1903, the seventh son in a family of seventeen. People said he was born with the gift of music. His father, a fisherman, was of Irish and Scottish descent and his mother was Acadian so he learned both French and English songs. He fished and farmed as a youth, worked in a saw mill, lumbercamps, a mine, and even on farms in western Canada. Ronald Labelle describes Kelly's life and his songs for the record *Suivant l' étoile du nord*, which includes versions of 'The False Knight on the Road' and 'The Cruel Mother'.

Amby Thomas was born in 1906 in the little fishing village of Deep Cove, Cape Breton. He had a problem with his sight and for a time went to a school for the blind in Halifax. He worked in a lobster factory, fished, cut timber, and finally settled in Halifax, where he sang his songs and told his stories to Ron McEachern. Amby says he learned 'The Wreck of the *John Harvey*' when he was six, and that his mother used to sing 'Patrick Sheehan' and 'The Moncton Tragedy'. He sings one unusual song, 'When I First Went to Caledonia', which combines lyric stanzas from an old love song with local verses about mining.

Ontario has also had many fine singers, mostly of Irish ancestry, although the finest and most representative, **Oliver John Abbott** (1872-1962), was born in England. He came to Canada as a young boy and worked on farms in the Ottawa Valley, learning many songs from the Irish settlers; then he went to the lumbercamps, where he picked up more. He knew over 120 songs, including some that are rare in North America like 'The Barley Grain for Me', 'The Cruiskeen Lawn', 'Nellie Coming Home from the Wake', 'Skibbereen', and 'The Mower'. 'The Weaver' and 'By the Hush Me Boys' seem unique in oral tradition, and his 'The Plains of Waterloo' has become a favourite in British folk clubs.

LaRena LeBarr Clark—Mrs Gordon Clark—has an amazing repertoire of some five hundred songs learned from her parents and grandparents. Born in 1917 at Pefferlaw on the Black River, she has the most unusual background of any Ontario singer: her ancestry includes French, English, Irish, Pennsylvania Dutch, and Indian strains, which are reflected in her songs. Rare items in her repertoire are Child ballads ('Lord Gregory' and 'Fair Annie'), old British songs ('The Old County Fair', 'The Faggot Cutter', 'I'll Go See My Love', 'The Rifle Boys', and 'Thyme 'Tis a Pretty Flower'), and lumbering songs ('Hurry up Harry', 'Fine Times in Camp Number Three', and 'The Raftsmen's Song'). These are mixed in with a lot of popular songs of the late nineteenth and early twentieth centuries.

Tom Brandon, a Peterborough singer born in 1927, learned songs from both his Irish parents, and picked up more while working in the woods and on Great Lakes ships. He sings 'The Spree', 'The Rambling Irishman', a fine version of 'The *Flying Cloud*', 'Patrick Sheehan', 'The Twelfth of July' about a riot in Montreal, and old bawdy songs—'Derby Town' and 'The Long Peg and Awl'.

Grace MacDonald Fraser—Mrs Arlington Fraser—was born in Glengarry County in 1910. Unlike most Ontario singers whose songs came from the lumbercamps, she learned hers from her mother who was half Scottish and half Irish. They include Scottish items like 'The Braes of Yarrow', 'Burns and His Highland Mary', 'Johnny Cope', and the unusual 'Young Munro' and 'Hey Arise and Come Along', as well as Irish songs like 'Groyle Machree', 'The Dawning of the Day', and 'Come All You True Lovers'—and one of Canada's few native love songs, 'The Jolly Raftsman O':

> I am sixteen I do confess,
> I'm sure I am no older O.
> I've placed my mind, it never shall move,
> It's on a jolly raftsman O.

> To hew and score it is his plan
> And handle a broad-axe neatly O.
> It's lay the line and mark the pine
> And do it most completely O.

Carrie Grover is an unusual singer who documented her many songs herself. Born in Nova Scotia in the 1880s, she lived there till she was twelve, and then her family moved to Maine. She became known as a folksinger and Alan Lomax recorded her for the Library of Congress. To preserve them for her children she began to write down the songs she had learned in her Nova Scotia childhood, indicating from what family member they came. Some 140 of them appear in *A Heritage of Songs*—an amazingly rich collection that shows how songs were preserved and used in a family where traditional singing was a natural part of life.

Another Nova Scotia singer, **Clarence Blois** (1904-85), was not known outside his local community around Upper Nine Mile River, Hants County, but Martin Lovelace's description of him throws light on the way singers react to their songs. Most of his songs came from his father who was a great singer, and, as Dr Lovelace puts it, they dealt mainly 'with the classic themes of Anglo-American folksong: love, separation, and death'. Clarence felt that the songs counteracted loneliness and that they had a civilizing influence on the men in the lumbercamps. He also had interesting comments about the scenes he 'saw' in his mind's eye as he sang, and how he interpreted the song 'Down by the Laney Side'.

THE SINGER-SONGMAKERS

Edward Ives' books about three outstanding Maritime songmakers help us to understand how folksongs are created and how they reflect the temperaments of their creators and the social climate of their communities.

The most famous of these, **Larry Gorman** (1846-1917)—known all through the eastern lumberwoods as 'the man who made the songs'—was, in W.M. Doerflinger's words, 'the most appealing and most important figure in the eastern woods minstrelsy from the 1870s into the present century'. Old-time woodsmen of New

Brunswick and Maine are still singing his songs, and they say that in Larry's own day the news that he was working in a camp was enough to make shantyboys from miles around join the same crew. His lyrics, usually satirical, were of life in the camps and individuals he encountered. His most popular songs are 'The Boys of the Island', 'The Gull Decoy', 'The Scow on Cowden Shore', and 'The Winter of Seventy-Three'. He is remembered also for his cante-fables—originally stories incorporating songs, but later humorous anecdotes ending with a satirical verse like this grace:

> Oh, Lord above, look down on us
> And see how we are forgotten,
> And send us meat that is fit to eat
> Because by Christ this is rotten.

Lawrence Doyle (1847-1907), 'the farmer-poet of Prince Edward Island', depicted community events in his songs. Like Gorman he was of Irish ancestry, but unlike Gorman he was good-natured in dealing with people. However, as a Grit he lambasted the Tory government in one of his best-known songs, 'Prince Edward Isle, Adieu'. Other popular ones were 'The Picnic at Groshaut' and 'When I Went Ploughing for Kearnon'.

Joe Scott (1867-1918) was born of a farming family in New Brunswick but left for the Maine lumberwoods before he was twenty. He was jilted in 1894 and that inspired his best known ballad, 'The Plain Golden Band'. A surprising number of his songs were about men who died violent deaths—'Guy Reed' killed in a log jam, 'John Ladner' killed by falling logs, and 'Howard Carey' who hanged himelf. These and a few others—like 'Benjamin Deane', who killed his sweetheart, and 'The Norway Bum', whose wife and child were burned to death—survived in tradition, partly because Scott sold broadsides of them.

5

MINOR GENRES

Traditional words, expressions, or names are the simplest forms of verbal folklore and are important factors distinguishing folk groups. This is true both for Canadians as a whole and for various regions and groups within the country. In *The Literary History of Canada* M.H. Scargill notes:

> Hundreds of words of various origins have made their way into the Canadian language either directly or through the United States. New names for new conditions of life, for new flora and fauna, for new peoples, new politics, new weather, all have joined the vocabulary of the New World to that of the Old in Canadian English and given it a vitality and variety that few other languages know.

Foremost among Canadianisms are words from French and Indian languages. *Habitant, voyageur, coureur de bois,* and Métis are recognized by all Canadians, as are such common French borrowings as portage, prairie, cache, lacrosse, and charivari. From the native tribes we have adopted parka, pemmican, muskeg, igloo, kayak, tepee, toboggan, mackinaw, and moccasin, to mention some of the best-known terms. Names from the animal kingdom include caribou, buffalo, muskox, prairie dog, gopher, chipmunk, moose, wolverine, dew worm, goldeye, and whisky jack. Some words used only in certain regions include saskatoons (berries), Chinook (wind), sockeye (salmon), chuck (water) or salt chuck (ocean) from the West, and tickle (narrow channel), cracky (little dog), and barrelman (lookout on a ship) from Newfoundland. Some words have different meanings in different provinces: bluff means a clump of trees in Saskatchewan, a cliff in Ontario. A banker works in a bank in most of Canada; in Newfoundland he is a Grand Banks fisherman.

Among the terms for natives of various regions are Bluenose (N.S.), Herring-Choker (N.B.), peasouper (Que.), Bison (Man.), Spud Islander (P.E.I.), Maritimer, and Newfie. Items prominent in our history include the Red River cart, York boat, Durham boat, Bennett buggy, Quebec heater, Fife wheat, and McIntosh apple. Canadian political terms include reeve, riding, premier, acclamation, Grit, Socred, and Confederation.

One of the most valuable of the books surveying Canadian speech is Henry Alexander's *The Story of Our Language.* Also important is *A Dictionary of Canadianisms on Historical Principles* edited by Walter S. Avis, and Scargill's article on 'The Growth of English' in *The Literary History of Canada.* A few earlier items of interest are John D. Higinbotham's pioneer article on 'Western Vernacular' as he heard it in Alberta in the 1880s, and the *Western Canadian Dictionary and Phrase-Book* that John Sandilands produced in 1913. The colourful terms they list include tenderfoot, spade brand, sourdough, sowbelly, flapjacks, slicker, grubstake, gunnysack, and haywire. Also of interest are several articles and pamphlets dealing with Chinook jargon, the trade language used by *voyageurs* dealing with West Coast Indians. There are also works dealing with the French-Canadian folk dialect known as *joual.*

A distinctive regional dialect that has been explored in detail is that of Newfoundland. George Patterson published some early 'Notes on the Dialect of the People of Newfoundland' in the *Journal of American Folklore* back in the 1890s, and in 1937 P.K. Devine compiled an interesting pamplet: *Devine's Folklore of Newfoundland in Old Words, Phrases and Expressions: The Origin and Meaning.* Beginning in 1968, Memorial University issued an occasional small journal, *RLS: Regional Language Studies . . . Newfoundland,* and after some twenty years' work, three Memorial professors—G.M. Story, W.J. Kirwin, and J.D.A. Widdowson— produced the *Dictionary of Newfoundland English,* a fascinating study of the history and culture of Newfoundlanders as revealed through their distinctive language. This is by far the most important publication dealing with language in Canada. Along with the words created in the island it lists words that have survived later there than elsewhere, many that date back to Elizabethan times, and ones that have taken on different forms or meanings among the islanders. Each item is traced from its earliest appearance through many sources: literary and historical writing, newspapers, pamphlets, ballads, charts and maps, and early glossaries. Of particular interest to folklorists are the many examples from oral materials the editors collected themselves or drew from the Memorial University Folklore and Language Archive.

It is not surprising that Newfoundland should have the most distinctive dialect of any Canadian region. Its separation from the mainland and the isolation of the hundreds of tiny outports around its coast created the kind of situation that promotes and preserves colourful language, as well as making it the richest Canadian source of folktales, songs, and other types of folklore.

T.K. Pratt's *Dictionary of Prince Edward Island English* (1988) contains some thousand entries of non-standard or dialect words. Less extensive than the Newfoundland volume, it still provides a good introduction to the smaller island's historical and sociological life. Among the unusual terms Pratt lists are 'fustle'—fussing about the house too much, 'tweeker'—a small child, and 'worpy'—stale or sour food.

In addition to its distinctive vocabulary, Canadian folk speech also involves pronunciations that differ from those of England and the United States. The Irish dialect is persistent, especially in folk song: many singers whose ancestors came here back in the 1820s speak as though they had recently landed from Cork. In Newfoundland, and in the speech of some Ontarians of Irish descent, the 'o' in many words becomes 'i', for example, 'b'y' for boy: 'I'se the b'y that builds the boat'. A ballad about 'Johnny Doyle' first became 'Johnny D'yle' and then 'Johnny Stiles'. Mourned and reared become 'merned' and 'rared'; arms and harm are usually 'arrums' and 'harrum'; 'parients' and 'lovyers' turn up in many ballads; the 'h' is often dropped in words like death; the first syllable in 'fatal' sounds like 'fat', and 'bonny' often sounds like 'boney'. An English dialect is also obvious in singers who drop or add initial 'h's'. The Newfoundland singer Joshua Osborne pronounces the curse in 'The Cruel Mother' as

> 'Eaven is 'igh and 'ell is low
> And when you die to 'ell you will go.

A more widespread characteristic of Canadian pronunciation that Americans often notice is the way some of us pronounce words like 'out' and 'house', which they hear as 'oot' and 'hoose'. Our pronunciations vary between those of England and the United States, and some words like 'khaki' and 'vase' have different pronounciations in Canada than in either country. And Canadians are generally believed to add 'eh' at the end of every sentence.

PLACE NAMES

Place names are another good indication of the diversiy of elements in our Canadian population. Again to quote M.H. Scargill: 'It is in its vocabulary that Canadian English is most distinctive; and it is in its varied names that Canadian English is most appealing. . . . This profusion of colourful names, American Indian, French, Scottish, English, was noticed early by travellers. . .' He could have added Irish, Greek, Spanish, German, and Italian. There are also many names drawn from history: Frontenac, Cartier, Simcoe, Victoria, Regina, Selkirk, Vancouver, Carleton, Charlottetown, Dorchester. More interesting are the many local names that are linked to local legends—like Moose Jaw, 'place where the white man mended his cart with the jawbone of a moose'; Kicking Horse Pass, where Dr James Hector was kicked by his horse when exploring the Rockies; Medicine Hat, where a Cree medicine man is said to have lost his headdress in a fight with a Blackfoot; Qu'Appelle, memorialized in Pauline Johnson's poem 'The Legend of the Qu'Appelle'; Windigo Lake haunted by cannibal spirits; and even Canada— one theory says it originated with Spanish sailors who, disappointed in not finding gold, cried 'Aca nada': nothing here.

Of the many publications dealing with place names, the most comprehensive is George H. Armstrong's *The Origin and Meaning of Place Names in Canada*. Various articles and books survey the place names of every province, and more specialized studies deal with names of Scottish, Doukhobor, Ukrainian, West African, Slavic, Kwakiutl, Algonkian, Micmac, and Inuit origin. The most extensive of these is J.B. Rudnyc'kyj's *Manitoba Mosaic of Place Names*.

Again, the most numerous studies are from Newfoundland, one of the most important being E.R. Seary's *Place Names of the Avalon Peninsula*. A glance at a map reveals a multitude of colourful names like Harbour Grace, Joe Batt's Arm, Cow Head, Tickle Cove Pond, Conception Bay, Come By Chance, Parson's Pond, Topsail, Seldom Come By, Quiddy Viddy, Maggoty Cove, Bay of Despair, Heart's Delight, Heart's Desire, Heart's Content, and Little Heart's Ease. Many of these suggest their history and the conditions that inspired them.

A few writers have discussed special aspects of folk speech. Helen Creighton writes of nicknames in Nova Scotia, citing such colourful ones as 'Maggie the Lighthouse'—not because she was tall and angular but because her father kept the light; 'Hughie the Hide'—because he tried to steal one; and a family known as the Skunks because the father painted his boat black with a white stripe. Another compilation is W.L. McAtee's study of the folk names of birds. In two analytic articles William Kirwin discusses folk etymology in relation to linguistic problem solving, and Robert Klymasz looks at the way Slavic surnames become Canadianized—but such studies are rare. So is material on folk sayings and proverbs in Canada, although folklorists in other countries have studied them thoroughly.

PROVERBS

Proverbs—described as 'The wisdom of many in the wit of one'—are in common use in Canada, but rarely collected. The sparse examples include Charles Dunn's article on Gaelic proverbs from

Nova Scotia, and sections in a few general collections. W.J. Wintemberg gives some German proverbs from Ontario's Waterloo County, and Creighton, Devine, and Halpert provide several examples from both Nova Scotia and Newfoundland.

Most of the proverbs heard in Canada are common in other countries, but some unusual ones reflect the culture of the region. For example, from Creighton's Lunenburg collection come: 'Talk is cheap but fish is scarce', 'Better a small fish than an empty dish', 'A new broom sweeps clean but an old one knows the corners best'. Devine gives a few examples of distinctive Newfoundland proverbs and folk sayings, such as 'Long may your big jib draw', 'The dirt of a squid can be washed off but the dirt of a tongue sticks and stays', or 'As hard to tell as the mind of a gull'. Other colourful sayings include 'Mean enough to skin a louse for its hide and tallow', 'As cold as a stepmother's breath', 'A person so worthless he couldn't make a jib-boom sail for a wheelbarrow', and 'Why don't you throw over the anchor and stay?' meaning 'sit down'.

Halpert's *A Folklore Sampler from the Maritimes* cites some vivid insults: 'He's got the face of a north-bound horse going south', 'She walks like a chicken about to lay an egg', 'If brains were manure, you wouldn't have enough to grow grass out your ears!' and Higinbotham gives some colourful ones from the West: for example, 'Them coal-miners have hearts so small that you could pack them into the kernel of a mustard seed, and so hard that they'd punch a hole in the buzz-saw of a mosquito.'

Dr Halpert also gives examples of sayings known as 'dites' which resemble proverbial phrases but are not considered folk wisdom. As Halpert notes, 'They are chiefly traditional metaphors of the kind often used by parents to explain weather phenomena to young children.' In the Maritime collection rain is said to be 'God crying', thunder is 'angels bowling' or 'God rolling potatoes downstairs', snow is 'God's dandruff' or 'the feathers from Mother Goose'.

RIDDLES

Today riddles circulate mainly among children, and they emphasize humorous or nonsensical questions. But riddles have an ancient and honourable history. In primitive times adults solved them to demonstrate their wit, to appease the gods, to win contests, and sometimes to save their lives. They were featured in classical legends and myth—the riddle the Sphinx posed to Oedipus ('What walks on four legs in the morning, two legs at noon, and three legs at night?') has survived to modern times, and the Bible records Samson's riddle to the Philistines ('Out of the eater came forth meat, and out of the meat came forth sweetness').

Tales and songs preserve riddles, some dating from the Middle Ages. 'The Shepherd Substituting for the Priest Answers the King's Questions' is one of the most famous international tales, usually known in English as 'The King and the Abbot of Canterbury', and often termed 'Ride with the Sun', for the answer to one of its riddles. Several of the Child ballads are based on riddles, and one of these, 'The False Knight on the Road'—in which a little schoolboy confounds the Devil by answering his questions—has been preserved in Nova Scotia, as has a later more light-hearted one about 'Captain Wedderburn's Courtship'.

True riddles—those that have a logical answer—are rarely heard in Canada any more, but they were posed in earlier times. In his 1918 article in the *Journal of American Folklore* F.W. Waugh cites some from Ontario, commenting, 'Riddles were formerly told, and are still to some extent, as a means of entertainment in the evening, particularly in the winter. Like many other folk-customs, the telling of riddles is falling into disuse with the introduction of more modern amusements.'

The largest Canadian collection of riddles appears in Fauset's *Folklore of Nova Scotia*, a smaller group in Creighton's *Folklore of Lunenburg County*, and some rhymed examples in Fowke's *Ring Around the Moon*. They include various true riddles that are widely known, like 'Humpty Dumpty', 'Little Nancy Etticoat', and 'Old Lady Twitchett', along with more poetic examples:

> In spring I am gay in handsome array,
> In summer more clothing I wear.
> When colder it grows, I throw off my clothes,
> And in winter quite naked appear. (A tree)

Many conundrums and trick riddles also circulate, like 'What is the difference between a ball and a prince?' (One is thrown in the air and the other is heir to the throne), or 'When is a cat not a cat?' (When it's a kitten).

Again some of the best examples are from Newfoundland. Elisabeth Greenleaf found that many old riddles were still in use on the island, along with some composed in Sally's Cove. These are of particular interest for the light they throw on island customs. For example,

> Through a narrow path of wood I went,
> Between two waters I came back,

is based on a local custom--girls place a wooden hoop through the handles of their full pails of water to hold them away so their skirts won't get wet when they carry them. Another,

> Jim's is in under,
> Joe's is on top;
> Our little dory
> Goes over the lop (waves),

pictures two men sawing planks to make a dory: the log rests on a platform and one man stands on top and the other underneath.

From the Ontario singer LaRena Clark comes an unusual version of a 'neck riddle'; tradition held that to save his neck a condemned prisoner had to pose a riddle that no one could solve. This one is the focus of an international tale, 'Out-Riddling the Judge', and is widely known as a story. LaRena's version is unusual in being posed in a song:

> A princess was I in a castle high,
> A princess was I in a castle high,
> A princess was I in a castle high,
> King Henry has set me free.
>
> 'Twas from the dead the living came,
> 'Twas from the dead the living came,
> 'Twas from the dead the living came,
> King Henry has set me free.

> Oh, six there were, and seven there'll be,
> Oh, six there were, and seven there'll be,
> Oh, six there were, and seven there'll be,
> King Henry has set me free.

The answer is that there was a bird's nest in a horse's skull; six young birds had hatched, and an egg was still to be hatched.

CHILDLORE

Children's lore is another area that has not been explored in much detail in Canada. This is surprising, for it is probably the easiest type of folklore to collect. Children form a distinctive folk group, and their lore survives better than most adult types. Their games and their skipping, ball-bouncing, and counting-out rhymes are handed down from one child generation to another, mainly between the ages of five and eleven. For the most part these do not come from parents or teachers but are picked up from slightly older children, who in their turn learned them from children before them.

Most children's lore has its roots in the distant past. Many games can be traced back to ancient Greece or Rome and are played in much the same way in many countries. Very few games or rhymes originated in Canada: most came from Britain, where they have circulated for centuries, and some later items have been imported from the United States.

Items from the past have survived here in remarkably consistent forms. Most common are the multitudinous rhymes used for skipping. Although singing games like 'London Bridge', 'Here Come Three Dukes A-Riding', and 'The White Ship Sails through the Alley Alley O' are still played occasionally, they are less popular today than in former times. Instead, skipping rhymes are now by far the most common form of children's lore, and some of the old singing games are used for skipping. ('Skipping rhymes' is the Canadian term; in the United States they are called 'jump-rope rhymes'.) Many are comical or nonsensical, like:

> Salami was a dancer: she danced for the king,
> And every time she danced she wiggled everything.
> 'Stop!' said the king, 'You can't do that in here.'

'Pooh!' said Salami and kicked him in the rear.

Some of the best known are more poetic:

> The wind, the wind, the wind blows high,
> Blowing Janie through the sky.
> She is handsome, she is pretty,
> She is the girl from the Golden City.
> He comes courting, one two, three,
> May I ask her, who is he?

and:

> On a mountain stands a lady.
> Who she is I do not know.
> All she wants is gold and silver.
> All she needs is a nice young man.
> So call in my Nora dear, Nora dear, Nora dear,
> So call in my Nora dear while I go out to play.

Local and modern references may have crept in and a few Canadian firms have acquired unpaid commercials:

> Tip Top Tailor,
> My father was a sailor.
> He went to sea and he broke his knee,
> Tip Top Tailor!

and

> Don't go to Eaton's any more!
> There's a big fat policeman at the door.
> He will take you by the collar and make you pay a dollar
> So don't go to Eaton's any more.

An old skipping rhyme, 'In came the doctor, in came the nurse, in came the lady with the alligator purse', has a modern verse:

> 'Penicillin,' said the doctor,
> 'Penicillin,' said the nurse,
> 'Penicillin,' said the lady
> With the alligator purse.

Place names creep in too, and more recent cartoon characters and movie stars replace earlier ones, but the patterns remain constant. Where earlier chants told of Charlie Chaplin or Tillie the Toiler, a more modern one celebrates Ramjet, a superhero in an animated television series:

> Roger Ramjet is his name,
> The hero of our nation.
> The only problem with him is
> Mental retardation.

There are always minor variations, but for the most part Anglo-Canadian children share their lore with the rest of the English-speaking world. Considered together, the various rhymes and songs form the folk poetry of childhood. They show children's love of rhyme and their delight in playing with words, their natural instinct for rhythm, and their flights of fancy. They chant of Christopher Columbus, Cowboy Joe, Donald Duck, Popeye the Sailor Man, a little Dutch girl, and a girl in a golden city. They reflect many changing moods: in turn romantic, realistic, imaginative, prosaic, sentimental, and saucy. Some of them are crude or bawdy—parents would be shocked if they heard some of the rhymes most children know. A mild example is a 'tease' verse:

> Mary had a steamboat, the steamboat had a bell.
> Mary went to heaven, the steamboat went to —
> Hello operator, give me number nine,
> And if you disconnect me I'll kick you from
> Behind the iron curtain Mary had a piece of glass
> And when she sat upon it she hurt her little —
> Ask me no more questions, I'll tell you no more lies —
> The boys are in the bathroom doing up their flies.

Parodies are also very popular, some showing a perhaps unexpected awareness of sexual matters:

> My bonnie lies over the ocean,
> My bonnie lies over the sea.
> My father lies over my mother
> And that's how I came to be.

A few Ontario children's games were among the earliest Anglo-Canadian folklore items reported. As mentioned earlier, Alexander Chamberlain and Alice Leon published brief articles on children's lore in the *Journal of American Folklore* in 1895, and Wintemberg, Waugh, and Bleakney all included some from Ontario in the 1918 issue. Later Fauset and Creighton noted some from Nova Scotia; Herbert Halpert collected skipping rhymes in Alberta, and reported various children's rhymes from the Maritimes; and Vicki Schultz gives skipping rhymes from Manitoba.

My *Sally Go Round the Sun* gives 300 singing games, skipping, counting-out, ball-bouncing, and nonsense rhymes known in Canada, and *Ring Around the Moon* contains riddles, rounds, tongue-twisters, nonsense verses, and various children's songs. *Red Rover, Red Rover: Children's Games Played in Canada* surveys the non-singing games mostly played outdoors, classifying them in fifteen sections according to the kinds of actions involved. Among the most popular have been 'Red Rover, Red Rover', 'What Time Is It, Mr. Wolf?' 'Red Light, Green Light', 'Mother May I?' and 'Ante Ante Over the Shanty'. Also widespread are hopscotch and various games played with jacks and marbles. In 1980 Robert Cosbey published a valuable study, *All in Together, Girls: Skipping Songs from Regina, Saskatchewan*, which discusses the sources, transmission, and changes of the rhymes, describes the different patterns, and analyses the texts. He notes that the children follow rigid rules: everybody gets a turn, and there is no competition. Some of the rhymes are used to foretell events, others express anxieties about sickness and death. There is a somewhat satirical attitude to adults:

> Mr Brown and Mrs Green
> Went to the movies and watched the screen.
> Doctor Black and Mrs White
> Went to bed and turned off the light,

and a complete naturalness about sexual encounters:

> Down in the meadow where the green grass grows
> There sat Suzy without any clothes.

> Along came Johnny swinging on a chain,
> Down went his zipper and out it came.
> Three months later Suzy began to swell,
> Six months later you could really tell.
>
> Nine months later out they came:
> Two little greasers swinging their chains.

The student who gave Dr Cosbey this rhyme told him, 'It was not that the song was bad, but the adults always took it the wrong way. They took it literally, while we took it as just another skipping song.'

A minor children's pastime is the writing of verses in autograph albums. Again, it is remarkable how consistent they are. Items circulating in Saskatchewan in the 1920s are nearly all known in Ontario in the 1980s. An attractive collection compiled by Meguido Zola, *By Hook or By Crook: My Autograph Book*, lists many that are familiar throughout Canada. They include expressions of friendship: 'If you love me like I love you/ No knife can cut our love in two'; metaphors: 'In the woodbox of your memory/ May I always be a chip'; good wishes: 'May you have just enough clouds in your life to make a glorious sunset'; advice: 'Don't take life too seriously,/ You won't come out alive anyway'; and friendly insults: 'Blushing is red, nausea is green, / My face is funny but yours is a scream.'

Another children's activity that has become very popular lately is the playing of string games. These have very old and widespread patterns that are known in many countries. Diamond Jenness noted them among the Canadian Inuit, and Camilla Gryski has published a series of books beginning with *Cat's Cradle, Owl's Eyes* that have fascinated modern children.

ADULT GAMES

Related to childlore but often involving teenagers or adults are various types of parlour games like charades or 'Murder', and pranks and practical jokes. Sheldon Posen and John Scott write about pranks, practical jokes, and games in summer camps and the seal fishery, and Maurice Tremblay describes French-Canadian parlour games played on Île Verte. Some of these are unusual and reflect the region's culture. For example, Scott notes that sealers sometimes play football with a bag of duff: a standard food on sealing ships made out of flour that hardens shortly after it is cooked.

Similarly, the games that Tremblay describes represent various aspects of French-Canadian culture. 'Arracher la souche' (Pulling Up the Stump) relates to clearing the forests for the settlers' farms; 'Sauter le rapide' (Shooting the Rapid) relates to the travels of the *coureurs de bois*; 'Le jugement dernier' (The Last Judgement), 'La demande de graces à la Sainte-Vièrge' (Asking Favours from the Holy Virgin), and 'La Sainte-enfance' (The Holy Child) reflect the religious feeling so dominant in early Québécois society; and 'Plonger le loup marin' (Diving like a Seal) was probably inspired by the seals that were common around Île Verte.

A modern type of folklore exists in the photocopied jokes and cartoons that circulate anonymously among office workers. These—sometimes called xerox lore—are modern counterparts of graffiti, a very old type of comment dating back at least to Roman times. Alan Dundes and Carl Pagter give many examples in their *Urban Folklore from the Paperwork Empire* (1975). Jennifer Connor collected some Canadian examples, many of which are parodies of government memos or notices—one gives a 'Simplified Income Tax Return': 'How much did you earn? $---. Send it in.' Most are variants of American items but some have a Canadian slant satirizing government policy—for example, a notice suggests that the government is changing the country's emblem from a maple leaf to a 'French safe'.

And so it goes. From games with patterns known in ancient Greece and Rome and sayings that have circulated for hundreds of years to recent jokes and satires spread by modern machines, folklore continues to pass from person to person, wandering and changing but always reflecting the culture in which it spreads.

6

POPULAR BELIEFS AND SUPERSTITIONS

Superstitions and popular beliefs form an important part of folklore. Where folktales and folksongs have become less common today, folk beliefs are still very much a part of everyday life. *Webster's Dictionary* defines superstition as 'Any belief or attitude that is inconsistent with the known laws of science or with what is generally considered in the particular society as true or rational—especially a belief in charms, omens, or the supernatural, and any action or practice based on such a belief or attitude.' That is about as good as any definition, although folklorists today tend to quote Alan Dundes, who says: 'Superstitions are traditional expressions of one or more conditions and one or more results, with some of the conditions signs, and others causes.' For example, 'If bubbles rise to the top of a cup of coffee (sign), you will be rich (result)'. Often, however, superstitions are not expressions but actions: for example, 'If you spill salt you must throw some of it over your left shoulder to avert misfortune.' Also, many 'traditional expressions' that conform to Dundes's definition are not superstitions: 'First comes love, then comes marriage (cause), then comes Mary with a baby carriage (result),' or 'All work and no play (cause) makes Jack a dull boy' (result).

Today folklorists tend to speak of folk or popular beliefs rather than superstitions, for the latter term implies that they lack validity, and some folk beliefs embody folk wisdom. However, those that are obviously false are still called superstitions. They are usually beliefs or practices that lack scientific proof or result from faulty reasoning, and most involve assumptions based on cause and effect. Sometimes these assumptions are valid, but often they are based on misleading coincidences.

It is difficult to separate folk beliefs from other types of folklore. They turn up in legends and related narrative forms, and are reflected in the motifs of ancient ballads—for example, 'The Unquiet Grave' expresses the belief that mourning disturbs the dead. They are even found in proverbs— 'Lightning never strikes twice in the same place'— and children's rhymes—'Step on a crack,/ Break your mother's back.'

It used to be thought that superstitions circulated only among primitive or ignorant peoples, but it has become evident that even today practically everyone shares at least some vestiges of superstition. Many beliefs concerned with ensuring good luck or averting bad luck are still current in modern society. Folklorists note that irrational beliefs tend to cling to a culture long after common sense has dismissed them, and superstitious practices outlive the beliefs that inspired them. The superstition that thirteen is bad luck is so ingrained that it is still common for the floors in buildings to be numbered from twelve to fourteen, and some people hesitate to begin a journey on Friday the thirteenth. Few today actually believe that touching wood will avert ill fortune, but many still do it.

The only Canadian book devoted entirely to folk beliefs is Helen Creighton's *Bluenose Magic*. Next in importance is Fauset's section in *Folklore from Nova Scotia* of 366 items that he terms 'Folk Notions'. Fraser and Wintemberg include some beliefs in their general surveys, Halpert cites some in his *Folklore Sampler,* and Wintemberg and Waugh list some in the 1918 issue of the *Journal of American Folklore.*

The American folklorist Wayland Hand classified folk beliefs under fourteen categories, of which the two largest deal with weather and folk medicine. Many weather beliefs are based on observations of natural phenomena, and those skilled in judging them—like farmers and fishermen—can often foretell rain, fog, winds, or storms at least as accurately as our supposedly scientific weather forecasters.

Bluenose Magic reflects the seaman's concern with weather in sayings like:

> Mackerel skies and mare's tails
> Make lofty ships lower their sails,

and

> Red sky in morning,
> Sailors take warning.
> Red sky at night,
> Sailors' delight.

Folk medicine beliefs are particularly interesting. There are two types: natural beliefs in cures based on natural substances like herbs, plants, and minerals; and magical beliefs in cures involving charms or symbolic actions. Natural folk medicine includes the old-fashioned household cures handed down from generation to generation, some of which have been proved effective. For example, foxglove, long used for heart disease, is the source of digitalis, now a recognized heart medicine, and willow-bark, a folk treatment for arthritis, is a source of salicin, now a common medical ingredient. Some of the folk treatments Dr Creighton cites that are probably helpful include onion or mustard poultices for chest colds, cough medicine made of lemons and flax seed, and tea leaves, which contain tannin, for burns.

Less effective and often dangerous are many beliefs classed as magico-religious. These involve healings supposedly brought about by God or various saints, blood-stoppers, pow-wow doctors, conjurors, faith-healers, relics and holy places, charms, or symbolic rituals. Dr Creighton describes a charm that is general in Nova Scotia: 'Use the three highest words in the Bible. Make a cross on the back of your hand with the forefinger of the other hand and each time say over one of the three names (Father, Son, and Holy Ghost).' The belief is that disease is sent by evil forces that can be overcome by counterspells, but the danger is that trusting in magical cures may prevent a sufferer from getting needed medical treatment. Some may be directly harmful, like beliefs that you should treat the instrument that causes a wound rather than the wound itself. One example from Nova Scotia says that when wounded by a rusty nail you should put the nail in a stove or an oil barrel to take the infection out—a practice that could let the victim get lockjaw.

Ailments for which doctors do not have reliable cures are especially likely to be treated by folk remedies. Rheumatism, cancer, sties, cold-sores, hiccups, and warts all have inspired many imaginative treatments. There are probably more recommended cures for warts than for any other ailment, and these are a good illustration of how superstitions start—from faulty reasoning based on coincidence. Warts frequently disappear spontaneously, so anything the sufferer did just before they went away is automatically accepted as a reliable cure.

Wart treatments found in Canada illustrate some of the devices upon which magical cures are based. For example, 'measuring' by knots in a string or notches in a stick is supposed to indicate the extent to which a disease may go before it is stopped. One wart cure advises: 'Go to a running stream, get a twig, cut as many notches as you have warts. Throw the twig into the stream, never look back, and the warts will go away.' Another device, 'transference', holds that you can rid a person of a disease by transferring it to another person, animal, plant, or object. For example, rub corn on warts and feed the corn to turkeys, or rub a potato on them and throw the potato away. Still another device, 'plugging', is supposed to render diseases harmless by plugging them up. Hence you prick a wart, wipe a drop of blood off with a rag, bore a hole in an oak, and put a peg in to hold the rag in place.

Publications on special aspects of folk medicine include *Why Faith Healing?* by Michael Jones, which deals with the reasons patients seek the services of a faith healer; and *Roles of Magic and Healing: The Tietaja in the Memorates and Legends of Canadian Finns* by Matt T. Salo.

An important article, Luc Lacourcière's 'A Survey of Folk Medicine in French Canada from Early Times to the Present', begins with the oldest folk remedy noted in the New World: the drink made from cedar bark that the Indians gave to Cartier to cure scurvy. The early settlers prayed to various saints who were supposed to cure specific diseases; consulted bone-setters, faithhealers, blood-stoppers, midwives, and 'wisewomen'; and used a great many folk remedies often based on magic rituals.

The Indians' cure for scurvy is only one of many native cures that have been noted. Doctors and anthropologists—like Arthur Van

Wart, Sally Weaver, and Wilson Wallis—have reported on the medicines used by various tribes.

An interesting article of value to modern medical men is David Hufford's 'A New Approach to the "Old Hag": The Nightmare Tradition Re-Examined'. The 'Old Hag' refers to bad dreams usually about being chased by an evil creature, and the feelings of hearing or seeing something come into the room, being pressed on the chest and nearly suffocated, and being unable to move or cry out. Through questonnaires Dr Hufford found that such experiences were more widespread than previously thought, and probably originate from altered states of consciousness, possibly related to narcolepsy.

Superstitions about 'Love, Courtship, and Marriage', one of Wayland Hand's fourteen classes, are still widely observed. Every bride is sure to wear 'Something old, something new, something borrowed, and something blue', and the bridegroom is not allowed to see the bride on the wedding day before the ceremony. Girls who put a piece of the wedding cake under their pillow will dream of their future husband, and the girl who catches the bride's bouquet will be the next to marry.

'Death and Funeral Customs', another of the classes, also includes beliefs still current. Many signs are supposed to foretell a death, such as a dog howling, an owl hooting near the house, a rooster crowing between sundown and midnight, or a bird in the house.

Innumerable actions or accidents are supposed to bring bad luck. Some common ones reported in both Ontario and Nova Scotia and probably known all across Canada include opening an umbrella in the house, breaking a mirror, spilling salt, singing or whistling in bed, walking under a ladder, starting anything on Friday, and cutting fingernails on Sunday. There seem to be fewer things that bring good luck, but a few common ones are finding a four-leaf clover, wearing a birth-stone, being born with a caul, putting a horseshoe above the door, or having a cricket in the house.

Many Canadians believe in water witching—a process of finding water underground by holding a forked stick in both hands until it dips downward over a spot where there is supposed to be water.

Farmers have frequently hired water diviners to tell them where to dig their wells.

While most folk beliefs found in Canada exist in other countries, some typical ones reflect regional conditions. For example, Nova Scotians have an unusual number of superstitions dealing with sailors and ships because their lives are so bound up with the sea. An unusual one that is fairly widespread in the Maritimes holds that if you say the word 'pig' it makes the wind blow. One fisherman warned: 'Never say the word "pig" on a vessel. If you must speak of it call it Gruff. The reason the word must not be spoken is because pigs can see the wind.'

Other well-known maritime beliefs hold that you should always put money under the mast of a ship when it is being built, and that to turn a loaf of bread upside down upsets a ship at sea. It is bad luck to whistle on a boat or have a woman aboard, to turn a boat against the sun, to take a black suitcase aboard, and to wear coloured mittens on a vessel.

Many superstitions result from people's desire to believe in some magic formula that will help them to control their lives. There is also an inherent tendency to believe in the supernatural, so many interesting superstitions—involving ghosts, poltergeists, *doppelgängers*, witches, fairies, goblins, spells, hexes, amulets, and the evil eye—have been fairly widespread in Canada, as elsewhere. Creighton and Fraser both list many such beliefs that were current in Nova Scotia, Wintemberg lists some from the Pennsylvania Germans of Ontario, and in *Vampires, Dwarves, and Witches among the Ontario Kashubs* Jan Perkowski shows that strange beliefs from the Old World have survived among Canadian gypsies.

Dr Creighton, who has had some supernatural experiences herself, notes that forerunners—supernatural warnings of approaching death—are very common in Nova Scotia. One of the most common is hearing three knocks when there is nobody to knock. Another is seeing a *doppelgänger*—a person's own ghost. There are reports of hearing someone sawing wood for a coffin, or the rumble of a death wagon passing. She also cites many examples of persons with second sight, and of people who are convinced they were hexed by witches.

Canada has its share of strange supernatural tales. Champlain and the Jesuits gave observers' accounts of the phenomenon known as the shaking tent of the Indian medicine men. Poltergeist hauntings are responsible for several famous cases. Twenty-six witnesses attested to the strange happenings that took place at John T. McDonald's Ontario farm at Baldoon from 1829 to 1831. They saw stones and bullets come through windows and doors, kettles and other objects flying through the air, and fires breaking out many times a day, finally destroying both the house and barns.

In 1878 the home of Daniel Teed in Amherst, Nova Scotia, became the focus for what has been termed Canada's best ghost story. Teed's two unmarried sisters, Jane and Esther, lived with him. After an unpleasant experience with a suitor named Bob McNeal, Esther began having strange attacks in which her whole body swelled, only to deflate when several loud reports were heard. Many peculiar manifestations followed: odd noises, objects flying through the air or disappearing mysteriously, writings on walls, and ghosts communicating through a code of knocks. Fires broke out, and followed Esther when she moved to different homes, sometimes occurring as often as forty-five times in a day. Finally Esther was convicted of arson and sent to jail, which ended her 'manifestations'.

Hauntings have also been reported from Clarendon on the Quebec side of the Ottawa River, and Caledonia Mills near Antigonish, Nova Scotia. R.S. Lambert describes these and other strange phenomena in *Exploring the Supernatural: The Weird in Canadian Folklore*.

There are also the widespread beliefs about monsters—Sedna and D'Sonoqua, the Windigo and the Sasquatch—that appear in legends mentioned earlier. In addition to the many first-person reports, they are the subject of a number of studies. Morton Teicher discusses *Windigo Psychosis: A Study of a Relationship Between Belief and Behavior among the Indians of Northeastern Canada*, and Marius Barbeau describes 'Supernatural Beings of the Huron and Wyandot'. Carole Henderson [Carpenter] writes of 'Monsters of the West: The Sasquatch and the Ogopogo', seeing them as 'vestiges of the retreating wilderness' and maintained by westerners 'partly because these creatures are something distinctive which Easterners do not have'. In *Manlike Monsters on Trial,* Marjorie Halpin and Michael Ames assemble essays—by physical and social scientists, folklorists, historians, and a psychoanalyst—that examine the reports and analyse the beliefs in these monsters to show their relationship to human culture.

Along the east coast there are many reports of ghost ships. Often people claim to have seen a burning vessel that is thought to be the *Teazer,* a privateer that was trapped by British warships off the coast of Nova Scotia in 1813 and set afire by its crew to avoid capture. Other phantom ships are identified with particular vessels sunk or burned, and many stories tell of ghosts that haunt ships. There are also many folk beliefs about pirates, a common one being that when they buried their treasure they always killed a man and left him as a ghost to guard it.

A widely held sea superstition holds that the spirits of men lost from a vessel will board that vessel at a later time. In a 1914 sealing disaster the *Newfoundland* lost seventy-seven men out of a crew of two hundred. MacEdward Leach's record *Songs from the Outports of Newfoundland* gives the story of sailors who swore they saw ghostly figures climb into the *Newfoundland* on the anniversary of the disaster. The same tradition inspired the popular east-coast ballad 'The Ghostly Sailors', which tells how the men who drowned in 1866, when the *Charles Haskell* sank the *Andrew Jackson,* boarded the *Haskell* when it returned to the same fishing grounds. Janet McNaughton, who analyses the beliefs it illustrates, argues that 'those who sing this song accept the ballad system in which the living and the dead co-exist', and they believe that the ghosts return to validate the tradition that ships are sacred, preserving sailors from the sea.

7

FOLKLIFE AND CUSTOMS

Folklife is a broad category that could include practically everything that has been written about pioneer life, the life of minorities, and customs within the many folk groups. Because the subject is so extensive, this survey will merely suggest its scope and mention some representative publications. It should be noted that most of the books in this area are by non-folklorists.

The chapter on 'Beginnings' mentioned the many anthropologists who studied the life and customs of the native peoples. It also noted that some of the earliest Anglo-Canadian folklore descriptions appeared in nineteenth-century books reflecting folklife in pioneer Ontario. More recently historians have described the way various groups lived in the past; among their many books Edwin C. Guillet's *Early Life in Upper Canada* and J.M.S. Careless's *The Pioneers: An Illustrated History of Early Settlement in Canada* give good general surveys. Also, most of the numerous oral history books that have been appearing in recent years describe aspects of folklife. Some of these were mentioned in the chapter on 'Tales' as illustrating personal narratives.

John Kenneth Galbraith writes of his Ontario Lowland Scots community in *The Scotch*, and Charles W. Dunn describes a quite different culture in *Highland Settler: A Portrait of the Scottish Gael in Nova Scotia*. Still another study covering a third group of Scots in Canada is more analytic: a collection of articles titled *Cultural Retention and Demographic Change: Studies of the Hebridean Scots in the Eastern Townships of Quebec* collected largely by Margaret Bennett Knight and edited by Laurel Doucette.

In another volume Laurel Doucette writes of her Irish-Canadian family in *Skill and Status: Traditional Expertise within a Rural Canadian Family*, while John Mannion takes a sociological approach in *Irish Settlements in Eastern Canada: A Study of Cultural Transfer and Adaptation.*

Descriptions in English of life in French Canada appear in a number of general books like Greenough's *Canadian Folk-Life and Folk-Lore*, Charles G.D. Roberts' translation of Phillipe-Aubert de Gaspé's *Les Anciens Canadiens, Canadians of Old*, and Marius Barbeau's *The Kingdom of the Saguenay* and *Quebec, Where Ancient France Lingers.* Horace Miner produced a more analytical study in *St Denis: A French-Canadian Parish.*

Again, as with the other folklore areas, some of the most important publications are from Newfoundland. Two autobiographical accounts—Victor Butler's *Little Nord Easter: Reminiscences of a Placentia Bayman* and Aubrey Tizzard's *On Sloping Ground: Reminiscences of Outport Life in Notre Dame Bay, Newfoundland*—reflect the different aspects of life in the outports as seen through the eyes of two men who lived in them. Broader in conception are two accounts by women: Hilda Murray's *More than 50%: Women's Life in a Newfoundland Outport 1900-1950* and Helen Porter's *Below the Bridge* about life in St John's. The Institute of Social and Economic Research (ISER) has published more analytic studies such as James Faris's *Cat Harbour: A Newfoundland Fishing Settlement*, Melvin Firestone's *Brothers and Rivals: Patrilocality in Savage Cove*, and John Szwed's *Private Cultures and Public Imagery: Interpersonal Relations in a Newfoundland Peasant Society.*

Somewhat fewer publications describe folklife in western Canada. Two good homesteading accounts, one early and one recent, are Samuel Strickland's *Twenty-Seven Years in Canada West* (1853), and R.D. Symons' *Where the Wagon Led* (1973). Many folklife descriptions from the Prairies deal with ethnic groups other than English and French because the Canadian Centre for Folk Culture Studies emphasizes multiculturalism. Its Mercury publications include Robert Blumstock's *Békévar: Working Papers on a Canadian Prairie Community* about Hungarians, Jan Brunvand's

Norwegian Settlers in Alberta, Ban Seng Hoe's *Structural Changes of Two Chinese Communities in Alberta,* Rolf Brednich's *Mennonite Folklife and Folklore,* G.J. Houser's *The Swedish Community at Eriksdale, Manitoba,* James Patterson's *The Romanians of Saskatchewan* and *The Greeks of Vancouver,* Frank Paulsen's *Danish Settlements on the Canadian Prairies,* and Koozma Tarasoff's *Traditional Doukhobor Folkways.* The Mercury series also documents the folkways of some ethnic groups in eastern Canada: Matt and Sheila Salo's account of a gypsy tribe in *The Kalderas in Eastern Canada,* and Linda Degh's discussion of Hungarian traditions, *People in the Tobacco Belt.*

A few other significant books on ethnic folklife are G. Elmore Reaman's *The Trail of the Black Walnut,* the story of the Pennsylvania Germans who left the United States to come north and settle in Ontario around Waterloo; Ken Adachi's *The Enemy That Never Was: A History of the Japanese Canadians,* describing their treatment during the Second World War; Mark Mealing's *Doukhobor Life,* about the history, religion, and customs of the Doukhobors in their western settlements; and Edna Staebler's *Sauerkraut and Enterprise,* describing the household traditions of the Mennonites.

The customs of various occupational groups present another aspect of folklore. Grace Nute's *The Voyageur* is one of several accounts of the men who first travelled Canada's many waterways. George England gives a vivid picture of the sealing industry in *Vikings of the Ice: Being the Log of a Tenderfoot on the Great Newfoundland Seal Hunt.* Two early and rare books, John Geikie's *George Stanley; or, Life in the Woods* and George S. Thompson's *Up to Date; or, The Life of a Lumberman,* give first-hand descriptions of lumbering in Ontario during the nineteenth century, and out west Ed Gould describes *British Columbia's Logging History.* On the prairies Grant MacEwan writes of ranchers in *Blazing the Old Cattle Trail* and *John Ware's Cow Country,* and of the early farmers in *The Sodbusters.* Those accounts are not by folklorists, but Robert McCarl, a folklorist who studies occupational groups, writes of 'The Communication of Work Technique' with particular reference to the fishing industry.

CUSTOMS

The two most important publications delineating customs in Canada come from Memorial University: *Christmas Mumming in Newfoundland* edited by Herbert Halpert and George Story, and *If You Don't Be Good: Verbal Social Control in Newfoundland* by J.D.A. Widdowson.

The volume on mumming—or 'mummering', as it is often called—is the first extensive study of a Canadian custom. There are many accounts of mumming in Britain, but its Canadian practice was comparatively unknown until Halpert and Story inspired various folklorists, anthropologists, sociologists, and historians to share their observations of mumming as practised on the island. They show that what was originally a folk play of death and resurrection has become a tradition of house-visits by disguised figures known as mummers, or as 'janneys' in some parts of Newfoundland where the custom is called 'janneying'. A common pattern in the house-visits requires the hosts to guess the identity of their disguised visitors, and sometimes the visitors expect to be given food or money.

Through their careful analysis of this tradition the contributors to *Christmas Mumming* show how it throws light on various aspects of the islanders' social and cultural life. In a later account, *The Newfoundland Mummers' Christmas House-Visit*, Margaret Robertson describes its significant patterns and suggests that these patterns are ritual symbols representing the cultural values in the outports.

Persons of German descent in Nova Scotia practised a similar custom known as 'belsnickling', and in Cape Sable Island a somewhat more elaborate practice was termed 'Santa Clawing'. As Herbert Halpert describes it in *A Folklore Sampler*, a group of men playing various musical instruments would perform skits and sing songs satirizing members of the community. He also notes that in two small islands off the Nova Scotia coast the mummers were known as sandys, and in some parts of Nova Scotia and New Brunswick a rowdy crowd of masked men were called Callithumpians.

Robert Klymasz describes another form of mumming that Ukrainians practised on the Prairies. It featured comic figures led by Malanak—a man dressed as a woman—and included songs and jokes that suggested unofficial matchmaking. Recently this practice has been revived as a form of New Year's supper dance.

The other major Newfoundland book on customs, Widdowson's account of the methods parents use to control children, outlines various threats and discusses the many frightening figures that turn up in them. Bogeymen, the Black Man, mermaids, or the Devil are invoked in attempts to keep children away from dangerous places, to bring them indoors, to get them to bed, or to prevent disobedience or naughty behaviour.

Although these are the only detailed studies of particular customs, innumerable articles describe other specific folkways. Some are about making maple sugar, building sod shanties, and making dyes from plants; others deal with harvest customs and various festivals. Louis Fréchette writes of *Christmas in French Canada*, Bruce Giuliano analyses four Italian religious festivals, and Michael Taft describes 'The St Laurent Pilgrimage' in Saskatchewan. More recent celebrations held in Toronto every summer include Caribana based on West Indian carnival customs, and Caravan, a big multicultural festival.

Widespread in earlier times were such social customs as holding square dances in schools or private homes, and fowl suppers and Christmas concerts in the church. Bees were the means of accomplishing much community work, as people gathered to help their neighbours. There were house-raising and barn-raising bees, and smaller husking or quilting bees. Cape Breton held milling frolics—when a long web of newly woven cloth was beaten and pounded until it thickened—and Ontario had its paring bees to peel and dry apples for winter, or even pumpkin bees to prepare the pumpkins for storage. When the work was done a social evening would follow, often taking the form of a square dance.

There were also singing competitions, sometimes called singing bees. Roy Mackenzie tells of an old man who remembers one being held in a tavern when travellers were delayed by a storm, and Louise Manny describes how 'singers sang one song after another, all different, until only one man had something left to sing'. Such a competition provides the framework for Thomas Raddall's fine tale, 'Blind MacNair'.

Dr Manny also cites Mrs Jared McLean's description of several New Brunswick customs. The annual work of blueberry picking became a festival of song—the pickers drove to the blueberry barrens in big hay-wagons, sang as they picked to pass the time, and sang all the way home, driving out of their way to circle 'The Square' in Newcastle 'singing and whooping as a triumphant finale to their day of toil'. Picking potatoes in the fall was also a sort of neighbourhood celebration in which whole families took part, and the stalks were always burned on Hallowe'en. They also held pancake parties at which they played cards—forty-fives, cribbage, snap, old maid—while the women cooked the pancakes; then they danced and ate and sang.

The Newfoundland 'times'—parties with singing and dancing corresponding to the old-country ceilidhs—are common. Elisabeth Greenleaf tells of one that took the form of an all-day fair to raise money for the schoolhouse and the church. Featured were the 'guess cakes' in which the unmarried girls concealed something that the prospective purchasers had to guess. They paid five cents for each guess until someone got it right and won the cake.

Many customs fall into one of two groups: those connected with the rites of passage, and those related to the cycle of the year. The rites of passage are the ceremonies that mark changes in the life cycle. In primitive societies these were designed to help a person pass safely from one stage of life to the next: from pre-existence to life, from childhood to adulthood, from a single to a married state, and from life to the afterlife. These stages are less emphasized today, but there are still customs relating to them. Birth customs include the father handing out cigars, friends giving baby showers, dressing boys in blue and girls in pink, and so on. Jewish boys have their Bar Mitzvah, and college students hold initiations. Customs relating to marriage involve exchanging rings, showers, stag parties, throwing rice, and decorating the newlyweds' car. Death is marked by drawn blinds and black bows on the door, black clothing or black armbands, floral tributes, holding a wake, etc. Few have written about these customs in Canada, but Anne-Kay Buckley and Christine Cartwright studied customs associated with death in Newfoundland.

The charivari, sometimes termed shivaree, was a typical Canadian custom associated with weddings in pioneer times. As Susanna Moodie describes it, when the community did not approve of a particular marriage, the young men in the neighborhood would disguise themselves and proceed to the bridegroom's house where they made a racket and beat on the door until the bridegroom gave them money or drink.

In a Newfoundland wedding custom that Elisabeth Greenleaf describes, the bridal party had to walk from the church to the bride's home between two lines of people, while the young men shot off their guns as close to the wedding couple as they could. Mrs Greenleaf was told that this was because using firearms was a privilege restricted to Protestants, so they loved to fire off guns just to show that they could. Today the custom of playing pranks on newlyweds still continues—Monica Morrison describes some typical tricks played in New Brunswick.

Similarly, there are many customs relating to the cycle of the year. New Year's Eve parties, sending valentines, colouring Easter eggs, 'trick or treat' visits at Hallowe'en, the Thanksgiving dinner, and Christmas carolling and gift-giving are a few common ones. Helen Creighton mentions Lunenburg practices for Christmas, New Year's, Good Friday, Easter, and Hallowe'en. There are quite a few accounts of Christmas customs, but folklorists are just beginning to study some of the other festivals and rituals. Mary Kaye-Roil writes of Easter customs in 'A Time of Restraint: A Survey of the Good Friday Traditions in Newfoundland' and Darryl Hunter writes of Hallowe'en customs as they were known to a Saskatchewan woman; Robert Klymasz discusses funeral rhetoric among Ukrainians in the West, and Laurel Doucette describes a Gatineau Valley church picnic.

It is rather surprising to find that the most complete survey of Canada's special days and the customs associated with them appear in a book for children: Caroline Parry's *Let's Celebrate!* She notes the name-days associated with saints, the spring and the autumn equinoxes and the summer and the winter solstices, May Day and Labour Day, Boxing Day and New Year's Eve, Twelfth Night, Mardi Gras, Shrove Tuesday, Ash Wednesday, Valentine's Day, April Fool's Day, Victoria Day, Mother's and Father's Days, Midsummer's Eve, Yom Kippur, Hannukah, and many festivals celebrated by Canada's various ethnic groups. Most of the customs associated with these are yet to be studied by folklorists.

8

FOLK ARTS AND CRAFTS

Although people usually think of folklore in terms of oral tradition (folktales, folksongs, folk speech), it also emcompasses traditional methods of working and making things, and the objects made. These aspects are generally referred to as folk arts and crafts, or more broadly as material culture.

Folk arts and crafts normally cover artifacts that are created for personal use and pleasure, or sometimes for sale within a community. They are usually thought to be hand-made rather than machine-made, and home-made rather than factory-made, although as time goes on they may be produced by more modern methods. But, as Marius Barbeau noted, they are 'opponents of the serial nunber, the stamped product, and the patented standard'. They usually show design elements belonging to a local tradition, and have qualities that appeal to the people who use them.

Folk crafts refer to the making of useful articles: items created for a particular purpose, such as providing clothing, food, shelter, bedding, tools, or utensils. Folk arts refer to articles created for aesthetic reasons—food for the soul rather than for the body. In practice, items created for use—crafts—are often decorated in ways that make them also appreciated as folk art.

Material culture is very broad, including—in addition to the items we normally think of as arts and crafts—such things as furniture, bread ovens, fences, covered bridges, grave markers, and the folk architecture of houses and barns. Jean-François Blanchette, René Bouchard, and Gerald Pocius list the many publications in this field in 'A Bibliography of Folk Material Culture in Canada 1965-1982', published in a special issue of *Canadian Folklore canadien* titled 'People and Things'.

The arts and crafts of Canada are of particular interest because of the blending of two concepts: the transference of traditions from the lands from which Canadians came, and the adaptation of those traditions to the Canadian scene. Michael Bird, who has written extensively of Mennonite and Doukhobor arts, notes in his article on 'Doukhobor Folk and Decorative Arts':

Few Western countries are blessed with so rich a mixture of cultural traditions as Canada, and probably still fewer are distinguished by the continuation to such late date of ethnically unique folk and decorative art traditions. It is interesting to observe that nearly all of the national folk art traditions illustrated in H.J. Hansen's monumental *European Folk Art* can be found in one form or another somewhere in Canada. From the earliest votive art of New France to the domestic art forms of the Scandinavians, Germans, Ukrainians, and others who settled in western Canada in the late nineteenth and early twentieth centuries, not to mention the wealth of indigenous art produced by Canada's diverse native peoples, there is a working panorama of ethnically or religiously infused artistic expression.

Today folklorists are showing increased interest in material culture, perhaps because more job opportunities have been opening up in museums, pioneer villages, and historical buildings. Until recently, however, most studies in this field were by non-folklorists: historians, art critics, anthropologists, and museum curators. More specialized studies of material culture have lately begun to appear. Folklorists have written of mills, bread ovens, bridges, gravestones, shipbuilding, potteries, saunas, baskets, bottles, toys, duck decoys, and of articles made of iron, wood, glass, and silver. Costumes and food are also considered part of material culture.

The National Museum of Man, recently renamed the Canadian Museum of Civilization, has been influential in collecting and studying folklore artifacts through the Canadian Centre for Folk Culture Studies. It attempts to depict Canada's diversified heritage through the display of textiles, costumes, folk art, furnishings, and musical instruments, many of which are described in its Mercury series.

THE NATIVE PEOPLES

As with the other folk genres, the arts and crafts of the native peoples have been more thoroughly explored than those of any other group. Inuit sculpture and prints, Indian masks and totem poles, have inspired innumerable publications. A few important works are Barbeau's volumes on *Totem Poles* and *Haida Art, Kwakiutl Art* by Audrey Hawthorn, *Art of the Northwest Coast Indians* by R.B. Inverarity, *Eskimo Prints* by James Houston, and *Sculpture of the Eskimo* by George Swinton. Those books are largely descriptive, but Bill Holm and William Reid take a more analytical approach in *Indian Art of the Northwest Coast: A Dialogue on Craftsmanship and Aesthetics*. Most writers have dwelt on the arts of the West Coast Indians and the Inuit, but some have described and studied many other artifacts of the native peoples, including canoes, kayaks, stone boats, sleds, snowshoes, costumes, baskets, blankets, and jewelry. Ian and Patricia Bradley's *A Bibliography of Native Arts* gives a useful list.

FRENCH CANADIANS

French-Canadian folk art reflects the historic influence of the church on every aspect of life. This is particularly obvious in the early religious carvings of Madonnas, apostles, saints, angels, and crucifixes. Other carvings are realistic, based on animals, birds, flowers, and human figures. Useful objects like maple sugar and butter moulds were highly decorative, and so were such textiles as the Assomption sashes made for the *voyageurs,* embroidered robes and altar cloths, and hooked rugs. From metal the French Canadians made weathervanes, crosses, agricultural tools, and much silverwork. Illustrations of many of these appear in Barbeau's *I Have Seen Quebec*. Recently an Acadian folklorist, Ronald Labelle, discusses a narrower aspect in 'A Case Study of Folk Religion Among Quebec's Stone Cutters'.

Naturally most French-Canadian studies dealing with material culture are in French, but a few important ones in English are Jean Palardy's *The Early Furniture of French Canada,* Ramsay Traquair's *The Old Architecture of Quebec,* Lise Boily's *The Bread Ovens of Quebec,* and Jay Anderson's 'The Early Development of French-Canadian Foodways'. The *Bibliography of the Material Culture of New France* by Barbara Alexandrin and Robert Bothwell provides a useful survey of early publications.

ANGLO-CANADIANS

Pioneer settlers in English Canada shared much of their material culture with the French. Their craftsmen produced beds, chairs, chests, cradles, cupboards, desks, and tables, which Philip Shackleton describes in *The Furniture of Old Ontario,* and Scott Symons provides *A Romantic Look at Early Canadian Furniture.*

Pioneer housewives spun wool from their sheep and wove the yarn into cloth. They made their own clothes by sewing and knitting, and used scraps of cloth or worn-out clothing to make hooked or braided rugs, and quilts of widely varied patterns. Some of the quilts were simple strips sewn together, but others had more complicated geometric arrangements, and sometimes pictorial or symbolic designs. Common traditional patterns include the Log Cabin, Lone Star, Wedding Ring, Rose and Thistle, True Lover's Knot, and Double Irish Chain. Harold and Dorothy Burnham describe pioneer textiles in '*Keep Me Warm One Night'': Early Handweaving in Eastern Canada*, and Dorothy Burnham expands this in *The Comfortable Arts: Traditional Spinning and Weaving in Canada.* Gerald Pocius describes the *Textile Traditions of Eastern Newfoundland* and Edwin C. Guillet gives a good overview in *Pioneer Arts and Crafts.*

As mentioned in the 'Folklife' chapter, neighbours co-operated in building houses and barns, and the results are studied as 'vernacular achitecture'—the ordinary buildings of a region. Marion MacRae and Anthony Adamson write of *The Ancestral Roof: Domestic Architecture of Upper Canada*, Eric Arthur and Dudley Witney study *The Barn: A Vanishing Landmark in North America,* and Anthony Adamson and John Willard describe *The Gaiety of Gables: Ontario's Architectural Folk Art*. Janice Tyrwhitt writes of mills, and Richard and Lyn Harrington of covered bridges in central and eastern Canada.

Other studies deal with more varied aspects of material culture. David Taylor describes *Boat Building in Winterton, Trinity Bay, Newfoundland*, Eustella Langdon writes of *Pioneer Gardens at Black Creek Pioneer Village*, and Muriel Newton-White describes an early architectural feature of the pioneer landscape in *Back houses of the North*. Humanity's final craft is the subject of Deborah Trask's *Life How Short, Eternity How Long: Gravestone Carving and Carvers in Nova Scotia* and Carole Hanks' *Early Ontario Gravestones*, while Gerald Pocius takes a more analytical approach in 'Eighteenth- and Nineteenth-Century Newfoundland Gravestones: Self-Sufficiency, Economic Specialization, and the Creation of Artifacts'.

OTHER ETHNIC GROUPS

Among other culture groups the folk arts and crafts of the Pennsylvania Germans, Ukrainians, and Doukhobors are particularly rich and have inspired the largest number of publications.

Especially distinctive is Fraktur, the decorative calligraphy combined with painted embellishment that characterizes the Mennonite art of southwestern Ontario. Samplers, watercolour hangings, Bible registers, and bookplates incorporate illuminated texts with traditional motifs of birds, hearts, and flowers. Michael Bird describes *Ontario Fraktur: A Pennsylvania German Folk Tradition in Early Canada*, and Reginald Good writes of the work of one Mennonite artist, Anna Weber. The Mennonites are also noted for their needlework, woodworking, and decorative painting, which Nancy-Lou Patterson describes in *Swiss-German and Dutch-German Mennonite Traditional Art in the Waterloo Region, Ontario*. Michael Bird and Terry Kobayashi present a broader view in *A Splendid Harvest: German Folk and Decorative Arts in Canada*, and Edna Staebler describes the foodways of the Waterloo region in several books, beginning with *Food That Really Schmecks*.

The decoration of Easter eggs is a distinctive Ukrainian art form. Originally the decoration involved waxing and dyeing by a batik method, but today the eggs are sometimes made of wood and painted. Early Ukrainian churches are striking, capped with bulbous domes and ornamental wrought-iron crosses, while inside they exhibit elaborately embroidered altar-cloths, processional banners, painted wooden icons, and carved wooden crosses.

The Ukrainians are also noted for sheepskin coats and richly embroidered shirts, sashes, and wrap-around skirts decorated with the characteristic cross-stitch patterns, described in Nancy Ruryk's *Ukrainian Embroidery Designs and Stitches.* Ukrainians' love of music is emphasized by their unusual musical instruments: a many-stringed lyre called a bandura, a type of dulcimer called a cymbaly, an old-country violin, and a flute known as a sopilka. Robert Klymasz surveys their arts and describes the changes that have taken place in *Continuity and Change: The Ukrainian Folk Heritage in Canada,* and Savella Stechishin describes their distinctive food in *Traditional Ukrainian Cookery.*

The Doukhobors are noted for their woodworking—ladles, sugar bowls, and spinning wheels—and for their spinning, knitting, needlework, and rugs, which Koozma Tarasoff describes in *Traditional Doukhobor Folkways.* They have also produced distinctive furniture and buildings. Michael Bird notes that while Doukhobor furniture shares characteristics with that of the Ukrainians and Mennonites, it is marked by more complex surface decoration involving carving, inlay, and painting. The carved ornamentation is particularly distinctive, taking the form of either relief carving or fretwork.

Two articles relating to other ethnic groups are Michael Taft's account of lace-making by a Belgian family in Saskatchewan and Charles Sutya's of the Finnish sauna in Manitoba.

GENERAL

Despite the plethora of cookbooks, few deal with Canadian food customs. Those that do concentrate on ethnic cooking. Edna Staebler's and Savella Stechishin's books on Mennonite and Ukrainian cooking are almost the only ones that provide more than recipes. More descriptive are Jay Anderson's article on French-Canadian foodways, Thelma Barer-Stein's *You Eat What You Are: A Study of Ethnic Food Traditions*, Beulah Barss's *The Pioneer Cook: A Historical View of Canadian Prairie Food*, and Edith Rowles' 'Bannock, Beans, and Bacon: An Investigation of Pioneer Diet'.

Costumes can tell us much about the culture of various communities, but so far this subject has inspired fewer accounts than rugs and quilts. Madeleine Doyon-Ferland has researched French-Canadian costumes and published extensively in French. There is only one major book in English, Peggy Tyrchniewicz's *Ethnic Folk Costumes in Canada*, and a few pamphlets like Katherine Brett's *Modest to Mod: Dress and Undress in Canada, 1780-1967* and Eileen Collard's *Early Clothing in Southern Ontario.*

Several books give good over-all surveys of folk art: Michael Bird's *Canadian Folk Art: Old Ways in a New Land*, R.H. Field's *Spirit of Nova Scotia: Traditional Decorative Folk Art 1780-1930*, and Ralph and Patricia Price's *'Twas Ever Thus: A Selection of Eastern Canadian Folk Art.* A special issue of *artscanada* deals with the rather neglected area of 'Prairie Folk Art'.

Some of the best works on folk arts and crafts are catalogues for museum and gallery exhibitions. One of the few produced by folklorists, *From the Heart: Folk Art in Canada*, features items from the Canadian Centre for Folk Culture Studies. Its four sections illustrate artifacts from pioneer farming and logging; local motifs, symbols, icons, and talismans; works of imagination, humour and fantasy; and the work of four typical folk artists. Its compilers feel that folk art is in transition: from tradition to innovation, from functionality to pure form, from collective representation to individuality, and from ethnic patterns to greater universality.

Recently folklorists have been focusing on traditional craftspeople like David Horst, a St Jacobs woodcarver; Walter Cameron, a Fallbrook blacksmith, woodcarver, and storyteller; Edith Clayton, a Nova Scotia basket-maker; George Cockayne, an Ontario woodcarver; and Patrick Murphy, a Newfoundland artist. In describing them the folklorists try to show how their work relates to their community. In a more personal account, novelist Adele Wiseman describes her mother's hobby of making dolls, presenting a fascinating character study she calls *Old Woman at Play*.

The field of material culture has become increasingly important to folklorists. They are beginning to publish studies that add contextual and interpretative insights to the earlier descriptive accounts, and to increase the scope from pioneer times to the present. Gerald Pocius, a folklore professor at Memorial University, is Canada's leading scholar in this field. He has written several articles relating material folklore to social structure: for example, 'Hooked Rugs in Newfoundland. The Representation of Social Structure in Design'. He notes that historians, anthropologists, folklorists, and researchers in art history, cultural geography, and architectural history have recognized that artifacts are important in developing historical and contemporary insights. He finds it ironic that artifact studies in Canada have focused on central Canada, and particularly on pioneer life in Ontario, because most people think of folklore as belonging to non-English groups, and he argues for broadening material culture studies to include urban and modern artifacts to supplement the past emphasis on pre-industrial culture.

9

A FEW FINAL WORDS

The concept of folklore has enlarged enormously in the last half-century. Earlier scholars thought of it as primarily from the past—the 'popular antiquities' for which William Thoms substituted the term 'folklore'. It was considerd the lore of the rural countryside preserved by peasants and the uneducated. Today we recognize that all people have folklore and that it exists everywhere. It is constantly taking new forms—the ancient tales and ballads are joined by lore stemming from movies, television, xerox machines, and many other things that make up modern life.

The basic stages in studying folklore are collection, classification, and analysis. The study of folklore in Canada is still young, but in the last thirty years it has begun to move from collecting and classifying towards analysis. Some areas still call for collecting. Because of the government's multicultural policy the National Museum has stressed minority cultures at the expense of major ones, so there is still a need to collect more Anglo-Canadian lore. Eastern Canada has been studied much more thoroughly than western Canada, and rural traditions more than urban. We need to pay more attention to occupational and children's lore, and we need more regional, national, and cross-cultural studies.

Scholars at Laval University have developed detailed classification systems for tales and songs and have begun to analyse their extensive archives. Memorial University scholars are collecting in context and producing a wide variety of analytical and theoretical studies. Now that the discipline has a firm grounding, it will develop rapidly in future years. There is a danger, however, that such development will emphasize theory at the expense of the human values that make folklore valuable. Scholars should never forget that they are dealing with people, and that the lore of people does not fit neatly into scientific patterns.

Folklore has a double set of values—for the folk who use it and for those who study it. Among the folk it has a variety of functions; as Alan Dundes notes in *The Study of Folklore:*

> Some of the most common ones include aiding in the education of the young, promoting a group's feeling of solidarity, providing socially sanctioned ways for individuals to act superior to or to censure other individuals, serving as a vehicle for social protest, offering an enjoyable escape from reality, and converting dull work into play.

When we study it, it can broaden our understanding of ourselves and our goals. The variety of our folklore—involving the rich lore brought from older countries, the customs, tales, and songs adapted to Canadian conditions, the new lore created here in the past, and the modern lore existing today—can help us to understand our culture and our people. Bertrand Bronson's comment on folksong applies to folklore in general:

> Folksong can be thought of as a rich deposit of our commom humanity, laid down centuries deep layer after layer, by generations of anonymous men and women, who have shared in the same cultural heritage. . . . Folksong serves as a precious touchstone to remind us how far away we get and to call us back to our common centre. . .

That emphasizes folklore's importance in helping us to understand our own cultural heritage. It has been said that we can't know where we are going until we know where we have been. As we learn more about our folklore we will see how it reflects our history and our ethnic, economic, and regional divisions, and by studying it we may gain knowledge that will help us to reduce the things that divide us. Many folklorists today emphasize the different groups that make up our pluralistic society, but, as William Wilson emphasizes in the *Journal of American Folklore*: 'The attempt to discover the uniqueness of the group is closely parallel to the romantic-nationalistic attempt, with all of its inherent dangers, to discover the uniqueness of a particular nation.' He holds that 'We transmit folklore not because we belong to a particular nation or to a particular group, but because we are human beings dealing with recurring human problems in traditional human ways.' Realizing this can help us to understand people of other countries, for much lore transcends cultural and linguistic barriers and thus reveals the common bonds that link us to all humankind. If such understanding were widespread it might lessen the tensions that cause so much misunderstanding and conflict between races and between nations.

SELECTED BIBLIOGRAPHIES

* = General reference books.

ABBREVIATIONS

JAF = *Journal of American Folkore*

CFMJ = *Canadian Folk Music Journal*

CCFCS = Canadian Centre for Folk Culture Studies

MS = Mercury Series

MUN = Memorial University of Newfoundland

ISER = Institute of Social and Economic Studies

UTP = University of Toronto Press

UP = University Press

Explorations = *Explorations in Canadian Folklore.* Ed. Edith Fowke and Carole H. Carpenter. Toronto, M & S, 1985.

Folklore of Canada = *Folklore of Canada.* Edith Fowke. Toronto: M & S, 1976.

Folklore Studies... Halpert = *Folklore Studies in Honour of Herbert Halpert: A Festschrift.* Eds Kenneth S. Goldstein, Neil V. Rosenberg, *et al.* St John's: MUN, 1980.

GENERAL
Bibliographies, Periodicals, Surveys

Alberta Folklore Quarterly. Edmonton, U of Alberta, 1945-1975.

Les Archives de Folklore, U Laval, Quebec, 1946—.

BARBEAU, MARIUS. *The Kingdom of the Saguenay.* Toronto, Macmillan, 1935. 167 pp.

———. *Quebec, Where Ancient France Lingers.* Toronto, Macmillan, 1936. 173 pp.

BARTER, GERALDINE. *A Critically Annotated Bibliography of Works Published Relating to the Culture of French Newfoundlanders.* St John's, MUN, 1977. 54 pp. (Mimeo.)

BLEAKNEY, F. EILEEN. 'Folk-Lore from Ottawa and Vicinity', *JAF* 31 (1918), 158-69.

Bulletin of the Folklore Studies Association of Canada. Quarterly. 1976—.

Canadian Ethnic Studies. Special issue, 'Ethnic Folklore in Canada' 7.2 (1975), 1-127.

Canadian Folklore canadien. Biannual, 1979—.

Canadian Folk Music Journal. Annual, 1973—.

Canadian German Folklore. Occasional. Pennsylania German Folklore Association of Ontario, 1961—.

Cape Breton's Magazine, Wreck Cove, N.S. Monthly, 1973—.

CARPENTER, CAROLE H. *Many Voices: A Study of Folklore Activities in Canada and Their Role in Canadian Culture.* CCFCS MS 26. Ottawa, National Museum, 1979. 484 pp.

CHIASSON, ANSELME. *Cheticamp, History and Acadian Traditions.*Trans. Jean Doris LeBlanc. Portugal Cove, Breakwater, 1986. 316 pp.

CREIGHTON, HELEN. *Folklore of Lunenburg County, Nova Scotia*. National Museum Bull. 117, 1950. Toronto, McGraw-Hill, 1976. 163 pp.

———. 'Folklore of Victoria Beach, Nova Scotia', *JAF* 63 (1950), 131-46.

Culture & Tradition, MUN and U Laval. Annual, 1976—.

*DUNDES, ALAN. *The Study of Folklore*. Englewood Cliffs, NJ, Prentice-Hall, 1965. 481 pp.

DYCK, RUTH. 'Ethnic Folklore in Canada: A Preliminary Survey', *Canadian Ethnic Studies* 7 (1975), 90-101.

FAUSET, ARTHUR H. *Folklore from Nova Scotia*. Memoir Series 24. New York, American Folklore Society, 1931. 204 pp.

'Folklore Theses at Memorial University', *Bulletin of the Folklore Society of Canada* 9.3/4 (1985), 27-9.

FOWKE, EDITH. 'Canadian Folklore in English', *The Oxford Companion to Canadian Literature*, ed. William Toye. Toronto, Oxford, 1983, 261-4.

———. Folklore of Canada. Toronto, M & S, 1976. 349 pp.

———. 'Folktales and Folk Songs', *Literary History of Canada*. Ed. Carl F. Klinck. 2nd edn. Toronto, UTP, 1975. I, 177-87.

FOWKE, EDITH, and CAROLE H. CARPENTER, comps. *A Bibliography of Canadian Folklore in English*. Toronto, UTP, 1981. 272 pp.

———, eds. *Explorations in Canadian Folklore*. Toronto, M & S, 1985. 400 pp.

FRASER, MARY L. *Folklore of Nova Scotia*. N.p., n.d. (1931). Rpt. Antigonish, N.S., Formac, 1975. 115 pp.

GOLDSTEIN, KENNETH S., ed. *Canadian Folklore Perspectives*. St John's, MUN, 1978. 68 pp.

GOLDSTEIN, KENNETH S., NEIL V. ROSENBERG, *et al.*, eds. *Folklore Studies in Honour of Herbert Halpert: A Festschrift*. St John's, MUN, 1980. 395 pp.

GREENOUGH, WILLIAM P. *Canadian Folk-Life and Folk-Lore*. New York, Richmond, 1897. 186 pp.

HALPERT, HERBERT. *A Folklore Sampler from the Maritimes*. With a Bibliographical Essay on the Folktale in English. St John's, MUN, 1982. 273 pp.

HALPERT, HERBERT, and NEIL ROSENBERG. *Folklore Studies at MUN: Two Reports*. St John's, MUN, 1978. 16 pp.

JAF. *Journal of American Folklore,* Canadian Issues 63.2 (1950); 67.2 (1954)

KLYMASZ, ROBERT B. *A Bibliography of Ukrainian Folklore in Canada, 1902-64*. Anthropology Paper 21. Ottawa, National Museum, 1969. 53 pp.

LABELLE, RONALD. *Inventaire des sources en folklore acadien*. Moncton, U de Moncton, 1984.

LACOURCIÈRE, LUC. 'The Present State of French-Canadian Folklore Studies', *JAF* 74 (1961), 378-81. Rpt. *Folklore Research Around the World,* ed. Richard M. Dorson. Bloomington, Indiana UP, 1961, 86-95.

LANDRY, RENÉE. 'Archival Sources: A List of Selected Manuscript Collections at the Canadian Centre for Folk Culture Studies, National Museum of Man, Ottawa', *Canadian Ethnic Studies* 7 (1975), 73-89.

Laurentian Review. Special issue, 'Folklore and Oral Tradition in Canada' 8.2 (1976), 1-147.

*LEACH, MARIA, ed. *Funk & Wagnalls Standard Dictionary of Folklore, Mythology, and Legend*. 2 vols. New York, Funk & Wagnalls, 1949. 1196 pp.

LYSENKO, VERA. *Men in Sheepskin Coats*. Toronto, Ryerson, 1947. 312 pp.

ROY, CARMEN. *An Introduction to the Canadian Centre for Folk Culture Studies*. CCFCS MS 7. Ottawa, National Museum, 1973. 88 pp.

RUDNYC'KYJ, J.B. *Readings in Canadian Slavic Folklore*. Vol 2, Texts in English Translation. Winnipeg, U of Manitoba P, 1961.

———. *Ukrainian-Canadian Folklore*. Texts in English Translation. Winnipeg, Ukrainian Free Academy of Sciences, 1960. 232 pp.

Sound Heritage, British Columbia Provincial Archives, 1972—.

STONE, KAY, comp. *Prairie Folklore*. Winnipeg, U of Winnipeg, 1976. 284 pp. (Mimeo.)

TAFT, MICHAEL. *Discovering Saskatchewan Folklore: Three Case Studies*. Edmonton, NeWest, 1983. 150 pp.

THOMAS, GERALD. 'Folklore in French', *The Oxford Companion to Canadian Literature*, ed. William Toye. Toronto, Oxford, 1983, 264-7.

WAUGH, F. W. 'Canadian Folk-Lore from Ontario', *JAF* 31 (1918), 4-82.

WILSON, WILLIAM A. 'The Deeper Necessity: Folklore and the Humanities'. *JAF* 101 (1988), 156-67.

WINTEMBERG, W. J. 'Folk-Lore Collected at Roebuck, Grenville County, Ontario', *JAF* 31 (1918), 135-53.

———. 'Folk-Lore Collected in the Counties of Oxford and Waterloo, Ontario', *JAF* 31 (1918), 154-7.

———. *Folk-Lore of Waterloo County, Ontario*. Bull. 116. Ottawa, King's Printer, 1950. 68 pp.

WINTEMBERG, W.J., and KATHERINE H. WINTEMBERG. 'Folk-Lore from Grey County, Ontario', *JAF* 31 (1918), 83-124.

YUZYK, PAUL. 'The Ukrainian Canadian Cultural Pattern', *The Ukrainians in Manitoba. A Social History*. Toronto: UTP, 1953, 160-75.

BIOGRAPHY

BARBEAU, MARIUS. *My Life in Recording Canadian-Indian Folklore*. Folkways 7229, 1956.

BECK, JANE C. ' "Enough to charm the heart of a wheelbarrow and make a shovel dance": Helen Creighton, Pioneer Collector', *Canadian Folklore canadien* 7 (1985), 5-20.

BELAND, MARIO. *Marius Barbeau et l'art au Quebec*. CELAT. Quebec, U Laval, 1985. 139 pp.

BEN-AMOS, DAN. 'Elli-Kaija Köngäs-Maranda (1932-82)', *Canadian Folklore canadien* 5 (1983), 86-92.

BERGER, JEAN DU. 'Felix-Antoine Savard (1899-1982)', *Canadian Folklore canadien* 3 (1981), 153-4.

BERGERON, YVES. 'Portrait de Robert-Lionel Séguin', *Culture & Tradition* 8 (1984), 111-25.

———. 'Simonne Voyer', *Culture & Tradition* 9 (1985), 68-89.

BOAZ, FRANZ. 'In Memoriam, A.F. Chamberlain', *JAF* 27 (1914), 326-7.

———. 'Obituary of James A. Teit', *JAF* 36 (1923), 102-3.

BOULTON, LAURA. *The Music Hunter: The Autobiography of a Career*. Garden City, NY, Doubleday, 1969. 513 pp.

BRONSON, BERTRAND H. 'Maud Karpeles, 1886-1969', *JAF* 83 (1970), 455-65.

CREIGHTON, HELEN. *A Life in Folklore*. Toronto, McGraw-Hill, 1975. 244 pp.

CREIGHTON, HELEN, GRAHAM GEORGE, *et al*. 'Marius Barbeau (1883-1969)', *CFMJ* 12 (1984), 42-59.

DONALD, BETTY. 'Edith Fulton Fowke', *Profiles*. Ed. Irma McDonough. Ottawa, Can. Library Assn., 1975, 69-72.

DROLET, LISÉ, et CLAUDE MARTINEAU. 'Marius Barbeau', *Culture & Tradition* 8 (1984), 7-19.

DUPONT, JEAN-CLAUDE, ed. *Mélanges en l'honneur de Luc Lacourcière: Folklore français d'-Amerique*. Québec, Leméac, 1978. 'Hommages', 9-68.

FOWKE, EDITH. 'A Personal Odyssey and Personal Prejudices', *Bull. of the Folklore Studies Assn. of Canada* 2 (Sept./Nov. 1978), 7-13.

HENDERSON, M. CAROLE (Carpenter). 'Arthur Huff Fauset--A Biographical Sketch', *Black Gods of the Metropolis*. Arthur H. Fauset. Philadelphia, U of Pennsylvania P, 1971, 127-8.

KATZ, ISRAEL. 'Marius Barbeau, 1883-1969' (With 'Bibliography of Ethnomusicological Works'), *Ethnomusicology* 14 (1970), 129-42.

LAFORGE, VALERIE. 'Madeleine Doyon-Ferland', *Culture & Tradition*, 9 (1985), 12-30.

LAWS, G. MALCOLM, JR. 'W. Roy Mackenzie, 1883-1957', *Ballads and Sea Songs from Nova Scotia*. W. Roy Mackenzie. Hatboro, PA, Folklore Associates, 1963, i-ix.

LOVELACE, MARTIN. 'Roy Mackenzie as a Collector of Folksongs', *CFMJ* 5 (1977), 5-11.

LOWIE, ROBERT H. 'Franz Boas (1958-1942)', *JAF* 57 (1944), 59-70.

MacKINNON, RICHARD. 'Obituary (Christine Cartwright)', *Culture & Tradition* 8 (1984), 4-6.

MANDRYKA, M.I. *Bio-bibliography of J.B. Rudnyc'kyj*. Winnipeg, Ukrainian Free Academy of Arts and Sciences, 1961. 72 pp.

MOREAU, MARIE-EVE, et JULES CARON. 'Edouard-Zotique Massicotte', *Culture & Tradition* 8 (1984), 40-51.

MUNGALL, CONSTANCE. 'Charlotte Cormier, Ethnomusicologist', *Chatelaine* July 1977, 33, 50.

OUIMET, LOUISE. 'Carmen Roy', *Culture & Tradition* 9 (1985), 41-57.

PEERE, ISABELLE. 'Elisabeth Greenleaf: An Appraisal', *CFMJ*, 11 (1985), 20-31.

ROSENBERG, NEIL V. 'Herbert Halpert, A Biographical Sketch' and 'The Works of Herbert Halpert, A Classified Bibliography', *Folklore Studies . . . Halpert*, 1-30.

SWAYZE, NANSI. *Canadian Portraits: The Man Hunters*. Diamond Jenness, Marius Barbeau, W.J. Wintemberg. Toronto, Clarke, 1960. 178 pp.

WICKWIRE, WENDY C. 'The Contribution of a Colonial Ethnographer: Charles Hill-Tout, 1858-1944', *Canadian Folklore canadien* 2 (1980), 62-7.

TALES

*AARNE, ANTTI, and STITH THOMPSON. *The Types of the Folktale*. Helsinki, Scientiarum Fennica, 1961. 588 pp.

AUBRY, CLAUDE. *The Magic Fiddler and Other Legends of French Canada*. Trans. Alice Kane. Toronto, Martin, 1968. 98 pp.

BARBEAU, MARIUS. *The Tree of Dreams*. Toronto, Oxford, 1955. 112 pp.

BARBEAU, MARIUS, and MICHAEL HORNYANSKY. *The Golden Phoenix and Other French-Canadian Fairy Tales*. Toronto, Oxford, 1958. 144 pp.

BARTER, GERALDINE. 'The Folktale and Children in the Tradition of French Newfoundlanders', *Canadian Folklore canadien* 1 (1979), 5-12.

BEAUGRAND, HONORÉ. *La Chasse-Galerie and Other Canadian Stories*. Montreal, Pelletier, 1900. 101 pp.

BEDORE, BERNIE. *Tall Tales of Joe Mufferaw*. Toronto, Consolidated Amethyst, 1979. 64 pp.

BROADFOOT, BARRY. *The Pioneer Years 1895-1914*. Toronto, Doubleday, 1976. 403 pp.

BUCHANAN, ROBERTA. 'Some Aspects of the Use of Folklore in Harold Horwood's *Tomorrow Will Be Sunday*', *Culture & Tradition* 8 (1984), 87-100.

BUTLER, GARY. 'Folklore and Folk Discourse: The Function of Shared Knowldge in Intra-Cultural Communication', *Le Conte*. Ed. Pierre Leon and Paul Terron. Ottawa, Didier, 1987, 55-67.

———. 'Participant Interaction, Truth, and Belief in the Legend Process', *Culture & Tradition* 5 (1980), 67-78.

Canadian Folklore canadien. Special issue, 'Folktales in Canada' 1 (1979), 1-78.

COLDWELL, JOYCE-IONE HARRINGTON. 'Folklore as Fiction: The Writings of L.M. Montgomery', *Folklore Studies . . . Halpert,* 125-36.

COLOMBO, JOHN ROBERT. *Windigo: An Anthology of Fact and Fantastic Fiction*. Saskatoon, Western Producer, 1982. 207 pp.

CREIGHTON, HELEN. *Bluenose Ghosts*. Toronto, Ryerson, 1957. Rpt. McGraw-Hill, 1976. 280 pp.

CREIGHTON, HELEN, and EDWARD D. IVES. *Eight Folktales from Miramichi as Told by Wilmot Mac-Donald*. Orono, ME, *Northeast Folklore* 4 (1962), 3-70.

DE GASPÉ, PHILIPPE-AUBERT, père. *Canadians of Old*. Trans. C.G.D. Roberts, 1890. Rpt. Toronto, M & S, 1974. 364 pp.

DORSON, RICHARD M. 'Canadiens', *Bloodstoppers and Bearwalkers*. Cambridge, Harvard UP, 1959, 69-102.

———. 'Canadiens in the Upper Peninsula of Michigan', *Archives de Folklore* 4 (1949), 17-27.

———. 'Dialect Stories of the Upper Peninsula', *JAF* 61 (1948), 117-50.

ELBAZ, ANDRÉ E. *Folktales of the Canadian Sephardim*. Toronto, Fitzhenry & Whiteside, 1982. 192 pp.

FANNING, W. WAYNE. 'Storytelling at a Nova Scotia General Store', *Culture & Tradition* 3 (1978), 57-67.

FOWKE, EDITH. ' "Blind MacNair": A Canadian Short Story and Its Sources', *Folklore Studies . . . Halpert* 173-86.

———. *Folktales of French Canada*. Toronto, NC Press, 1979. 144 pp.

———. 'In Defence of Paul Bunyan', *New York Folklore* 5 (Summer 1979), 43-52. Rpt. *Explorations*, 189-99.

———. 'The Tale of Anson Minor: An Ontario Camp Legend', *Canadian Folklore canadien* 3 (1981), 1-9.

———. *Tales Told in Canada*. Toronto, Doubleday, 1986. 174 pp.

FRASER, C.A. 'Scottish Myths from Ontario', *JAF* 6 (1893), 185-98.

GARD, ROBERT E. *Johnny Chinook: Tall Tales and True from the Canadian West*. London, Longmans, 1945. Rpt. Edmonton, Hurtig, 1967. 360 pp.

GEDALOF, ROBIN (McGRATH). *An Annotated Bibliography of Canadian Inuit Literature*. Ottawa, Indian and Northern Affairs, 1979. 108 pp.

———. *Paper Stays Put: A Collection of Inuit Writing*. Edmonton, Hurtig, 1980.

GOLDIE, TERRY. 'Folklore in the Canadian Novel', *Culture & Tradition* 3 (1981), 93-101.

GREEN, JOHN. *Sasquatch: The Apes Among Us*. Saanichton, Hancock, 1978. 492 pp.

GREENHILL, PAULINE. ' "The Family Album": A Newfoundland Women's Recitation', *Canadian Folklore canadien* 6 (1984), 39-62.

———. *Lots of Stories: Maritime Narratives from the Creighton Collection*. CCFCS MS 57. Ottawa, National Museum, 1985. 232 pp.

HALPERT, HERBERT. '"The Cut-Off Head Frozen On": Some International Versions of a Tall Tale', *Canadian Folklore canadien* 1 (1979), 13-23. Rpt. *Explorations*, 159-73.

———. 'Ireland, Sheila and Newfoundland', *Literature and Folk Culture, Ireland and Newfoundland*. Eds. Alison Feder and Bernice Schrank. St John's, MUN, 1977, 141-71.

———. 'Tall Tales and Other Yarns from Calgary, Alberta', *California Folklore Quarterly* 4 (1945), 29-45. Rpt. *Folklore of Canada*, 171-89.

HALPERT, HERBERT, and J.D.A. WIDDOWSON. 'Folk-Narrative Performance and Tape Transcription, Theory versus Practice', *Lore and Language* 5.1 (1986), 39-50.

HOE, BAN SENG. 'Folktales and Social Structure: The Case of the Chinese in Montreal', *Canadian Folklore canadien* 1 (1979), 25-36.

HUNTER, DON, and RENE DAHINDEN. *Sasquatch*. Toronto, M & S, 1973. 192 pp.

IVES, EDWARD D. ' "The Man Who Plucked the Gorbey": A Maine Woods Legend', *JAF* 74 (1961), 1-8. Rpt. *Explorations*, 174-88.

JAF Canadian issues. 'Contes populaires canadiens', *JAF* 29.1 (1916); 30.1 (1917); 32.1 (1919); 36.3 (1923); 39.4 (1926); 44.3 (1931); 53.3 (1940).

JANES, L.W., ed. *The Treasury of Newfoundland Stories*. St John's: Maple Leaf Mills, n.d. 158 pp.

KERFONT, ANGELA. *Folktales from Western Newfoundland*. Coll. Marie-Annick Desplanques. Mont-Saint-Aignan, U de Rouen, 1985.

KIRSHENBLATT-GIMBLET, BARBARA. 'A Parable in Context: A Social Interactional Analysis of a Storytelling Performance', *Folklore Performance and Communication*. Ed. Kenneth S. Goldstein and Dan Ben-Amos. The Hague, Mouton, 1975, 105-30. Rpt. *Explorations*, 289-319.

KLYMASZ, ROBERT B. 'The Ethnic Joke in Canada Today', *Keystone Folklore Quarterly* 15 (1970), 167-73. Rpt. *Explorations*, 320-8.

———. *Folk Narrative among Ukrainian-Canadians in Western Canada*. CCFCS MS 4. Ottawa, National Museum, 1975. 133 pp.

LABA, MARTIN. 'The Jokes and Joke-Telling of Jim Dawe', *Culture & Tradition* 1 (1976), 33-43.

LACOURCIÈRE, LUC. 'The Analytical Catalogue of French Folktales in North America', *Laurentian Review* 8 (Feb. 1976), 123-8.

———. *Le Catalogue raisonné du conte populaire français en Amerique du Nord*. Quebec, U Laval.

LACOURCIÈRE, LUC, and BARBARA KIRSHENBLATT-GIMBLETT. 'Canada', *Tales Told around the World*. Ed. Richard M. Dorson. Chicago: U of Chicago P, 1975, 429-77.

LEACH, MacEDWARD. 'Celtic Tales from Cape Breton', *Studies in Honor of Stith Thompson*. Ed. W. Edson Richmond. Bloomington, Indiana UP, 1957, 40-54.

LOW, MARGARET. 'The Motif of the External Soul in French-Canadian Folktales', *Laurentian University Review* 8 (Feb. 1976), 61-9. Rpt. *Explorations*, 266-76.

MacDONELL, MARGARET, and JOHN SHAW, colls. and eds. *Luirgean Eachainn Nill/ Folktales from Cape Breton.* Told by Hector Campbell. Stornoway, Lewis, Acair, 1981. 90 pp.

McGRATH, ROBIN GEDALOF. 'Inuit Literature', *The Oxford Companion to Canadian Literature.* Ed. William Toye. Toronto, Oxford, 1983, 390-1.

MacLEOD, C.I.N. *Stories from Nova Scotia.* Antigonish, Formac, 1974. 129 pp.

McNEIL, BILL. *Voice of the Pioneer.* 2 vols. Toronto, Macmillan, 1978; 1984. 157 pp.; 168 pp.

MacNEIL, JOE NEIL. *Tales Until Dawn. The World of a Cape Breton Gaelic Story-Teller.* Trans. and ed. John W. Shaw. Kingston, McGill-Queen's, 1986. 269 pp.

MONTEIRO, GEORGE. '*Histoire de Montferrand, l' athlete canadien* and Joe Mufraw', *JAF* 73 (1960), 23-34.

———. 'Montferrand Meets the McDonalds: Freezing One Frame in the Growth of a Legend', *Canadian Folklore canadien* 6 (1984), 93-101.

MOON, MARY. *Ogopogo, the Okanagan Mystery.* Vancouver, Douglas, 1977. 195 pp.

MURPHY, CLARA J. 'The Use of Fairy Lore in Margaret Duley's Novel *Cold Pastoral*', *Culture & Tradition* 7 (1983), 106-19.

PETRONE, PENNY. 'Indian Legends and Tales' and 'Indian Literature', *The Oxford Companion to Canadian Literature.* Ed. William Toye. Toronto, Oxford, 1983, 377-89.

POCIUS, GERALD L. 'Frank Williams, Newfoundland Joke-Teller', *Lore and Language* 2 (Jan. 1977), 16-29; 2 (July 1977), 11-21; 2 (Jan. 1978), 11-19; 2 (July 1978), 6-25.

*RADIN, PAUL. *The Trickster: A Study in American Indian Mythology.* 1945. New York, Longmans, 1969. 211 pp.

ROBERTSON, HEATHER. *Salt of the Earth.* Toronto, Lorimer, 1974. 228 pp.

ROBINS, JOHN D. 'Paul Bunyan', *Canadian Forum* 6 (1926), 145-50.

SCHWARTZ, HERBERT T. *Tales from the Smokehouse.* Edmonton, Hurtig, 1974. 104 pp.

SMITH, SUSAN. 'Urban Tales', *Folklore of Canada*, 262-8.

SPRAY, CAROLE. *Will o' the Wisp: Folk Tales and Legends of New Brunswick.* Fredericton, Brunswick, 1979. 132 pp.

STONE, KAY. 'Polish Folktales', *Prairie Folklore.* Ed. Kay Stone. Winnipeg, U of Winnipeg, 1976, 190-201.

SUDERMAN, MARLIES. 'Old Man Gimli Stories', *Prairie Folklore.* Ed. Kay Stone. Winnipeg, U of Winnipeg, 1976, 78-85.

TAFT, MICHAEL. *Tall Tales of British Columbia.* Sound Heritage Series No. 39. Victoria, Provincial Archives, 1983. 100 pp.

TEIT, JAMES A. 'Water-Beings in Shetlandic Folk-Lore, as Remembered by Shetlanders in British Columbia'. *JAF* 31 (1918), 180-201.

THOMAS, GERALD. *Les Deux Traditions: le conte populaire chez les Franco-Terreneuviens.* Montreal, Bellarmin, 1983.

———. 'The Folktale and Folktale Style in the Tradition of French Newfoundlanders', *Canadian Folklore canadien* 1 (1979), 71-8.

———. 'Newfie Jokes', *Folklore of Canada*, 142-53.

———. 'Other Worlds: Folktale and Soap Opera in Newfoundland's French Tradition', *Folklore Studies... Halpert*, 343-52.

———. *The Tall Tale and Philippe d'Alcripe*. St John's, MUN, 1977. 259 pp.

*T HOMPSON, ST I T H. *Motif Index of Folk Literature*. 6 vols. Bloomington, Indiana UP, 1966.

WAGNER, JUDY. 'Urban Belief Tales in a Junior High School', *Prairie Folklore*. Ed. Kay Stone. Winnipeg, U of Winnipeg, 1976, 30-40.

WAREHAM, WILFRED. 'The Monologue in Newfoundland', *The Blasty Bough*. Ed. Clyde Rose. St John's, Breakwater, 1976, 196-216.

WATSON, NANCY. '*Rockbound*, by Frank Parker Day: Novel and Ethnography', *Culture & Tradition* 6 (1982), 73-83.

SONGS, MUSIC, AND DANCE

BARBEAU, MARIUS. 'Canadian Folk-Songs', *University of Toronto Quarterly* 16 (1947), 183-7.

———. 'La Complainte de Cadieux, coureur-de-bois (*ca.* 1709)', *JAF* 67 (1954), 168-83.

———. 'The Ermatinger Collection of Voyageur Songs (ca. 1830)', *JAF* 67 (1954), 163-83.

———. *Folk Songs of Old Quebec*. Bull. 75. Ottawa, National Museum, 1935. 72 pp.

———. *Jongleur Songs of Old Quebec*. Toronto, Ryerson, 1962. 202 pp.

BARBEAU, MARIUS, and EDWARD SAPIR. *Folk Songs of French Canada*. New Haven, Yale UP, 1925. 216 pp.

BRASSARD, FRANÇOIS. 'French-Canadian Folk Music Studies: A Survey', *Ethnomusicology* 16 (1972), 351-9.

*BRONSON, BERTRAND H. *The Traditional Tunes of the Child Ballads*. 4 vols. Princeton, Princeton UP, 1959-72.

*BUCHAN, DAVID. *The Ballad and the Folk*. London, Routledge, 1968.

BUTLER, GARY R. 'Folksong Performance in French-Canadian Culture', *CFMJ* 14 (1986), 19-26.

CASEY, GEORGE J., NEIL V. ROSENBERG, and WILFRED W. WAREHAM. 'Repertoire Categorization and Performer-Audience Relationships: Some Newfoundland Folksong Examples', *Ethnomusicology* 16 (1972), 397-403.

CASS-BEGGS, BARBARA. *Eight Songs of Saskatchewan*. Toronto, Can. Music Sales, 1963. 15 pp.

———. *Seven Métis Songs of Saskatchewan*. Don Mills, BMI, 1967. 31 pp.

CAVANAGH, BEVERLEY. 'Annotated Bibliography: Eskimo Music', *Ethnomusicology* 16 (1972), 479-87.

*CHILD, FRANCIS JAMES. *The English and Scottish Popular Ballads*. 5 vols. Boston, Houghton, 1882-98. New York: Dover, 1965.

*COFFIN, TRISTRAM P., and ROGER DeV. RENWICK. *The British Traditional Ballad in North America*. Austin, U of Texas P, 1977. 297 pp.

COHEN, JUDITH. 'Judeo-Spanish Traditional Songs in Montreal and Toronto', *CFMJ* 10 (1982), 40-7.

———. 'The Lighter Side of Judeo-Spanish Traditional Song: Some Canadian Examples', *CFMJ* 15 (1987), 25-34.

COLOMBO, JOHN ROBERT, ed. *Poems of the Inuit*. Ottawa, Oberon, 1981. 117 pp.

――――. *Songs of the Indians*. 2 vols. Ottawa, Oberon, 1983.

COX, GORDON. *Folk Music in a Newfoundland Outport*. CCFCS MS 32. Ottawa, National Museum, 1980. 220 pp.

CRAWFORD, VENETIA, comp. *Treasures of the Pontiac in Song and Story*. Shawville, Que., Dickson, 1979. 153 pp.

CREIGHTON, HELEN. 'Ballads from Devil's Island', *Dalhousie Review* 12 (1933), 503-10. Rpt. *Explorations*, 105-16.

――――. 'Canada's Maritime Provinces—An Ethnomusicological Survey', *Ethnomusicology* 16 (1972), 404-14.

――――. 'Collecting Songs of Nova Scotia Blacks', *Folklore Studies . . . Halpert*, 137-44.

――――. *Folksongs from Southern New Brunswick*. CCFCS. Ottawa, National Museum, 1971. 238 pp.

――――. *Maritime Folk Songs*. Toronto, Ryerson, 1962. Rpt. St John's, Breakwater, 1979. 210 pp.

――――. *Songs and Ballads from Nova Scotia*. Toronto, Dent, 1932. Rpt. New York, Dover, 1966. 333 pp.

――――. 'The Songs of Nathan Hatt', *Dalhousie Review* 32 (1953), 259-66.

CREIGHTON, HELEN, and CALUM MacLEOD. *Gaelic Songs in Nova Scotia*. Bull. 198. Ottawa, National Museum, 1964, 1979. 302 pp.

CREIGHTON, HELEN, and DOREEN H. SENIOR. *Traditional Songs from Nova Scotia*. Toronto, Ryerson, 1950. 284 pp.

DIBBLEE, RANDALL, and DOROTHY DIBBLEE. *Folksongs from Prince Edward Island*. Summerside, P.E.I., Williams, 1973. 124 pp.

DOERFLINGER, W.M. 'Cruising for Ballads in Nova Scotia', *Canadian Geographical Journal* 16 (Feb. 1938), 91-100. Rpt. *Explorations*, 117-30.

――――. *Shantymen and Shantyboys*. New York, Macmillan, 1951. Rpt. as *Songs of the Sailor and Lumberman*, 1972. 374 pp.

DOUCETTE, LAUREL, and COLIN QUIGLEY. 'The Child Ballad in Canada: A Survey', *CFMJ* 9 (1981), 3-19.

DOYLE, GERALD S., comp. and pub. *Old-Time Songs and Poetry of Newfoundland*. St John's, 1927, 1940, 1955, 1966, 1978. 72 pp., 80 pp., 88 pp., 86 pp., 64 pp.

DOYON, MADELEINE. 'Folk Dances in Beauce County', *JAF* 63 (1950), 171-4.

DUNLAY, K.E., with D.L. REICH. *Traditional Celtic Fiddle Music of Cape Breton*. East Alstead, NH, Fiddlecase, 1986.

DZ'OBKO, J. *My Songs. A Selection of Ukrainian Folksongs in English Translation*. Winnipeg; Ukrainian Canadian Pioneer Library, 1958. 102 pp.

ENNIS, DAVID. 'Fiddling in Lanark County: A Medium for the Examination of Acculturation in Canadian Folk Music', *CFMJ* 15 (1987), 45-53.

Ethnomusicology. Canadian Issue. 16 (1971), 329-515.

FERGUSSON, DONALD A., ed. and pub. *Fad Air Falbh As Innse Gall. Beyond the Hebrides*. Including the Cape Breton Collection. Halifax, Lawson Graphics, 1977. 343 pp.

FOWKE, EDITH. 'American Cowboy and Western Pioneer Songs in Canada', *Western Folklore* 21 (1962), 247-56.

————. 'Anglo-Canadian Folksong: A Survey', *Ethnomusicology* 16 (1972), 335-50.

————. 'British Ballads in Ontario', *Midwest Folklore* 13 (1963), 133-62.

————. 'Folk Songs in Ontario', *Canadian Literature* 116 (Spring 1963), 28-42.

————. 'Irish Folk Songs in Canada', *The Untold Story: The Irish in Canada*. Ed. Robert O'Driscoll and Lorna Reynolds. Toronto, Celtic Arts, 1988, 699-710.

————. 'Labour and Industrial Protest Songs in Canada', *JAF* 82 (1969), 34-50.

————. *Lumbering Songs from the Northern Woods*. Memoir 55, American Folklore Society, 1970. Rpt. Toronto, NC Press, 1985. 232 pp.

————, ed. ' "Old Favourites": A Selective Index', *CFMJ* 7 (1979), 41-56.

————. *The Penguin Book of Canadian Folk Songs*. Harmondsworth, Penguin, 1973. Rev. edn. Markham, Ont., Penguin, 1986. 224 pp.

————. ' "The Red River Valley" Re-examined', *Western Folklore* 23 (1964), 247-56. Rpt. *Alberta Historical Review* 13 (Winter 1956), 20-5.

————. 'Romantic Ballads in North America', *New York Folklore* 13.3/4 (1987), 49-54.

————. 'A Sampling of Bawdy Ballads from Ontario', *Folklore and Society*. Ed. Bruce Jackson. Hatboro, PA, Folklore Associates, 1966. 45-61.

————. *Sea Songs and Ballads from Nineteenth-Century Nova Scotia: The William Smith and Fenwick Hatt Manuscripts*. New York, Folklorica, 1982. 118 pp.

————. *Traditional Singers and Songs from Ontario*. Hatboro, PA, Folklore Associates, 1965. 210 pp.

————. *A Reference List on Canadian Folk Music*. Calgary, Canadian Folk Music Society, 1984. 20 pp. Rpt. from *CFMJ* 6 (1983), 43-60.

FOWKE, EDITH, and ALAN MILLS. *Canada's Story in Song*. Toronto, Gage, 1960. New edn, *Singing Our History*. Toronto, Doubleday, 1984. 249 pp.

FOWKE, EDITH, and RICHARD JOHNSTON. *Folk Songs of Quebec/Chansons de Quebec*. Waterloo, Waterloo Music, 1957. 93 pp.

FRYE, NORTHROP. 'Turning New Leaves'. *Canadian Forum* 13 (1954), 89, 91. Rpt. *The Bush Garden: Essays on the Canadian Imagination*. Toronto: Anansi, 1971, 157-62.

GAGNON, ERNEST. *Chansons populaires du Canada*. 1865. Montreal, Beauchemin, 1947. 350 pp.

GLEDHILL, CHRISTOPHER. *Folk Songs of Prince Edward Island*. Charlottetown, Square Deal, 1973. 84 pp.

GLOFCHESKIE, JOHN M. *Folk Music of Canada's Oldest Polish Community*. CCFCS MS 33. Ottawa, National Museum, 1980. 89 pp.

GOLDSTEIN, KENNETH. S. 'Faith and Fate in Sea Disaster Ballads of Newfoundland Fishermen', *By Land and By Sea: Studies in the Folklore of Work and Leisure*. Ed. Roger D. Abrahams *et al.* Hatboro, PA, Legacy, 1985, 84-94.

GREENLEAF, ELISABETH B., and GRACE Y. MANSFIELD. *Ballads and Sea Songs of Newfoundland*. Cambridge, Harvard UP, 1933. Rpt. Hatboro, PA, Folklore Associates, 1968. 395 pp.

GRIGGS, MARY ANN. *The Folk-Song in the Traditional Society of French Canada*. Sudbury, La Societé Historique du Nouvel-Ontario, 1969. 22 pp.

GROVER, CARRIE. *A Heritage of Songs*. Bethel, ME, n.p., n.d. Rpt. Norwood, PA, Norwood, 1973. 216 pp.

GUEDON, MARIE-FRANÇOISE. 'Canadian Indian Ethnomusicology: Selected Bibliography and Discography', *Ethnomusicology* 16 (1972), 465-78.

HOGAN, DOROTHY, and HOMER HOGAN. 'Canadian Fiddle Culture', *Communique: Canadian Studies* 3 (Aug. 1977), 72-101.

HUTCHINSON, PATRICK. ' "You Never Think to Lose the 'Nyah'. . . .": Retention and Change in A Fiddler's Tradition, *Canadian Folklore canadien* 7 (1985), 121-8.

IVES, EDWARD D. 'The Ballad of John Ladner', *Folklore Studies . . . Halpert*, 239-58.

———. *Joe Scott, The Woodsman-Songmaker.* Urbana, U of Illinois P, 1979. 473 pp.

———. *Larry Gorman, The Man Who Made the Songs.* Bloomington, Indiana UP, 1964. 259 pp.

———. *Lawrence Doyle, The Farmer-Poet of Prince Edward Island.* Orono, U of Maine P, 1971. 269 pp.

———. *Twenty-one Folksongs from Prince Edward Island.* Orono, ME, *Northeast Folklore* 5 (1963) 1-87.

KALLMAN, HELMUT, GILLES POTVIN, KENNETH WINTERS, eds. *Encyclopedia of Music in Canada.* Toronto, UTP, 1981.

KARP, ELLEN, comp. *Many Are Strong among the Strangers: Canadian Songs of Immigration.* CCFCS MS 50. Ottawa, National Museum, 1984. 137 pp.

KARPELES, MAUD. *Folk Songs from Newfoundland.* London, Faber, 1971. 340 pp.

KLYMASZ, ROBERT B. *The Ukrainian-Canadian Immigrant Folksong Cycle.* Bull. 234. Ottawa, National Museum, 1970. 106 pp.

———. *The Ukrainian Winter Folksong Cycle in Canada.* Bull. 236. Ottawa, National Museum, 1970. 156 pp.

KLYMASZ, ROBERT B., and JAMES PORTER. 'Traditional Ukrainian Balladry in Canada', *Western Folklore* 33 (1974), 89-132.

LAFORTE, CONRAD. *Catalogue folklorique de la chanson française.* 6 vols. Quebec, U Laval, 1977-1986.

*LAWS, G. MALCOLM, JR. *American Balladry from British Broadsides.* Philadelphia, American Folklore Society, 1957. 315 pp.

* ———. *Native American Balladry.* Philadelphia, American Folklore Society, 1964. 298 pp.

LEACH, MacEDWARD. *Folk Ballads and Songs of the Lower Labrador Coast.* Bull. 201. Ottawa, National Museum, 1965. 332 pp.

LEACH, RUSTY. *The Rusty Leach Collection of Shanty Songs and Recollections of the Upper Ottawa Valley.* Shawville, Que., Dickson, 1984. 147 pp.

LEDERMAN, ANNE, ed. Special Issue, 'Fiddling in Canada', *Canadian Folk Music Bulletin* 19.3 (1985).

LEHR, GENEVIEVE, with ANITA BEST. *Come and I Will Sing You: A Newfoundland Songbook.* Toronto, UTP, 1985. 210 pp.

LIVESAY, FLORENCE R. *Songs of Ukrainia.* London, Dent, 1916. 175 pp.

LOVELACE, MARTIN. ' "Down by This Laney Side": Clarence Blois, Farmer and Singer', *CFMJ* 13 (1985), 3-12.

MacDONELL, MARGARET. *The Emigrant Experience: Songs of Highland Emigrants in North America.* Toronto, UTP, 1982. 229 pp.

MACKENZIE, W. ROY. *Ballads and Sea Songs from Nova Scotia.* Cambridge, Harvard UP, 1928. Rpt. Hatboro, PA, Folklore Associates, 1963. 421 pp.

———. *The Quest of the Ballad.* Princeton, Princeton UP, 1919. 247 pp.

MacLEOD, MARGARET ARNETT. *Songs of Old Manitoba.* Toronto, Ryerson, 1959. 93 pp.

McNAUGHTON, JANET. 'Variation and Stability in Two Murder Ballads of Placentia Bay, Newfoundland', *CFMJ* 12 (1984), 3-19.

MANNY, LOUISE, and JAMES R. WILSON. *Songs of Miramichi.* Fredericton, Brunswick, 1968. 330 pp.

MERCER, PAUL. *The Ballads of Johnny Burke: A Short Anthology.* St John's, Nfld. Historical Society, 1974. 40 pp.

———. *Newfoundland Songs and Ballads in Print 1842-1974: A Title and First-Line Index.* St John's, MUN, 1979. 343 pp.

MERCER, PAUL, and MAC SWACKHAMMER. ' "The Singing of Old Newfoundland Ballads and a Cool Glass of Beer Go Hand in Hand": Folklore and "Tradition" in Newfoundland Advertising', *Culture & Tradition* 3 (1978), 36-45.

MOULDEN, JOHN. ' "The Blooming Bright Star of Belle Isle": American Native or Irish Immigrant?' *CFMJ* 14 (1986), 3-9.

O'DONNELL, JOHN C. 'Labour's Cultural Impact on the Community: A Cape Breton Perspective', *CFMJ* 14 (1986), 49-59.

———. *Men of the Deeps.* Waterloo, Waterloo Music, 1975. 63 pp.

ORNSTEIN, LISA. 'Instrumental Folk Music of Quebec: An Introduction', *CFMJ* 10 (1982), 3-11.

PEACOCK, KENNETH. 'Folk and Aboriginal Music', *Aspects of Music in Canada.* Ed. Arnold Walter. Toronto, UTP, 1969, 62-89.

———. *A Garland of Rue: Lithuanian Folksongs of Love and Betrothal.* CCFCS, Ottawa: National Museum, 1971. 60 pp.

———. *Songs of the Doukhobors.* Bull. 231. Ottawa, National Museum, 1970. 167 pp.

———. *Songs of the Newfoundland Outports.* 3 vols. Bull. 197. Ottawa, Natinal Museum, 1965. 1035 pp.

———. *A Survey of Ethnic Folk Music Across Western Canada.* Anthropology Paper 5. Ottawa, National Museum, 1965. 13 pp.

———. *Twenty Ethnic Songs from Western Canada.* Bull. 211. Ottawa, National Museum, 1966.

PELINSKI, RAMON. 'The Music of Canada's Ethnic Minorities', *Canada Music Book* Spring/Summer 1975, 59-86.

POSEN, I. SHELDON. *'For singing and dancing and all sorts of fun': The Story of the Chapeau Boys.* Toronto, Deneau, 1988.

———. 'Tracking Down the Chapeau Boys', *Canadian Folk Music Bulletin* 19.4 (1985), 11-15.

PROCTOR, GEORGE A. 'Fiddle Music as a Manifestation of Canadian Regionalism', *Explorations*, 225-36.

———. 'Musical Styles of Gaspe Songs', Bull. 190. Ottawa, National Museum, 1960, 209-12.

———. 'Old-Time Fiddling in Ontario', Bull. 190. Ottawa, National Museum, 1960, 173-208.

QUIGLEY, COLIN. *Close to the Floor: Folk Dance in Newfoundland.* St John's, MUN, 1985. 128 pp.

RAHN, JAY. 'Guidelines for Harmonizing English-Language Folk Songs', *CFMJ* 14 (1986), 35-48; 15 (1987), 12-24.

———. 'Stereotyped Forms in English Canadian Children's Songs: Historical and Pedagogical Aspects', *CFMJ* 9 (1981), 43-53.

———. 'Text Underlay in Gagnon's Collection of French-Canadian Songs', *CFMJ* 4 (1976), 3-14.

RHODES, FRANK. 'Dancing in Cape Breton Island, Nova Scotia', Appendix, *Traditional Dancing in Scotland*. J.R. Fleet and T.M. Fleet. London, Routledge, 1961. Rpt. *Explorations*, 200-24.

ROGERS, T.B. 'The *Southern Cross*: A Case Study in the Ballad as History', *CFMJ* 10 (1982), 12-22.

ROSENBERG, NEIL V. *Country Music in the Maritimes, Two Studies*, St John's, MUN, 1976. 20 pp.

———. ' "It Was a Kind of Hobby": A Manuscript Song Book and Its Place in Tradition', *Folklore Studies . . . Halpert*, 315-34.

———. 'A Preliminary Bibliography of Canadian Old-Time Instrumental Music Books', *CFMJ* 8 (1980), 20-2.

RUBIN, RUTH. 'Yiddish Folk Songs Current in French Canada.' *Journal of the International Folk Music Council* 12 (1960), 76-8.

RYAN, SHANNON, and LARRY SMALL. *Haulin' Rope and Gaff: Songs and Poetry in the History of the Newfoundland Seal Fishery*. St John's, Breakwater, 1978. 192 pp.

SÉGUIN, ROBERT-LIONEL. *La danse traditionnelle au Québec*. Québec, Université du Québec, 1986. 176 pp.

SHIFRIN, ELLEN. 'Traditional French-Canadian Dance Iconography: A Methodology for Analysis', *Canadian Folklore canadien* 6 (1984), 127-40.

SMITH, GORDON. 'Ernest Gagnon's *Chansons populaires du Canada*: An Argument for Plainchant and Folksong', CFMJ 15 (1987), 3-11.

SONG, BAN-SONG. *The Korean-Canadian Folk Song: An Ethnomusicological Study*. CCFCS MS 10. Ottawa, National Museum, 1974. 225 pp.

SPALDING, DAVID A.E. 'What We Sang Down on the Farm: A Forgotten Manuscript on Western Canadian Singing Traditions', *CFMJ* 13 (1985), 37-53.

SZWED, JOHN F. 'Paul E. Hall: A Newfoundland Song-Maker and His Community of Song', *Folksongs and Their Makers*. H. Glassie, E.D. Ives, and J.F. Szwed. Bowling Green U Popular P, 1970, 147-69.

TAFT, MICHAEL. *A Regional Discography of Newfoundland and Labrador 1904-1972*. St John's, MUN, 1975. 102 pp.

THOMAS, AMBY. *Songs and Stories from Deep Cove, Cape Breton*. Ed. Ron MacEachern. Sydney, College of Cape Breton P, 1979. 49 pp.

THOMAS, GERALD, comp. *Songs Sung by French Newfoundlanders: A Catalogue*. St John's, MUN, 1978. 94 pp.

THOMAS, PHILIP J. *Songs of the Pacific Northwest*. North Vancouver, Hancock, 1979. 176 pp.

VOYER, SIMONNE. *La danse traditionnelle dans l'est du Canada: quadrilles et cotillons*. Quebec: Université Laval, 1986. 505 pp.

WALTON, IVAN H. 'Songs of the Great Lakes', *Folklore of Canada*, 196-212.

RECORDS

ABBOTT, O.J. *Irish and British Songs from the Ottawa Valley*. Coll. Edith Fowke. Folkways 4051, 1961.

ALLARD, JOSEPH. *Masters of French Canadian Dances*. Folkways RBF 110.

BENOIT, ÉMILE. *Emile's Dream*. Pigeon Inlet 732, 1979.

———. *It Comes from the Heart*. Pigeon Inlet 7311, 1982.

BOUCHARD, JOSEPH. *Violoneux Île d'Orleans*. Opus 221.

BOUDREAULT, LOUIS. *Old Time Fiddler of Chicoutimi, Quebec*. Voyageur 323-5, 1979.

BRUNEAU, PHILIPPE. 'Danses pour vieilles Canadiennes'. Philo 2006, 1974.

Canadian Folk Songs. Columbia World Libary of Folk and Primitive Music, Vol. 8. Ed. Marius Barbeau. Columbia SL 211, 1954.

CARIGNAN, JEAN. *Jean Carignan*. Philo 2001, 1973.

———. *Jean Carignan rend hommage à Joseph Allard*. Philo 2012, 1976.

———. *Old-Time Fiddle Tunes*. Folkways 3531.

CLARK, LaRENA. *LaRena Clark: Canadian Garland*. Topic 12T140, 1965.

———. *Songs of an Ontario Family*. Clark QC 903, c. 1968.

———. *Heritage of Folk Songs*. Clark QCS 1311, 1977.

———. *Family Legend in Song*. Clark LCS 106, 1978.

———. *Canada's Traditional Queen of Song*. Clark LCS 107, 1978.

———. *Authentic Canadian Folk Symbol*. Clark LCS 108, 1979.

———. *Canadian Folk Sound with LaRena*. Clark LCS 109, 1979.

———. *Canada at Turn of the Sod*. Clark LCS 110, 1979.

———. *LaRena Sings for Country Folk*. Clark LCS 112, 1980.

CLIFTON, ROY. *Square Dances with Calls*. Folkways 8825, 1960.

Come Hell or High Water. Songs of the Buchans Miners. Coll. Peter Narvaez. Breakwater 1001, 1977.

CORMIER, JOSEPH. *The Dances Down Home*. Rounder 7004.

The Doukhobors of British Columbia. Coll. Barbara Bachovseff. Folkways 8972, 1962.

The Eskimos of Hudson Bay and Alaska. Coll. Laura Boulton. Folkways 4444, 1954.

Far Canadian Fields: Companion to the Penguin Book of Canadian Folk Songs. Coll. Edith Fowke. Leader 4057, 1975.

FITZGERALD, WINSTON 'Scotty'. *Canada's Outstanding Scottish Fiddler*. Celtic CX 17.

Folk Music from Nova Scotia. Coll. Helen Creighton. Folkways 4006, 1956.

Folk Songs of Ontario. Coll. Edith Fowke. Folkways 4005, 1958.

Folksongs of Saskatchewan. Coll. Barbara Cass-Beggs. Folkways 4312, 1963.

Folksongs of the Miramichi. Folkways 4053, 1962.

Game Songs of French Canada. Sung by Montreal school children. Coll. Sam Gesser. Folkways 7214, 1956.

GUINCHARD, RUFUS. *Newfoundland Fiddler*. Breakwater 1001. c. 1978.

————. *Step Tunes and Doubles.* Pigeon Inlet 737, 1982.

Haida: Indian Music of the Pacific Northwest. Coll. Ida Halpern. 2 discs. Folkways 4525, 1986.

Indian Music of the Canadian Plains. Coll. Kenneth Peacock. Folkways 4464, 1965.

Indian Music of the Pacific Northwest Coast. Coll. Ida Halpern. 2 discs. Folkways 4527, 1970.

Island Folk Festival: Local and Traditional Songs and Music from Prince Edward Island. Fox House 001, 1985.

KELLY, ALLAN, et LEONTINE KELLY. *Suivant l' étoile du nord: La tradition acadienne.* Bilingual. Ed. Ronald Labelle. Moncton, Centre d'études acadiennes, 1985.

Kwakiutl: Indian Music of the Pacific Northwest. Coll. Ida Halpern. 2 discs. Folkways 4122, 1967.

Lumbering Songs from the Ontario Shanties. Coll. Edith Fowke. Folkways 4052, 1961.

Marie Hare of Strathadam, New Brunswick. Notes by Louise Manny and Edward D. Ives. Folk Legacy 9, 1962.

Maritime Folk Songs. Coll. Helen Creighton. Folkways 4307, 1962.

Merasheen Farewell: A Selection of Old Time House Party Songs from Merasheen Island (Nfld.). Merasheen Records P.C., 1985.

MILLS, ALAN, and JEAN CARIGNAN. *Songs, Fiddle Tunes and a Folktale from Canada.* Folkways 3532, 1961.

Music from French Newfoundland. Pigeon Inlet 734, 1980.

The Music of Cape Breton. 2 discs. Coll. John Shaw and Rosemary Hutchison. Topic 12T353, 12T354, 1978.

Nootka: Indian Music of the Pacific Northwest. Coll. Ida Halpern. 2 discs. Folkways 4524, 1974.

Old Native and Métis Fiddling in Manitoba. 2 vols, 4 discs. Coll. Anne Lederman. Falcon Productions 187 and 287, 1987.

SNOW, LEM. *The Great Lobster Boil.* Pigeon Inlet 7316, 1983.

Songs and Dances of Quebec. Coll. Sam Gesser. Folkways 6951, 1955.

Songs and Dances of the Great Lakes Indians. Coll. Gertrude Kurath. Folkways 4003, 1956.

Songs from Cape Breton Island. Coll. Sidney Cowell. Folkways 4450, 1955.

Songs from the Outports of Newfoundland. Coll. MacEdward Leach. Folkways 4085, 1966.

Songs of French Canada. Ed. Marius Barbeau. Folkways 4482, 1957.

Songs of the Great Lakes. Coll. Edith Fowke. Folkways 4018, 1964.

Songs of the Newfoundland Outports. Coll. Kenneth Peacock. Pigeon Inlet 7319, 1984.

Tom Brandon of Peterborough, Ontario. Coll. Edith Fowke. Folk Legacy 10, 1962.

Tradition: Songs, Stories and Tunes from Newfoundland & Labrador. Pigeon Inlet 7317, 1983.

'When Johnny Went Ploughin' for Kearon' and Other Traditional P.E.I. Folksongs. Sung by Tommy Banks and John Cousins. P.E.I. Heritage Foundation, 1976.

MINOR GENRES
Folk speech, naming, proverbs, riddles, children's lore

*ABRAHAMS, ROGER. *Jump-Rope Rhymes: A Dictionary.* Austin, U of Texas P, 1969. 228 pp.

*ABRAHAMS, ROGER, and LOIS RANKIN. *Counting-Out Rhymes: A Dictionary*. Austin, U of Texas P, 1979. 252 pp.

ALEXANDER, HENRY. *The Story of Our Language*. Toronto, Nelson, 1940. 242 pp.

ARMSTRONG, GEORGE H. *The Origin and Meaning of Place Names in Canada*. Toronto, Macmillan, 1930; 1972. 312 pp.

AVIS, WALTER S., ed. *A Dictionary of Canadianisms on Historical Principles*. Toronto, Gage, 1967. 927 pp.

BARBEAU, MARIUS. *Roundelays—Dansons à la ronde*. Bull. 151. Ottawa, National Museum, 1958. 104 pp.

BOYLE, DAVID. 'Canadian Folklore', *Globe* (Toronto), 13 Nov. 1897-8 Jan. 1898.

CHAMBERLAIN, ALEXANDER F. 'Folk-lore of Canadian Children', *JAF* 8 (1895), 252-5.

'Childlore: The Folklore of Children', *A Folklore Sampler from the Maritimes*. Ed. Herbert Halpert. St John's, MUN, 1982. 157-202.

CONNOR, JENNIFER J. 'Parodies of Administrative Communications: Some Canadian Examples', *Culture & Tradition* 10 (1986), 67-83.

COSBEY, ROBERT C. *All in Together, Girls: Skipping Songs from Regina, Saskatchewan*. Canadian Plains Research Center Paper No. 2. Regina, U of Regina, 1980. 101 pp.

DEVINE, P.K. *Devine's Folklore of Newfoundland in Old Words, Phrases and Expressions*. St John's, Robinson, 1937. 80 pp.

DUNN, CHARLES W. 'Gaelic Proverbs in Nova Scotia'. *JAF* 72 (1959), 30-5.

DURAND, LAURA. 'Play Rhymes of the Dominion', *Globe*, 13 Nov.-18 Dec. 1909.

FOWKE, EDITH. 'Autograph Verses from Saskatchewan', *Folklore of Canada*, 236-43.

———. *Red Rover, Red Rover: Children's Games Played in Canada*. Toronto, Doubleday, 1988. 160 pp.

———. *Ring Around the Moon*. Toronto, M & S, 1977. Rpt. NC Press, 1988. 160 pp.

———. *Sally Go Round the Sun: 300 Songs, Rhymes, and Games of Canadian Children*. Toronto, M & S, 1969. 160 pp.

GREENLEAF, ELISABETH B. 'Riddles of Newfoundland', *Marshall Review* 1 (March 1938), 5-20. Rpt. *Folklore of Canada*, 130-42.

GRYSKI, CAMELLA. *Cat's Cradle, Owl's Eyes: A Book of String Games*. Toronto, Kids Can, 1983.

HALPERT, HERBERT. 'Skipping Rhymes from Calgary, Alberta', *California Folklore Quarterly* 3 (1944), 154-5.

HIGINBOTHAM, JOHN D. 'Western Vernacular', *Alberta Historical Review* 10 (Autumn 1962), 9-17. Rpt. *Folklore of Canada*, 243-51.

HOWAY, F.W. 'The Origin of the Chinook Jargon', *B.C. Historical Quarterly* 6 (1942), 225-50.

JENNESS, DIAMOND. 'String Figures of the Eskimo', *Report of the Canadian Arctic Expedition, 1913-1918*. Vol. 13, Part B. Ottawa, King's Printer, 1924. 192 pp.

KIRWIN, WILLIAM. 'Folk Etymology: Remarks on Linguistic Problem-Solving and Who Does It', *Lore and Language* 4.2 (1985), 18-24.

KLYMASZ, ROBERT B. 'The Canadianization of Slavic Surnames. A Study in Language Contact', *Names* 11 (1963), 81-105, 182-95, 229-53.

McATEE, W.L. *Folk Names of Canadian Birds*. Bull. 149. Ottawa, National Museum, 1957. 74 pp.

*OPIE, IONA and PETER OPIE. *Children's Games in Street and Playground*. Oxford, Oxford UP, 1969. 371 pp.

* ———. *The Lore and Language of Schoolchildren*. Oxford, Oxford UP, 1959. 417 pp.

PATTERSON, GEORGE. 'Notes on the Dialect of the People of Newfoundland'. *JAF* 8 (1895), 27-40; 9 (1896), 19-37; 10 (1897), 203-13.

POSEN, I. SHELDON. 'Pranks and Practical Jokes at Children's Summer Camps', *Southern Folklore Quarterly* 38 (1974), 299-309.

PRATT, T.K. *Dictionary of Prince Edward Island English*. Toronto, UTP, 1988. 240 pp.

RLS: Regional Language Studies . . . Newfoundland. Occasional. St John's, MUN, 1968—.

ROBERTSON, MRS DONALD. 'Counting Out Rhymes from Shelburne County, Nova Scotia', *Northeast Folklore* 3 (1960), 27-32.

RUDNYC'KYJ, JAROSLAV B. *Manitoba Mosaic of Place Names*. Winnipeg, Can. Institute of Onomastic Sciences, 1970. 221 pp.

SANDILANDS, JOHN. *Western Canadian Dictionary and Phrase Book*. 1913. Rpt. Edmonton, U of Alberta, 1977. 64 pp.

SCARGILL, M.H. 'The Growth of Canadian English', *Literary History of Canada*. Ed. Carl F. Klinck. 2nd edn Toronto, UTP, 1976. I, 265-73.

———. *Modern Canadian English Usage*. Toronto, M & S, 1974. 143 pp.

———. *A Short History of Canadian English*. Victoria, Sono Nis, 1976. 63 pp.

SCHULTZ, VICKI. 'Children's Folklore', *Prairie Folklore*. Ed. Kay Stone. Winnipeg, U of Winnipeg, 1970. 8-11.

SCOTT, JOHN R. 'Play at the Newfoundland Seal Fishery', *Culture & Tradition* 1 (1976), 63-71.

———. 'Practical Jokes of the Newfoundland Seal Fishery', *Southern Folklore Quarterly* 38 (1974), 275-83.

SEARY, E.R. *Place Names of the Avalon Peninsula of the Island of Newfoundland*. Toronto, Pub. for MUN by UTP, 1971. 383 pp.

SEARY, E.R., G.M. STORY, and W.J. KIRWIN. *The Avalon Peninsula of Newfoundland: An Ethnolinguistic Study*. Bull. 218. Ottawa, National Museum, 1968. 115 pp.

STEVENS, VIRGINIA. 'Winnipeg Skipping Rope Rhymes', *Prairie Folklore*. Ed. Kay Stone. Winnipeg, U of Winnipeg, 1975. 12-29.

STORY, G.M., W.J. KIRWIN, and J.D.A. WIDDOWSON. *Dictionary of Newfoundland English*. Toronto, UTP, 1982. 625 pp.

*TAYLOR, ARCHER. *English Riddles from Oral Tradition*. Berkeley, U of California P, 1951. 959 pp.

* ———. *The Proverb and An Index to The Proverb*. Hatboro, PA, Folklore Associates, 1962. 105pp.

TREMBLAY, MAURICE. 'Nous irons jouer dans l'Isle', *JAF* 63 (1950), 163-70. Rpt. *Folklore of Canada,* 83-91.

ZOLA, MEGUIDO. *By Hook or By Crook: My Autograph Book*. Montreal, Tundra, 1987. Unpaged.

POPULAR BELIEFS AND SUPERSTITIONS

BARBEAU, MARIUS. 'Supernatural Beings of the Huron and Wyandot', *American Anthropologist* 16 (1914), 288-313.

BOAS, FRANZ. *The Religion of the Kwakiutl Indians.* 2 vols. New York, Columbia UP, 1930. 284 pp.; 288 pp.

CHILDS, RALPH DE S. 'Phantom Ships of the North-East Coast of North America', *New York Folklore Quarterly* 5 (1949), 146-65.

CONNOR, JENNIFER C. 'Folklore in Anglo-Canadian Medical Journals 1845-1897', *Canadian Folklore canadien* 7 (1985), 35-53.

CREIGHTON, HELEN. *Bluenose Magic.* Toronto, Ryerson, 1968. 297 pp.

DOERING, J. FREDERICK. 'Pennsylvania German Folk Medicine in Waterloo County, Ontario', *JAF* 49 (1936), 194-8.

DOERING J. FREDERICK, and EILEEN F. DOERING. 'Some Western Ontario Folk Beliefs and Practices', *JAF* 51 (1938), 60-8; 54 (1941), 197.

HAGAR, STANSBURY. 'Micmac Magic and Medicine', *JAF* 9 (1896), 170-7.

HALPIN, MARJORIE, and MICHAEL L. AMES, eds. *Manlike Monsters on Trial.* Vancouver, UBC P, 1980. 336 pp.

*HAND, WAYLAND D. *Popular Beliefs and Superstitions from North Carolina. The Frank C. Brown Collection of North Carolina Folklore*, Vols. 6 and 7. Durham, NC, Duke UP, 1961.

HENDERSON, M. CAROLE (Carpenter). 'Monsters of the West: The Sasquatch and the Ogopogo', *Folklore of Canada*, 251-60.

HUFFORD, DAVID J. 'A New Approach to the "Old Hag": The Nightmare Tradition Re-examined', *American Folk Medicine.* Ed. Wayland D. Hand. Berkeley, U of California P, 1976. 73-85.

JONES, MICHAEL O. *Why Faith Healing?* CCFCS MS 3. Ottawa, National Museum, 1972. 52 pp.

KINSELLA, J. PAYSON. *Some Superstitions and Traditions of Newfoundland.* St John's, Union, 1919.

LACOURCIÈRE, LUC. 'A Survey of Folk Medicine in French Canada from Early Times to the Present', *American Folk Medicine.* Ed. Wayland D. Hand. Berkeley, U of California P, 1976. 203-14.

LAMBERT, R.S. *Exploring the Supernatural: The Weird in Canadian Folklore.* 1955. Toronto, M & S, 1966. 198 pp.

LAYTON, MONIQUE. 'Magico-Religious Elements in the Traditional Beliefs of Maillardville, B.C.', *BC Studies* 27 (Autumn 1975), 50-61.

LEESON, ALICE M. 'Certain Canadian Superstitions', *JAF* 10 (1897), 76-8.

McDONALD, NEIL T. *The Baldoon Mysteries: A Weird Tale of the Early Scotch Settlers of Baldoon.* Wallaceburg, Ont, Colwell, 1871; 3rd edn, 1910. 62 pp.

McKECHNIE, ROBERT E. *Strong Medicine.* Vancouver: Douglas, 1972. 193 pp.

MARTIN, PEGGY. ' "Drop Dead": Witchcraft Images and Ambiguities in Newfoundland Society', *Culture & Tradition* 2 (1977), 35-50.

PERKOWSKI, JAN. *Vampires, Dwarves, and Witches Among the Ontario Kashubs.* CCFCS MS 1. Ottawa, National Museum, 1972. 85 pp.

RIDDELL, WILLIAM R. 'Popular Medicine in Upper Canada a Century Ago', *Ontario History* 25 (1929), 384-404.

ROSE, HERBERT J. 'Ontario Beliefs', *Folk-Lore* 24 (1913), 219-27.

SALO, MATT T. *Roles of Magic and Healing: The Tietaja in the Memorates and Legends of Canadian Finns.* Ottawa, National Museum, 1973. 21 pp.

STEPHENSON, PETER H. 'Hutterite Belief in the Evil Eye', *Culture, Medicine and Psychiatry* 3 (1979), 247-65.

TEICHER, MORTON. *Windigo Psychosis: A study of a relationship between belief and behavior among the Indians of Northeastern Canada.* Seattle, U of Washington P for the American Ethnological Society, 1971. 129 pp.

VAN WART, ARTHUR F. 'The Indians of the Maritime Provinces: Their Diseases and Native Cures', *Canadian Medical Association Journal* 59 (1948), 573-8.

WALLIS, WILSON D. 'Medicine Used by the Micmac Indians', *American Anthropologist* 24 (1922), 24-30.

WEAVER, SALLY. *Medicine and Politics among the Grand River Iroquois.* Ottawa: National Museum, 1972. 182 pp.

WIDDOWSON, J.D.A., and J.H. MOSS. 'Figures Used for Threatening Children, 1: A Newfoundland Example', *Lore and Language* 1.7 (1972), 20-4.

WINTEMBERG, W.J. 'German Canadian Folk-Lore', *Ontario History* 3 (1901), 86-94.

FOLKLIFE AND CUSTOMS

ADACHI, KEN. *The Enemy That Never Was: A History of the Japanese Canadians.* Toronto, M & S, 1976. 456 pp.

BARBEAU, MARIUS. 'Maple Sugar', *Canadian Geographical Journal* 38 (Apr. 1949), 176-89.

BARBER, MARY, and FLORA MacPHERSON. *Christmas in Canada.* Toronto, Dent, 1959. 134 pp.

BARTLETT, ROBERT B. 'The Sealing Saga of Newfoundland', *National Geographic* 56 (1929), 91-130.

BAUMAN, RICHARD. 'Belsnickling in a Nova Scotia Island Community', *Western Folklore* 31 (1972), 229-43.

————. 'The LaHave Island General Store: Sociability and Verbal Arts in a Nova Scotia Community', *JAF* 85 (1972), 330-41.

BENNETT, MARGARET. 'A Codroy Valley Milling Frolic', *Folklore Studies . . . Halpert*, 99-110.

BLAKE, VERSCHOYLE B., and RALPH GREENHILL. *Rural Ontario.* Toronto: UTP, 1969. 173 pp.

BLUMSTOCK, ROBERT. *Békévar: Working Papers on a Canadian Prairie Community.* CCFCS MS 31. Ottawa: National Museum, 1979. 314 pp.

BREDNICH, ROLF WILH. *Mennonite Folklife and Folklore.* MS 22. Ottawa, National Museum, 1977. 116 pp.

BRUNVAND, JAN. *Norwegian Settlers in Alberta.* CCFCS MS 8. Ottawa, National Museum, 1973. 71 pp.

BUCKLEY, ANNE-KAY, and CHRISTINE CARTWRIGHT. 'The Good Wake: A Newfoundland Case Study', *Culture & Tradition* 7 (1983), 6-16.

BUTLER, VICTOR. *The Little Nord Easter: Reminiscences of a Placentia Bayman.* Ed. Wilfred W. Wareham. St John's, MUN, 1975. Rpt. Portugal Cove, Breakwater, 1977. 262 pp.

CARELESS, J.M.S. *The Pioneers. An Illustrated History of Early Settlement in Canada.* Toronto, M & S, rev. 1973. 127 pp.

DE GELDER, WILLEM. *The Dutch Homesteader on the Prairies*. Toronto, UTP, 1973. 92 pp.

DEGH, LINDA. *People in the Tobacco Belt: Four Lives*. CCFCS MS 13. Ottawa, National Museum, 1975. 277 pp.

DICKIE, GORDON. 'Cultural Origins in Colonial Life', *Dalhousie Review* 37 (1957), 41-51, 165-74.

DOUCETTE, LAUREL, ed. *Cultural Retention and Demographic Change: Studies of the Hebridean Scots in the Eastern Townships of Quebec*. CCFCS MS 34. Ottawa, National Museum, 1980. 170 pp.

———. 'Folk Festival: The Gatineau Valley Church Picnic', *Culture & Tradition* 1 (1976), 55-62.

———. *Skill and Status: Traditional Expertise within a Rural Canadian Family*. CCFCS MS 28. Ottawa, National Museum, 1979. 177 pp.

DUNN, CHARLES W. *Highland Settler: A Portrait of the Scottish Gael in Nova Scotia*. Toronto, UTP, 1953, 1968. 179 pp.

ENGLAND, GEORGE A. *Vikings of the Ice, Being the Log of a Tenderfoot on the Great Newfoundland Sea Hunt*. 1924. Rpt. as *The Greatest Hunt in the World*. Montreal, Tundra, 1969. 323 pp.

FARIS, JAMES C. *Cat Harbour: A Newfoundland Fishing Settlement*. ISER. St John's, MUN, 1972. 185 pp.

FARROW, MOIRA. *Nobody Here But Us: Pioneers of the North*. Vancouver: Douglas, 1972. 219 pp.

FIRESTONE, MELVIN. *Brothers and Rivals: Patrilocality in Savage Cove*. ISER. St John's, MUN, 1967. 143 pp.

FOSTER, ANNIE H., and ANNE GRIERSON. *High Days and Holidays in Canada*. Toronto, Ryerson, 1938; rev. 1956. 95 pp.

FRÉCHETTE, LOUIS H. *Christmas in French Canada*. Toronto, Morang, 1899. 261 pp.

GALBRAITH, JOHN KENNETH. *The Scotch*. Toronto, Macmillan, 1964. 145 pp.

GEIKIE, JOHN C. *George Stanley; or, Life in the Woods*. London, Routledge, 1864. 408 pp.

GIULIANO, BRUCE S. *Sacro o Profano? A Consideration of Four Italian-Canadian Religious Festivals*. CCFCS MS 17. Ottawa National Museum, 1976. 60 pp.

GLAZEBROOK, G.P. de T. *Life in Ontario: A Social History*. Toronto, UTP, 1968. 316 pp.

GOULD, ED. *Logging: British Columbia's Logging History*. Saanichton: Hancock, 1975. 224 pp.

GRANT, TED, and ANDY RUSSELL. *Men of the Saddle: Working Cowboys of Canada*. Scarborough, Van Nostrand Reinhold, 1978. 192 pp.

GUILLET, EDWIN C. *Early Life in Upper Canada*. 1933. Rpt. Toronto, UTP, 1964. 782 pp.

HALPERT, HERBERT, and GEORGE M. STORY, eds. *Christmas Mumming in Newfoundland*. Toronto, Pub. for MUN by UTP, 1969. 246 pp.

HENRY, LORNE J., and GILBERT PATERSON. *Pioneer Days in Ontario*. Toronto: Ryerson, 1938. 234 pp.

HISCOCK, PHILIP. 'The Mass Media in the Folk Culture of Newfoundland', *Culture & Tradition* 8 (1984), 20-39.

HOE, BAN SENG. 'Chinese Community and Cultural Tradition in Quebec City', *Canadian Folklore canadien* 7 (1985), 5-20.

———. *Structural Changes of Two Chinese Communities in Alberta, Canada*. CCFCS MS 19. Ottawa, National Museum, 1976. 385 pp.

HOUSER, GEORGE J. *The Swedish Community at Eriksdale, Manitoba*. CCFCS MS 14. Ottawa, National Museum, 1976. 112 pp.

HUNTER, DARRYL M. 'No "Malice in Wonderland": Conservation and Change in the Three Hallowe'ens of Ann Mesko', *Culture & Tradition* 7 (1983), 37-53.

KAY-ROIL, MARY. 'A Time of Restraint: A Survey of the Good Friday Traditions in Newfoundland', *Culture & Tradition* 10 (1986), 14-22.

KLYMASZ, ROBERT B. 'The Letter in Canadian Ukrainian Folklore', *Journal of the Folklore Institute* 6 (1969), 39-49.

———. ' "Malanka": Ukrainian Mummery on the Prairies', *CFMJ* 13 (1985), 32-6.

———. 'Speaking at/about/with the Dead: Funerary Rhetoric among Ukrainians in Western Canada', *Canadian Ethnic Studies* 7.2 (1975), 50-6.

McCARL, ROBERT S., Jr. 'The Communication of Work Technique', *Culture & Tradition* 3 (1978), 108-16.

MacEWAN, J.W. GRANT. *Blazing the Old Cattle Trail*. Saskatoon: Western Producer, 1962. 248 pp.

———. *Hoofprints and Hitching Posts*. Saskatoon, Modern, 1964. 249 pp.

———. *John Ware's Cow Country*. Edmonton: Institute of Applied Art, 1960. 261 pp.

———. *The Sodbusters*. Toronto, Nelson, 1948. 240 pp.

MacKAY, DONALD. *The Lumberjacks*. Toronto, McGraw-Hill, 1978. 319 pp.

MacLENNAN, GORDON. 'A Contribution to the Ethnohistory of Saskatchewan's Patagonian Welsh Settlement', *Canadian Ethnic Studies* 7.2 (1975), 57-72.

MANNION, JOHN J. *Irish Settlements in Eastern Canada: A Study of Cultural Transfer and Adaptation*. Toronto, UTP, 1974. 219 pp.

MATTHEWS, RALPH. *'There's No Better Place Than Here': Social Change in Three Newfoundland Communities*. Toronto, Martin, 1976. 164 pp.

MEALING, F. MARK. *Doukhobor Life: A Survey of Doukhobor Religion, History, and Folklife*. Castlegar, B.C., Cotinneh, 1975. 67 pp.

MINER, HORACE. *St Denis: A French-Canadian Parish*. Chicago, U of Chicago P, 1939. 283 pp.

MINHINNICK, JEANNE. *At Home in Upper Canada*. Toronto, Clarke, 1970. 227 pp.

MORGAN, E.C. 'Pioneer Recreation and Social Life', *Saskatchewan History* 18 (Spring 1965), 41-54.

MORRISON, MONICA. 'Wedding Night Pranks in Western New Brunswick', *Southern Folklore* 38 (1974), 285-97.

MURRAY, HILDA C. *More than 50%: Women's Life in a Newfoundland Outport 1900-1950*. St John's, Breakwater, 1979. 160 pp.

NUTE, GRACE L. *The Voyageur*. New York, Appleton, 1931. 289 pp.

PARRY, CAROLINE. *Let's Celebrate! Canada's Special Days*. Toronto, Kids Can, 1987. 256 pp.

PATTERSON, G. JAMES. *The Greeks of Vancouver: A Study in the Preservation of Ethnicity*. CCFCS MS 18. Ottawa, National Museum, 1976. 169 pp.

———. *The Romanians of Saskatchewan: Four Generations of Adaptation*. CCFCS MS 23. Ottawa, National Museum, 1977. 85 pp.

PAULSEN, FRANK M. *Danish Settlements on the Canadian Prairies*. CCFCS MS 11. Ottawa, National Museum, 1974. 114 pp.

PHILBROOK, TOM. *Fisherman, Logger, Merchant, Miner: Social Change and Industrialism in Three Newfoundland Communities*. ISER. St John's, MUN, 1966. 212 pp.

PORTER, HELEN. *Below the Bridge*. St John's, Breakwater, 1979. 126 pp.

REAMAN, G. ELMORE. *The Trail of the Black Walnut*. Toronto, M & S, 1957. 256 pp.

ROBERTSON, MARGARET R. *The Newfoundland Mummers' Christmas House-Visit*. CCFCS MS 49. Ottawa, National Museum, 1983. 181 pp.

SALO, MATT T., and SHEILA M.G. SALO. *The Kalderas in Eastern Canada*. CCFCS MS 21. Ottawa, National Museum, 1977. 278 pp.

SHAKESPEARE, MARY, and RODNEY H. PAIN. *West Coast Logging 1840-1910*. History Div. MS 2. Ottawa, National Museum, 1977. 84 pp.

STAEBLER, EDNA. *Sauerkraut and Enterprise*. Toronto, M & S, 1979. 318 pp.

STEAD, ROBERT J.C. 'The Old Prairie Homestead', *Canadian Geographical Journal* 7 (July 1933), 13-22.

SYMONS, R.D. *Where the Wagon Led*. Toronto, Doubleday, 1973. 343 pp.

SZWED, JOHN F. 'Gossip, Drinking and Social Control: Consensus and Communication in a New-foundland Parish', *Ethnology* 5 (1966), 434-41.

————. *Private Cultures and Public Imagery: Interpersonal Relations in a Newfoundland Peasant Society*. ISER. St John's, MUN, 1966. 188 pp.

TAFT, MICHAEL. 'The Itinerant Movie-Man and His Impact on the Folk Culture of the Outports of Newfoundland', *Culture & Tradition* 1 (1976), 107-19.

TARASOFF, KOOZMA J. Traditional Doukhobor Folkways: An Ethnographic and Biographic Record of Prescribed Behaviour. CCFCS MS 20. Ottawa, National Museum, 1977. 307 pp.

THOMPSON, GEORGE S. *Up to Date; or, The Life of a Lumberman*. Peterborough, Ont., Times Print., 1895. 126 pp.

TIZZARD, AUBREY M. *On Sloping Ground: Reminiscences of Outport Life in Notre Dame Bay*, New-foundland. Ed. J.D.A. Widdowson. St John's, MUN, 1979. 390 pp.

VAN LENT, PETER. 'La Vie de l'Habitant: Quebec's Folk Culture of Survival', *New York Folklore* 7 (Winter 1981), 57-65. Rpt. *Explorations*, 329-39.

WIDDOWSON, JOHN D.A. *If You Don't Be Good: Verbal Social Control in Newfoundland*. ISER. St John's, MUN, 1977. 345 pp.

FOLK ARTS AND CRAFTS

ADAMSON, ANTHONY, and JOHN F. WILLARD. *The Gaiety of Gables: Ontario's Architectural Folk Art*. Toronto, M & S, 1974. 128 pp.

ALEXANDRIN, BARBARA, and ROBERT BOTHWELL. *Bibliography of the Material Culture of New France*. History Series 4. Ottawa, National Museum, 1970. 32 pp.

ANDERSON, JAY A. 'The Early Development of French-Canadian Foodways', *Folklore of Canada*, 91-9.

ARTHUR, ERIC, and DUDLEY WITNEY. *The Barn: A Vanishing Landmark in North America*. Toron-to, M & S, 1972. 256 pp.

BARBEAU, MARIUS. *Assomption Sash*. Bull. 93. Ottawa, National Museum, 1939, 1972. 51 pp.

————. *Haida Carvers in Argillite*. Bull. 139. Ottawa, National Museum, 1957; 1974. 214 pp.

————. *I Have Seen Quebec*. Toronto, Macmillan of Canada, 1957. Unpaged.

———. *Totem Poles*. 2 vols. Bull. 119. Ottawa, National Museum, 1950. 880 pp.

BARER-STEIN, THELMA. *You Eat What You Are: A Study of Ethnic Food Traditions*. Toronto, M & S, 1979. 624 pp.

BARSS, BEULAH M. *The Pioneer Cook: A Historical View of Canadian Prairie Food*. Calgary, Detselig, 1980. 134 pp.

BARSS, PETER. *Older Ways: Traditional Nova Scotia Craftsmen*. Toronto, Van Nostrand Reinhold, 1980.

BELAND, MARIO. *Marius Barbeau et l'art au Québec. Bibliographie analytique et thématique*. Québec, Outils de recherche du CELAT, No. 1, 1985. 139 pp.

BIRD, MICHAEL. *Canadian Folk Art, Old Ways in a New Land*. Toronto, Oxford, 1983. 121 pp.

———. 'Doukhobor Folk and Decorative Arts', *Canadian Folklore canadien* 4 (1982), 43-66.

———. *Ontario Fraktur: A Pennsylvania German Folk Tradition in Early Canada*. Toronto, Feheley, 1977. 144 pp.

BIRD, MICHAEL S., and TERRY KOBAYASHI. *A Splendid Harvest: Germanic Folk and Decorative Arts in Canada*. Toronto, Van Nostrand Reinhold, 1981. 240 pp.

BLANCHETTE, JEAN-FRANÇOIS, ed. *People and Things*. Special issue of *Canadian Folklore canadien* including 'A Bibliography of Folk Material Culture in Canada 1965-1982', 4 (1982), 107-46.

BOILY, LISÉ, and JEAN-FRANÇOIS BLANCHETTE. *The Bread Ovens of Quebec*. Ottawa, National Museum, 1979. 135 pp.

BRADLEY, IAN L., and PATRICIA B. BRADLEY. *A Bibliography of Canadian Native Arts*. Victoria, GLC Pub., 1977. 109 pp.

BRETT, KATHERINE B. *Modesty to Mod: Dress and Undress in Canada, 1780-1967*. Toronto, Royal Ontario Museum, 1967. 71 pp.

BURNHAM, DOROTHY K. *The Comfortable Arts: Traditional Spinning and Weaving in Canada*. Ottawa, National Gallery, 1981. 238 pp.

BURNHAM, HAROLD B., and DOROTHY K. BURNHAM. *'Keep Me Warm One Night': Early Handweaving in Eastern Canada*. Toronto, UTP, 1972. 416 pp.

CLEMSON, DONOVAN. *Living with Logs: British Columbia's Log Buildings and Rail Fences*. Saanichton, Hancock, 1974. 94 pp.

COLLARD, EILEEN. *Early Clothing in Southern Ontario*. Burlington, Collard, 1969. 27 pp.

CONROY, MARY. *300 Years of Canada's Quilts*. Toronto, Griffin, 1976. 133 pp.

DOBSON, HENRY, and BARBARA DOBSON. *The Early Furniture of Ontario and the Atlantic Provinces*. Toronto, Feheley, 1974. 200 pp.

DUFF, WILSON, WILLIAM REID, and WILLIAM HOLM. *Arts of the Raven*. Vancouver, Art Gallery, 1967. 112 pp.

ENNALS, PETER M. 'Nineteenth Century Barns in Southern Ontario'. *Canadian Geographer* 16 (1972), 256-70.

ENNALS, PETER, and DERYCK HOLDSWORTH. 'Vernacular Architecture and the Cultural Landscape of the Maritime Provinces: A Reconnaissance', *Acadiensis* 10.2 (1981), 86-106.

Eskimo Art. Beaver Autumn 1967. 98 pp.

Eskimo Art Issue. North/Nord 22 (Mar. Apr. 1974). 53 pp.

The Eskimo World. artscanada 162/163 (1971/1972), 29-121.

FIELD, RICHARD H. *Spirit of Nova Scotia: Traditional Decorative Folk Art 1780-1930*. Hamilton, Dundurn, 1986. 224 pp.

From the Heart: Folk Art in Canada. Ottawa, M & S and National Museum, 1983. 256 pp.

GIBBONS, ROY W. *The CCFCS Collection of Musical Instruments*. 3 vols. CCFCS MS 43, 44, 45. Ottawa, National Museum, 1981. 161 pp.; 121 pp.; 267 pp.

GOOD, E. REGINALD. *Anna's Art: The Fraktur Art of Anna Weber, a Waterloo County Mennonite Artist 1814-1888*. Kitchener, Pochauna, 1976. 48 pp.

GOWANS, ALAN. *Building Canada: An Architectural History of Canadian Life*. Toronto, Oxford, 1966. 412 pp.

'Grass Roots Art'. Special issue of *artscanada* 138/139 (1969).

GREEN, H. GORDON. *A Heritage of Canadian Handicrafts*. Toronto, M & S, 1967. 222 pp.

GUILLET, EDWIN C. *Pioneer Arts and Crafts*. 1940. Rpt. Toronto, UTP, 1968. 97 pp.

HANKS, CAROLE. *Early Ontario Gravestones*. Toronto, McGraw-Hill, 1974. 94 pp.

HARPER, J. RUSSELL. *A People's Art: Primitive, Naive, Provincial and Folk Art Painting in Canada*. Toronto, UTP, 1974. 176 pp.

HARRINGTON, LYN, and RICHARD HARRINGTON. *Covered Bridges of Central and Eastern Canada*. Toronto, McGraw-Hill, 1977, 100 pp.

HAWTHORN, AUDREY. *Kwakiutl Art*. Vancouver, Douglas, 1979. 320 pp.

HOLM, BILL. *Northwest Coast Indian Art, An Analysis of Form*. 1965. Vancouver, Douglas, 1978. 116 pp.

HOLM, BILL, and WILLIAM REID. *Indian Art of the Northwest Coast: A Dialogue on Craftsmanship and Aesthetics*. Vancouver, Douglas, 1976. 265 pp.

HOUSTON, JAMES. *Canadian Eskimo Art*. Ottawa, Queen's Printer, 1966, 1972. 40 pp.

———. *Eskimo Prints*. Toronto, Longman, 1967; 1971. 112 pp.

INGLIS, STEPHEN. *'Something Out of Nothing': The Work of George Cockayne*. CCFCS MS 46. Ottawa, National Museum, 1983. 112 pp.

INVERARITY, R.B. *Art of the Northwest Coast Indians*. Los Angeles, U of California P, 1950. 236 pp.

KLYMASZ, ROBERT B. *Continuity and Change: The Ukrainian Folk Heritage in Canada*. Ottawa, CCFCS, 1972. 56 pp.

KOBAYASHI, TERRY, MICHAEL BIRD, and ELIZABÉTH PRICE. *Folk Treasures of Historic Ontario*. Ontario Heritage Foundation and Dundurn Press, 1986. 128 pp.

LABELLE, RONALD. 'A Case Study of Folk Religion Among Quebec's Stone Cutters', *Laurentian Review* 12 (1979), 51-63.

LANGDON, EUSTELLA. *Pioneer Gardens at Black Creek Pioneer Village*. Toronto, Holt, Rinehart & Winston, 1972. 64 pp.

McKENDRY, RUTH. *Quilts and Other Bed Coverings in the Canadian Tradition*. Scarborough, Van Nostrand Reinhold, 1979. 240 pp.

MacLAREN, GEORGE. *Antique Furniture by Nova Scotia Craftsmen*. Toronto, McGraw-Hill Ryerson, 1975. 146 pp.

MacRAE, MARION, and ANTHONY ADAMSON. *The Ancestral Roof: Domestic Architecture of Upper Canada*. Toronto, Musson, 1963. 258 pp.

Material History Bulletin, 1972—.

MILLS, DAVID S. 'The Development of Folk Architecture in Trinity Bay, Newfoundland', *The Peopling of Newfoundland*. Ed. John J. Mannion. ISER. St John's, MUN, 1977. 77-101.

MUSSON, PATRICIA, *et al. Mennonite Furniture: The Ontario Tradition*. Toronto, Lorimer, 1977. 96 pp.

NEWTON-WHITE, MURIEL E. *Backhouses of the North*. Cobalt, Highway Book Shop, 1972. 38 pp.

PAIN, HOWARD. *The Heritage of Upper Canadian Furniture*. Toronto, Van Nostrand Reinhold, 1978. 548 pp.

PALARDY, JEAN. *The Early Furniture of French Canada*. Toronto, Macmillan, 2nd edn, 1965. 410 pp.

PATTERSON, NANCY-LOU. *Swiss-German and Dutch-German Mennonite Traditional Art in the Waterloo Region, Ontario*. CCFCS MS 27. Ottawa, National Museum, 1979. 216 pp.

POCIUS, GERALD L. 'Eighteenth- and Nineteenth-Century Newfoundland Gravestones: Self-Sufficiency, Economic Specialization, and the Creation of Artifacts', *Material History Bulletin* 12 (1981), 1-16.

——. 'Hooked Rugs in Newfoundland. The Representation of Social Structure in Design', *JAF* 92 (1979), 273-84.

——. 'Material Folk Culture Research in English Canada: Antiques, Aficionados, and Beyond', *Canadian Folklore canadien* 4 (1982), 27-42.

——. *Textile Traditions of Eastern Newfoundland*. CCFCS MS 29. Ottawa, National Museum, 1979. 89 pp.

'Prairie Folk Art', *artscanada* 230/231 (1979), 1-19.

PRICE, RALPH, and PATRICIA PRICE. *'Twas Ever Thus: A Selection of Eastern Canadian Folk Art*. Toronto, Feheley, 1979. 87 pp.

ROWLES, EDITH. 'Bannock, Beans, and Bacon: An Investigation of Pioneer Diet.' *Saskatchewan History* 5 (Winter 1952), 1-15.

RURYK, NANCY R., comp. *Ukrainian Embroidery Designs and Stitches*. Winnipeg, Ukrainian Women's Assn, n.d. 130 pp.

RUSH, ANITA. 'Changing Women's Fashion and Its Social Context, 1870-1905', *Material History Bulletin* 14 (1982), 27-45.

Sculpture of the Inuit. Toronto, UTP, 1971. 494 pp.

SHACKLETON, PHILIP. *The Furniture of Old Ontario*. Toronto, Macmillan, 1973. 399 pp.

STAEBLER, EDNA. *Food That Really Schmecks*. Toronto, M & S, 1968. 297 pp.

STECHISHIN, SAVELLA. *Traditional Ukrainian Cookery*. Winnipeg; Trident, 1957. 498 pp.

SUTYLA, CHARLES M. *The Finnish Sauna in Manitoba*. CCFCS MS 24. Ottawa, National Museum, 1977. 117 pp.

SWINTON, GEORGE. *Sculpture of the Eskimo*. Toronto, M & S, 1965; rev. 1972. 255 pp.

SYMONS, HARRY. *Fences*. Toronto, Ryerson, 1958. 155 pp..

SYMONS, SCOTT. *Heritage: A Romantic Look at Early Canadian Furniture*. Toronto, M & S, 1971. 220 pp.

TAYLOR, DAVID A. *Boat Building in Winterton, Trinity Bay, Newfoundland*. CCFCS MS 41. Ottawa, National Museum, 1982. 270 pp.

TILNEY, PHILIP V.R. *Artifacts from the CCFCS Collection*, MS 5. Ottawa, National Museum, 1973. 61 pp.

TRAQUAIR, RAMSAY. *The Old Architecture of Quebec*. Toronto, Macmillan, 1947. 324 pp.

TRASK, DEBORAH. *Life How Short, Eternity How Long: Gravestone Carving and Carvers in Nova Scotia*. Halifax, N.S. Museum, 1978. 100 pp.

TYE, DIANE. 'Folk and Tourist Art in the Life of Patrick Murphy', *Culture & Tradition* 7 (1983), 54-67.

TYRCHNIEWICZ, PEGGY. *Ethnic Folk Costumes in Canada*. Winnipeg, Hyperion, 1979. 229 pp.

TYRWHITT, JANICE. *The Mill*. Toronto, M & S, 1976. 224 pp.

WISEMAN, ADELE. *Old Woman at Play*. Toronto, Clarke, 1978. 148 pp.

ZIMMERLY, DAVID, Ed. *Contextual Studies of Material Culture*. Ethnology MS 43. Ottawa, National Museum, 1978. 58 pp.

SELECTIVE INDEXES

(Indexes do not include every mention of persons or subjects. Many simply listed or mentioned incidentally are omitted.)

AUTHORS, INFORMANTS, PERSONALITIES

Aarne, Antti, 26
Abbott, O.J., 72-3
Adachi, Ken, 100
Adamson, Anthony, 109, 110
Alcock, F.J., 14
Alexander, Henry, 77
Alexandrin, Barbara, 109
Allard, Joseph, 65
Anderson, Jay A., 112
Armstrong, George H., 80
Arsenault, Georges, 50
Arthur, Eric, 109
Aubry, Claude, 35
Avis, Walter S., 77

Bâby, Stanley, 62
Barbeau, Marius, 1-2, 6, 7, 10, 12, 14-16, 18, 23, 35, 36, 49, 50, 69, 96, 99, 108
Barer-Stein, Thelma, 112
Barss, Beulah M., 112
Barter, Geraldine, 37
Beaugrand, Honoré, 10, 34
Beaverbrook, Lord, 20
Bedore, Bernie V., 36
Bemer, John, 37
Benoit, Emile, 66
Best, Anita, 60
Bird, Michael S., 107, 110, 111, 112
Blanchette, Jean-François, 106
Blois, Clarence, 74
Blumstock, Robert, 99
Boas, Franz, 10
Boily, Lise, 109
Bothwell, Robert, 109
Bouchard, Joseph, 66
Bouchard, René, 106

Boudreau, Daniel, 50
Boudreault, Louis, 66
Boulton, Laura, 48
Boyle, David, 12
Bradley, Ian L. and Patricia, 108
Brandon, Tom, 73
Brassard, François, 50
Brébeuf, Father Jean de, 9
Brednich, Rolf W., 100
Brett, Katherine B., 112
Broadfoot, Barry, 42
Bronson, Bertrand H., 51, 115
Brown, Geordie, 40
Bruneau, Philippe, 66
Brunvand, Jan, 99-100
Buchanan, Roberta, 47
Buckley, Anne-Kay, 104
Burke, John, 13
Burnham, Dorothy K. and Harold, 109
Butler, Gary R., 37, 50
Butler, Victor, 99

Cadieux, 49-50
Cameron, Walter, 112
Campbell, Hector, 43-4
Careless, J.M.S., 98
Carignan, Jean, 65
Carpenter, Carole H., 7, 8, 96
Cartwright, Christine, 104
Casey, George J., 62
Cass-Beggs, Barbara, 50, 62
Chamberlain, Alexander F., 10, 12, 87
Champlain, Samuel de, 96
Chiasson, Anselme, 7, 50
Child, F.J., 51
Clark, LaRena, 73, 83-4
Clayton, Edith, 112

Cockayne, George, 112
Cohen, Judith, 64
Coldwell, Joyce, 47
Collard, Eileen, 112
Colombo, John Robert, 33, 48
Connor, Jennifer C., 89
Cormier, Charlotte, 50
Cormier, Joseph, 66
Cosbey, Robert C., 87-8
Costard, Josephine, 50
Crawford, Venetia, 62
Creighton, Helen, 18-20, 37, 38, 42, 59, 70-1, 80, 81, 91-3, 95, 104

Dawe, Jim, 42
De Gaspé, Philippe-Aubert, 10, 35,99
Degh, Linda, 100
Deschênes, Donald, 50
Desplanques, Marie-Angélique, 36
Devine, P.K., 77, 81
Dibblee, Dorothy and Randal, 61
Dornan, Angelo, 71
Dorson, Richard M., 2-3, 16-17, 36
Doucette, Laurel, 98, 99, 104
Doyle, Gerald S., 58
Doyle, Lawrence, 75
Doyon-Ferland, Madeleine, 112
Dundes, Alan, 89, 115
Dunn, Charles W., 80, 98
Dupont, Jean-Claude, 6
Durand, Laura, 12

Elbaz, André E., 45
England, George A., 100
Ermatinger, Edward, 11

Falcon, Pierre, 50
Fanning, Wayne, 42
Faris, James C., 99
Farrow, Moira, 42
Fauset, Arthur Huff, 8, 24-5, 26, 38, 40, 45, 82, 91
Fergusson, Donald, 63
Field, R.H., 112

Firestone, Melvin, 99
Fitzgerald, Winston, 66
Fletcher, Alice C., 48
Fowke, Edith, 8, 36, 41, 45, 47, 61, 62, 87
Fraser, Mrs Arlington, 73-4
Fraser, C.A., 45
Fraser, Mary L., 8, 24, 38, 91
Fréchette, Louis H., 102
Frye, Northrop, 53

Gagnon, Ernest, 11
Galbraith, John Kenneth, 98
Gard, Robert E., 39, 40
Geikie, John C., 100
Giuliano, Bruce S., 102
Gledhill, Christopher, 61
Glofcheskie, John, 64
Goldie, Terry, 47
Goldstein, Kenneth S., 60, 62
Good, Reginald, 110
Gould, Ed, 100
Gorman, Larry, 74-5
Greenhill, Pauline, 42
Greenleaf, Elisabeth Bristol, 21-2, 59-60, 83, 103, 104
Greenough, William P., 11, 34-5, 99
Grey, Jim, 40
Griggs, Mary Ann, 50
Grover, Carrie, 74
Gryski, Camilla, 88
Guillet, Edwin C., 67, 98, 109
Guinchard, Rufus, 66

Hall, Paul, 62
Halpern, Ida, 48
Halpert, Herbert, 7, 8, 38-9, 40, 42, 43, 81, 87, 91, 101
Halpin, Marjorie M., 97
Hand, Wayland, 91
Hanks, Carole, 110
Hare, Marie, 21, 71-2
Harrington, Richard and Lyn, 110
Harris, Kenneth, 33

Hartlan, Enos, 70
Hatt, Fenwick, 61
Hatt, Nathan, 71
Hawthorn, Audrey, 108
Henneberry, Ben, 19-20, 71
Higinbotham, John D., 77
Hinds, Dick, 70
Hoe, Ban Seng, 100
Hogan, Dorothy and Homer, 65
Holm, Bill, 108
Hornyansky, Michael, 35-6
Horst, David B., 112
Houser, George J., 100
Houston, James, 108
Hufford, David J., 94
Hunter, Darryl, 104

Inverarity, R.B., 108
Ives, Edward D., 21, 37, 41, 61, 62, 74-5

Jameson, Anna, 12
Janes, L.W., 38
Jenness, Diamond, 88
Jones, Michael O., 93

Kane, Paul, 9
Karp, Ellen, 64
Karpeles, Maud, 60
Kaye-Roil, Mary, 104
Kelly, Allan, 72
Kerfont, Angela, 36
Kirshenblatt-Gimblett, Barbara, 46
Kirwin, W.J., 77, 80
Klymasz, Robert B., 41, 45, 63, 64, 80, 102, 104, 111
Knight, Margaret Bennett, 40, 98
Kobayashi, Terry, 110
Kurath, Gertrude P., 48

Laba, Martin, 42
Labelle, Ronald, 50, 72, 108
Lacourcière, Luc, 6, 11-12, 14, 16-17, 18, 34, 35, 50, 93

Laforte, Conrad, 14, 50
Lambert, R.S., 96
Langdon, Eustella, 110
Langille, Bob, 70
Langille, Ned, 69-70
LaRue, Hubert, 11
Laws, Malcolm, Jr, 17, 18
Leach, MacEdward, 5, 22, 44, 60, 97
Leach, Russell, 62
Lederman, Anne, 65
Leechman, Douglas, 23
Leeson, Alice, 12
Lehr, Genevieve, 60
Lemieux, Germain, 7, 50
LeMoine, James M., 10
Leon, Alice, 12, 87
Lescarbot, Marc, 10
Livesay, Florence, 63
Lovelace, Martin, 74
Low, Margaret, 36, 37

MacAskill, Angus, 44
McAtee, W.L., 80
McCarl, Robert, 100
MacDonald, John T., 96
MacDonald, Wilmot, 37, 71
MacDonell, Margaret, 43, 63
McDougall, Dave, 40
MacEachern, Ron, 59
MacEwan, J.W. Grant, 100
McGrath, Robin Gedalof, 33
McIntyre, Paul, 63
Mackenzie, W. Roy, 17-18, 59, 69-70, 102
MacLean, Mrs Jared, 103
MacLeod, Calum I.N., 43-4, 63
MacLeod, Margaret Arnett, 50
McNaughton, Janet, 97
McNeill, Bill, 42
MacNeil, Joe Neil, 43-4
MacRae, Marion, 109
Mannion, John J., 99
Manny, Louise, 20-1, 60-1, 71, 102-3
Mansfield, Grace Yarrow, 21, 59

Mealing, F. Mark, 100
Mercer, H. Paul, 58, 59
Messer, Don, 65
Mills, Alan, 71
Miner, Horace, 99
Monteiro, George, 37
Montferrand, Joseph, 37
Moodie, Susanna, 12, 104
Morrison, Donald, 40
Morrisseau, Norval, 32
Moulden, John, 62
Murphy, Clara, 47
Murphy, James, 13
Murphy, Patrick K., 112
Murray, Hilda C., 99

Nazaire, 34
Newton-White, Muriel E., 110
Nute, Grace L., 100

Ornstein, Lisa, 65

Palardy, Jean, 109
Parry, Caroline, 104
Patterson, G. James, 100
Patterson, George, 12, 77
Patterson, Nancy-Lou, 110
Pattison, Jeanne, 37
Paulsen, Frank M., 100
Peacock, Kenneth, 48, 60, 63
Pelinski, Ramon, 64
Perkowski, Jan, 95
Petrone, Penny, 4, 33
Pocius, Gerad L., 43, 106, 109, 110, 113
Porter, Helen, 99
Posen, I. Sheldon, 40, 62, 88
Pratt, T.K., 78
Price, Ralph and Patricia, 112
Proctor, George A., 64

Quigley, Colin, 68

Raddall, Thomas H., 61, 103
Radin, Paul, 31

Rahn, Jay, 11
Rand, Silas T., 9-10
Reaman, Elmore, 100
Reid, Bill, 32, 108
Rhodes, Frank, 68
Robertson, Heather, 42
Robertson, Margaret R., 101
Robins, John D., 19, 22, 41
Rogers, Tim, 62
Rosenberg, Neil V., 58, 62
Rowles, Edith, 112
Roy, Carmen, 6
Rudnyc'kyj, Jaroslav B., 45, 80
Ruryk, Nancy R., 111
Ryan, Shannon, 60

Salo, Matt T., 93, 100
Saltman, Judith, 33, 34
Sandilands, John, 77
Scargill, M.H., 76
Schoolcraft, Henry R., 9
Schwartz, Herbert T., 33
Scott, Joe, 75
Scott, John, 88-9
Seary, E.R., 80
Séguin, Robert-Lionel, 68
Shackleton, Philip, 109
Shaw, John, 43
Shifrin, Ellen, 68
Simard, Louis, 69
Small, Lawrence G., 60
Smallwood, Joseph R., 40
Smith, Gordon, 11
Smith, Susan, 41
Smith, William, 61
Snider, C.H.J., 61-2
Song, Ban-Song, 63
Spray, Carole, 38, 40
Staebler, Edna, 100, 110
Stechishin, Savella, 111
Stone, Kay F., 45-6
Story, George M., 77, 101
Strickland, Samuel, 99
Suderman, Marlies, 41

Sutya, Charles M., 111
Swackhammer, Robert M., 59
Swinton, George, 108
Symons, R.D., 99
Symons, Scott, 109
Szwed, John F., 62, 99

Taché, J.C., 10
Taft, Michael, 39, 102, 111
Tarasoff, Koozma J., 100, 111
Taylor, Archer, 1
Taylor, David A., 110
Teed, Daniel, 96
Teicher, Morton, 96
Teit, James A., 10, 45
Thomas, Amby, 72
Thomas, Gerald, 36, 37, 41
Thomas, Philip J., 62
Thompson, George S., 100
Thompson, Stith, 26, 27, 28
Thoms, William J., 1
Tizzard, Aubrey, 99
Traill, Catharine Parr, 12
Traquair, Ramsay, 109

Trask, Deborah, 110
Tremblay, Maurice, 89
Tyrchniewicz, Peggy, 112
Tyrwhitt, Janice, 110

Voyer, Simonne, 68

Wagner, Judy, 41
Walton, Ivan H., 61
Wareham, Wilfred W., 30, 62
Watson, Nancy, 47
Waugh, F.W., 82, 87, 91
Weber, Anna, 110
Widdowson, John D.A., 42, 43, 77, 101
Willard, John, 110
Williams, Frank, 43
Wilson, J. Reginald, 61
Wilson, William, 115
Wintemberg, W.J., 8, 22-4, 81, 91
Wiseman, Adele, 113
Witney, Dudley, 109

Zola, Meguido, 88

SUBJECTS

American Folklore Society, 12, 15, 20, 23
animal tales, 26
architecture, 109-10
Archives de Folklore, 6, 16
autograph verses, 88

Baldoon, 96
bees, 102
belsnickling, 101
Black lore, 24-5, 38, 63
British broadsides, 52-3
Bunyan, Paul, 37, 40

camp legends, 30, 42
Canadian Centre for Folk Culture Studies (CCFCS), 6, 45

Canadian Folklore canadien, 7
Canadian Folk Music Journal, 7
Canadian Folk Music Society, 7, 15
cante fables, 75
CELAT, 6
charivari, 104
chasse galerie, 34
Child ballads, 51-2
childlore, 84-8
Chinook jargon, 77
clogging, 65
Corriveau, La, 35
costumes, 112
crafts people, 112-13
coureurs de bois, 10, 49, 50
Culture & Tradition, 7
customs, 101-5

cycle of the year, 104

dancing, 66-8
dites, 81
döppelgangers, 95
Doukhobor lore, 63, 100, 111
d'Sonoqua, 29

Easter eggs, 111
embroidery, 111
ethnic jokes, 28, 41

farming, 56
festivals, 102-3
feux-follets, 34
fiddlers, 64-5
fiddling, 64-6
folk arts and crafts, 106-13
folk beliefs, 90-7
folk groups, 3
folklife, 98-105
Folklore Studies Association of Canada, 7
folk medicine, 92-4
folk speech, 76-9
food, 111-12
forerunners, 95-6
formula tales, 28
Fraktur, 110
French-Canadian lore, 3-4, 6-7, 10-12, 34-7, 49-50, 68, 69, 76, 89, 99, 102, 108-9

Gaelic lore, 43-5, 63, 98
games, 84, 86-7, 88-9
German lore, 23, 38, 110
ghost ships, 97
ghosts, 45, 95, 97
gorbey legend, 38, 40-1

historical songs, 54-5, 61

Indians and Inuit, 4, 9-10, 31-3, 48, 76, 96-7, 108

Irish influence, 57, 65, 78

janneying, 101
Jewish lore, 45, 46, 64
jokes, 27-8, 42-3
joual, 77
Journal of American Folklore, 6, 12, 14, 15, 17, 23, 24-5, 77

Laval University, 6, 16, 114
legends, 28-30, 36, 38, 40-2
literary relationships, 46-7
loup-garous, 29, 34
lumbering, 100
lumbering songs, 55-6
lutins, 29, 34

Malanaka, 102
Märchen, 26-7, 38
material culture, 106-7
Memorial University, 7, 30, 60, 77, 114
Mennonite lore, 100, 110
mining songs, 56
Miramichi Folk Festival, 20-1
monologues, 30
motifs, 27
mouth music, 68
Mufferaw, Joe, 37, 39-40,
mumming, 101
murder ballads, 57
myths, 28, 31

Nanabozo, 9, 31
National Museum, 6, 14, 16, 19, 107
nicknames, 80

Ogopogo, 29-30, 96-7
'Old Favourites', 58

parables, 46
parlour games, 88-9
personal narratives, 30, 42
phonograph records, 69
place names, 79-80

poltergeists, 95, 96
proverbs, 80-1

ranching, 100
riddles, 81-4
rites of passage, 103

Sasquatch, 29, 96-7
sealing, 60, 100
sea songs, 55, 61-2
Sedna, 29
Sheila, 40
singers, 69-74
singer-songmakers, 74-5
singing games, 84, 86-7
skipping rhymes, 84-8
square dancing, 66-7
step dancing, 66

string figures, 88
superstitions, 90-7
tale types, 26-8
tall tales, 27, 39
textiles, 109, 112
Ti-Jean, 34
tricksters, 31

Ukrainian lore, 45, 63, 80, 102, 111
urban legends, 30, 42
voyageurs, 10, 11, 50
water witching, 95-6
weather beliefs, 91-2
Western Producer, The, 58
Windigo, 29, 33, 96
witches, 95
woodworking, 109

xerox lore, 89